RO RO MORSE: KILL OR BE KILLED

Ro Ro Morse: Kill or Be Killed

Tony DePaul

NewPlainsPress.com

Contents

In Philadelphia, there are two degrees of separation.
Everybody knows Everybody.

Story One: The King is Dead

Chapter One

Philadelphia Homicide Detective Rowena Morse twirls her shoulder length frosted blond hair around her right forefinger. She smiles her best flirt as Al the bar owner fills her cocktail glass with a fresh margarita.

"On me, Ro Ro."

Al stands six-four, a foot taller than Ro and weighs twice her hundred and forty-one pounds. Al is her contemporary at 52. Ro looks a dozen years younger.

"Thanks Al. You're the best."

Al has spent ten plus years trying to get her into the sack. She's been a widow for a minute and has already made the mistake of falling in love with a tall, handsome man with a sly smile and the moral fiber of a worm. Besides, Al is married.

The Happy Hour bell rings. O'Grady's fills with the raucous Mount Airy crowd. As if on cue, they pour in, scrambling for precious empty bar stools, preferably near a TV.

Ro Ro knows most of them and their families going back to her grammar school days at Holy Cross. The chatter at the bar ranges from arguments about politics to the Philadelphia Eagles, Flyers, Sixers, and Phillies.

She swirls her drink stir while saying hello to the treasured people who she's grown bored with. The gang is mainly Kool Aid drinking Catholics who consider original thought the original sin. They are endearing knuckleheads. Hearts of gold. Heads of lead.

She is the only female in the bar, and no man dares challenge her.

A new face appears in the doorway. Dark eyes, jet black hair, and a scowl running across his square face. Dressed in a full-length brown leather coat, a crimson turtleneck, and designer jeans, he crosses the room in three long strides, his leather boot heels echoing his presence. He settles into a corner booth. Ro Ro notices a slight bulge under his coat.

A minute later, the front door opens again. This time it's Jimmy "The Jumper" Roscoe, local bookie, card cheat, and renowned wielder of a switchblade. His gray fedora hangs tightly along his orange-red hair line. He nods to Al and swirls his finger in a circle above his head, a signal to buy the house. The grateful fools thank him for buying drinks with money they have already lost, and with enough vigor to drown a whale, and Jumper shakes hands with the crowd before settling into the booth with the stranger. They do not shake hands.

Then she realizes the stranger is "Germantown" John Mancuso. G Town John was his street name. Local legend has it that G Town Johnny was the toughest street fighter in Philly. Her dead ex-husband grew up with him.

Meeting in person means he's sending someone a message, Ro Ro internally reasons.

Normally she leaves by five-thirty, but home is far less interesting than watching two thugs in a booth from the mirror over the bar. Bottles of Tullamore Dew, Red Breast, John Powers, and Paddy's line the back bar. The Irish angels, Al calls them, for they make men sing "Danny Boy" and "Whiskey in the Jar" like they are solemn hymns.

Joey "The Moocher" McKee sidles his lithe sixty-year-old carcass toward the corner booth. Joey has not won a bet in decades, so it would not surprise Ro Ro if Joey were in debt over the top of his shock of gray hair. Joey walks to the table smiling but the smile melts away like snow in a rainstorm. He turns a whiter shade of pale as G Town John pats his chest bulge.

Al walks from behind the bar, motioning for the crowd to follow him. Twenty men surround Joey.

Al points to Jumper. "Leave Joey alone. He's got pancreatic cancer. Whatever he owes, we will cover it when he passes. And any bets you take from him from here on are on you."

The crowd murmurs their support. Then Tony "Little Boss" De Giacomo, walks in front of Al. Little Tony was a cousin of Al's and a worse loser than Joey. His pencil mustache and squinty eyes create the distinct impression of a weasel in a black pea coat, sneaky and out of season. He wears high top sneakers that squeak with each step. Tony has the smallest feet on record. The high tops are probably a kid's size ten. Growing up, Tony's pint-size shoes earned him nicknames like Wussy Foot, Mini Guinea, and Rapid Rabbit. Ro suspects he is showing up to deflect Jumper to focus on Joey. He creeps her out.

G Town pulls his gun and yanks Joey by his shirt collar across the table.

"Don't mess with us. Punk."

Joey cries out, "No, John G. I'll get the dough. I swear on my mother's eyes."

"Your mother is as dead as you'll be if you don't pay us," says Jumper.

Ro swings off her stool, pistol in hand, pointing the barrel square at G Town.

"Go back to Germantown!"

The bar turns deadly quiet. For a long moment no one moves. You could hear a fly burp.

"Who's the Chick?" asks G Town.

Al's lips curl into a snickering smile. "Mount Airy's finest cop. Screw with her and she'll spread your brains across the wall."

G Town slides the gun back into its hiding place. "This ain't over," he says.

"That's right," says Jumper.

G Town stops at the doorway. "There are dead beats here who owe us. We will collect. As for you Miss Annie Oakley, don't ever pull a gun on me again or maybe you'll get one of your tits shot off."

A few laughs from across the room but they suddenly muffle. Rowena glares laser beams at him. Her heart races like Smarty Jones down the stretch. "Go for it anytime, you grease ball."

G Town nods. "Wait, I remember you. You married Ricky Rawlings. Yeah. You were Ricky's broad. You are looking hot, Mrs. Rawlings."

"The name is Detective Morse."

"Yeah. A real hard head. That's what Ricky told me. Too bad about Ricky and that car accident. I miss him. Don't you?"

"If you miss him, then just go to Hell. His lying, cheating ass is there waiting for you."

"Touché tough lady. Ricky was small potatoes next to you."

G Town John blows her a kiss and walks out.

The bar erupts into cheers. Al hugs her, a little too closely.

"Drinks on the house," says Al.

The men gather around her singing, "For She's a Jolly Good Fellow."

"What a chorus of knuckle-heads," she says. The praise warms her like brandy pouring down her insides.

An hour later, her hand on her pistol, Ro walks three blocks to her twin stone and stucco home on East Mount Airy Avenue. The tree-lined street holds enough ambush opportunities to scare Super Woman.

She showers to relax her body, calm her mind. She admits to herself that she wants to shoot Germantown John, just like she wanted to shoot her dead husband Ricky when she caught him cheating on her with another skank from Germantown, Julie Monaco. She had a link to G Town. What was it?

At eleven thirty, she crawls into bed, feeling happy that she has stood up for Joey and backed down Germantown John. With her parents dead, she has no one with whom to share her pride. They had never encouraged her, anyway. They bullied her as surely as Germantown John had bullied Joey. Her mother would dine on steak while taunting her. "Hot dogs for you," mother would say, holding a forkful of prime rib. And her father never said a word in her defense. College was out of the question despite her record of straight As. "Girls don't need college. They need a good husband and lots of kids to keep them busy," said her mother at least eighty thousand times.

She'd left her childhood home at twenty, escaping like a lamb running from hungry wolves. For six months she lived at the YWCA on Chestnut Street in Center City, until she took a police exam and aced it. She was a survivor.

Satisfied with her fate, she closes her eyes and sleeps soundly until her cell phone blares at six-thirty. The caller ID reads "Malone."

Her affair with Bart ended months prior. He must be drunk.

Anxious, she pushes the big green button.

"Detective Morse."

"Ro Ro. It's Bart. I just found Al O'Grady shot dead in his bar. You better get over here."

Ro gasps, "What? Are you pulling my leg?"

"I am not that nuts. I called it in. CSU is on the way. The case is more than likely going to you, so get over here, pronto."

She races to the bathroom for a quick pee. She splashes water across her face. Her wrinkles are showing. No time for makeup. No time to shower. She plies her body with a bath gel and soft sponge. She rinses her teeth with a mouthful of Listerine, and glances at the mirror. She winces at the reflection of a baggy-eyed woman who looks past forty. She dresses in a dark gray pantsuit, in need of pressing. She straps on her double-sided holster. She's an expert with both hands. Rowena flees the house, jogging in flats toward O'Grady's, anxious to get after whoever shot Al, and curious as to why Bart called her directly.

All the way to O'Grady's, her mind swirls around one question. Had she gotten Aloysius Francis O'Grady murdered by antagonizing Germantown John? Wise guys don't like women who make them look bad. Al had stood up to the thug, too. And what is Bart Malone doing in O'Grady's so early?

She crosses the bumpy cobblestones on Germantown Avenue, barely grasping the inescapable fact that Al O'Grady is dead, and, with him, so too does part of Mount Airy die tonight. The King is dead. Somebody is going to pay.

Rowena kneels beside Al's body, supine on the ceramic tile floor next to the bar. His bloody shirt clinging to his corpse. The red badge of courage, she thought.

"I covered his face with a tablecloth after I closed his eyes," says Malone.

Rowena avoids looking at Bart aka "Black Bart," after the Old Western bandit who robbed Wells Fargo stagecoaches in California. Malone is a thief in his own right but a good-looking one.

She edges the tablecloth away from Al's face, fearful he will somehow see her and cast guilt upon her. He's been shot in the chest twice at close range. Upturned bar stools are set in a neat row along the bar, meaning he'd done a post close cleanup, so the murder had taken place sometime after two AM. Al would have locked the door, so he must have let the killer inside. The killer was somebody Al knew and trusted. Somebody she probably knows, as well.

One of the stools is slightly out of line. Al was meticulous and never left anything out of its place.

The CSU team arrives, headed by Dr. Charles "Docky" Poteet, a product of Sharpnack Street in lower Mount Airy. Docky played linebacker at Germantown High and at Temple. He has street smarts from his Dreadlocks down to his yellow Nike running shoes.

"What we got here, Sister Ro Ro?"

"Somebody put two in Al O'Grady. Bart found him."

"Hmmm. Al was a good dude. Let me get to work so I can cipher this riddle."

Rowena points to the row of stools. "One of those stools is out of sync. See if you can help me figure out why."

Bart smirks. "Typical Ro Ro. She just loves to make a mystery out of a miscue."

"Murder is not a miscue," she snaps.

Docky waves a finger under Bart's nose. "Don't piss her off, Bart. She owns a broadsword, I am told."

Rowena grins as she makes a chopping motion across the front of Bart's pants. She takes Bart by the arm. "Come with me. I need a statement."

"Sure thing."

Rowena glances once more at the out of place stool.

Bart's statement sheds no light. He'd worked all night on a carjacking of a female Uber driver that turned into a rape case. It seems he had an alibi. And needing a bourbon after an all-nighter is understandable. But she would verify his story with the district officers. She calls the Records Department and gets the address and phone number of Germanton John Mancuso.

He answers on the fourth ring.

"This is John."

"Mancuso. This is Officer Rowena Morse. I am coming to pay you a visit regarding the shooting death of Al O'Grady. I will be there in fifteen minutes."

"Take your time. I ain't leaving town. Sorry about O'Grady. Owning a bar is a dangerous occupation."

Rowena shakes her phone like she is wringing his neck. "Yeah. So is bookmaking, loan sharking, and murder. Do not leave your residence."

Mancuso chuckles. "I like feisty women. Come over, please."

Rowena hangs up. G Town's impunity rankles her. She has to control her anger before she gives in to the temptation of pistol whipping the arrogant bastard.

Chapter Two

Germantown John lives in a one-hundred-year-old, two-story stone home on West Gravers Lane in Chestnut Hill, a short ride up the trolley tracks and cobblestoned Germantown Avenue. "The Hill" is a town within the city. A vigilant Community Association scrutinizes all new store openings, renovations, and building projects. The Hill's newspaper prints weekly and reports on all things Chestnut Hill. Ro Ro wonders how a low life Germantown hood like G Town John is allowed to join the civilized gentry of The Hill.

He agrees to see her, sans lawyer. Ro wonders, "Is he being macho or is he showing scorn?" She relishes being underestimated.

She finds a parking spot four houses away under a tall maple tree. An elderly man dressed in baggy shorts and a faded University of Pennsylvania red and blue tee walks past her, eyeing her.

He probably thinks I am a hooker who made a wrong turn. Ro Ro gets out of the car, badge in hand. "Excuse me Sir. I am Detective Morse. May I ask you a question?"

The man stares at her badge and her breasts with equal interest.

"Sure Dear. My name is Gordon Shuster. I live a few doors down."

Ro Ro winces at the word, "Dear." Condescendence annoys her. "Do you know Mister John Mancuso?"

Shuster's bony fingers rub his gray chin stubble. "Oh, you mean the dago? He's a bit sleazy. People come and go to his house at all hours. Is he a mobster like on The Sopranos?"

Ro has the temptation to roll her eyes. "Tell me more about his visitors."

"Well, there is a short guy who was here last night. And then there is a red-haired man who wears a fedora. I noticed because I wear one myself. And there is also a fancy dresser. Always wearing suits even in the heat. Maybe he's a lawyer."

Little Tony, Jumper, and Bart. All on Germantown John's visitor list. Ro turns to walk away.

"Wait, Officer. I saw the television story about that bar owner who was shot. He was here last week."

Rowena holds back a gasp. "When exactly was he here?"

Shuster is now staring openly at her chest. Ro Ro wants to slap him.

"Tuesday. I remember because I play Mega Millions and I hit the Mega Ball for two whole dollars. I never win those darn things."

Rowena gives him her card. He cradles it like she has given him another winning lottery ticket.

"Please keep an eye on Mancuso and call me if any of these men reappear. Will you do that for me?"

"Sure will."

Rowena gently squeezes Shuster's arm as if to seal the deal.

"Thank you, Mister Shuster."

"Call me Gordy," he says and smiles like a school kid at a sophomore hop.

"And you can call me Officer Morse."

Gordy's smile evaporates.

Rowena turns on her heels as she heads toward G Town John's house. Her nostrils flare in anger. Bart has lied to her. Why?

John Mancuso is the son of a bricklayer who spent Saturdays losing more than half his paycheck at Garden State racetrack. By the time John had reached sixteen, he'd learned it was more profitable to take bets as a bookie than to try and pick winners. He never bet on an unfixed race. He made his bones by taking out one of gang boss Joey Merlino's assassins in a knife fight.

High hedges surround Casa Mancuso like a natural barrier. Ro Ro scales the six steps to a wooden porch where a hammock hangs from the wooden porch ceiling. A hand-written note "Out Back" is pinned to the front door. She tracks along a cement walk noting that the side of the house is shielded by hedges as well.

Luscious red, ripe tomatoes hang along a dozen stakes. Mancuso sweats under a broad straw hat. A sleeveless tee shirt clings to his hairy chest. His long, muscular legs stretch to his low-cut Nikes. His biceps bulge like a man who does chin ups for a living. He turns and flashes a broad, sexy smile, his blue eyes alight as the summer sky.

Rowena and Mancuso's eyes lock. She senses he is testing her, sizing up her mental strength.

"Hello Mister Mancuso. We meet again. I need to ask you questions about the murder of Al O'Grady."

Mancuso nodded. "Sure, Detective. Let's go inside. Where is your partner?"

"I have no partner. I work alone."

"Come on inside."

The kitchen has a retro-style stove, fridge, oven, sink, and dishwasher. A water softener is attached to the sink faucet. The appliances gleam under overhead LEDs. Mancuso takes a glass pitcher of iced tea with lemons from the fridge, two water glasses from the oak cabinets, and sets them on a butcher block table.

G Town John is no stereotypical hood, she ponders.

Mancuso pours two glasses full. "Enjoy," he says.

Rowena sits opposite Mancuso, mindful that his eyes remain fixed on hers and not on her body.

"Thanks for the iced tea. Where were you last night?" she asks him.

"Hah. You go right to the heart of the matter. I like directness. It does not work with every woman, but you are not typical. Ricky described you as unusual. To answer your question, I stayed home alone last night."

Why does he keep bringing up Ricky?

"So, do you have anyone who can corroborate that statement?"

"Nope."

"Why were you in O'Grady's bar yesterday afternoon?"

Mancuso holds up his left palm and scratches it with his manicured fingernails. "People who frequent the place owe me money."

"Who owes you money and how much do they owe you?"

"That's confidential."

"In a murder case everything is fair game. Shall I get a warrant to search this house, your tax records, bank accounts, credit card accounts?"

"Absolutely."

"Why not keep things simple, especially if you didn't do the shooting?"

"My business runs in the security of confidentiality. Clients don't want their business on the street. It's bad all around."

Mancuso swigs from his glass of iced tea, stalling she suspects.

"Look Ro Ro, or that's what Ricky called you. Anyhow, I want to cooperate because I have nothing to hide regarding who killed Al. If word gets out that I caved to the cops and shared certain names, I lose credibility. I will look very weak. No one wants a Tenuous Timmy in this business. Guys will move in on me and I will be dead or broke in a month. That is not a desirable outcome. However, a subpoena gets me off the hook. So, go do your subpoena so you look good, and I maintain my reputation as a standup guy. Ricky said you had a logical mind. I am sure you see the logic here."

Rowena nods, rocking in her chair. "I see your point. Answer me this. Why do you keep bringing up my dead ex?"

Mancuso refreshes his iced tea. "Ah, that is good tea. My mother used to brew tea and drop fresh mint leaves in it. God rest her soul. I didn't realize I talked about Ricky so much. You see, we were asshole buddies. I introduced him to Julie Monaco. You know the rest of the story. It's Julie who may have gotten him killed."

Rowena's heart skips three beats. "What?"

"Ricky could have made that curve on Cresheim Valley Drive with his eyes closed. He was side swiped into that tree by Julie's ex-boyfriend."

Blood rushes to Rowena's head. Dizzy, she grasps the edges of her chair. "Who? Damn it, who?"

Mancuso whispers, "Al O'Grady."

"I don't believe you."

"Make book on it. And if that word gets out, guess who is the prime suspect for killing Al? Y. O. U." The Police Department will take you off the case and strap your sweet ass to a desk in the basement of the Fourteenth District. I hear the rats in there like Brie."

Rowena pounds the table with both fists. "Liar. Liar, Liar."

"Germantown John tells no lies. What is your alibi for last night?"

"You bastard! You're a lying, conniving bastard."

"Do you want more iced tea?"

Rowena takes a deep breath to control her urge to slap G Town across his smiling face. He has her for the moment.

"Mancuso, I am not going to be intimidated by a bullshit artist like you. Expect subpoenas and surveillance. Go tell your lies to whomever may be dumb enough to believe it all."

"I will. Now get out of my home before I call the cops."

Rowena backs away from G Town's mocking laughter. Her gut tells her that the scumbag is telling the truth.

Rowena guns the engine and heads for the Fourteenth District on Haines Street in Germantown. Her phone rings, so she answers it hands free. Caller ID reads, "Lieutenant Jones." Her boss. Jonesy is tall, lean, and mean. She has known him since the eighth grade. He gives her lots of room to operate but she never crosses the line of taking too much rope, lest Harley Jones come down on her like an avalanche.

"Hello boss."

"Hello Rowena. What happened with G Town?"

"Lots. I just left his house. I learned a lot that I will report when I get there. Please send officers to pick up Joey, "The Moocher" McKee, "Little Tony" De Giacomo, and Jimmy "The Jumper" Roscoe. And please get Docky moving on his report. Mancuso pulled a strong-arm tactic on me. The rats are scared."

"Good. I can hardly wait to hear your report."

"See you in ten minutes, Boss."

Chapter Three

The hundred-year-old brick Fourteenth District building looks like a pre-World War One prison. A black wrought iron fence separates the building from the run-down houses and empty, trash strewn lots on its sides.

The front room serves as a Magistrate Court for DUI and minor offense cases. The Judge holds court from a raised seat backed by a six-foot by four and a half-foot American flag.

To the left, Police desks and offices are arranged behind secure plate glass protection. The site is simple but safe, non-pretentious.

Harley Davidson Jones, aka "Biker," welcomes Rowena into his office at the rear with a wave. Biker is a godsend of a boss. He makes sure she is not assigned a partner. Male partners spend too much effort trying to bed her. Women would spend too much time complaining. "Come in Ro Ro. Tell me about G Town's stunt and how it ties to you."

Biker always dresses like he is going to church. He sports cufflinks daily, usually gold. He despises his nickname, feeling it demeans his status as a police officer and family man.

Rowena settles into a round back wooden chair. "G Town implied that my ex's car accident was a murder and I had motive to kill Ricky. The troubling point is that I think he knows something. I want Docky to review the file. Maybe the previous CSU Examiner missed something. Anyway, I think we better be sure there is no way G Town can get me off this case."

Biker scratches his pencil thin mustache, a sign he is intrigued. "G Town is slicker than black ice. Okay, I will instruct Docky to check it out, since it may be relevant to O'Grady's murder in a roundabout way. What does your gut tell you about the motive for killing Al?"

Rowena takes a deep breath and sighs, not liking to answer a question when she is not sure of the answer. "At first, I thought it must have been a robbery gone bad, but now I think there is a subtle explanation. I cannot imagine Al having been in business with G Town. But Al liked the ponies. He used to say he was going to give me one for Christmas. Now I remember he gave me a toy palomino pony once as a way of fulfilling his promise. He said the pony was a blond like me. Al was as horny as he was corny. I thought it was a cheap trick to get me into bed with him. Perhaps my erstwhile knight in shining armor had a gambling problem that tarnished his armor. Bars are cash cows and great ways to launder money."

Biker taps the top of his desk with both fore fingers as if he is typing hunt and peck on a PC. "We will subpoena his bank records and question his CPA, or whoever did his taxes."

"Follow the money. The dollars are the breadcrumbs that lead you to the truth," remarks Rowena.

Biker's cell phone buzzes. "Jones," he says. "Good, bring him in and then go get the other two losers."

He turns off the phone. "We picked up Little Tony. ETA is ten minutes. Interview him in the rear conference room. It's hot in there. Sweat the punk until the grease soaks his shirt."

Rowena shoots him a thumbs-up. "Will do, Boss."

Little Tony De Giacomo barely stands five feet tall. Wiry, well-defined bicep muscles thrust from his black tee shirt, cut sharp from working out at Planet Fitness daily, he has nicknames ranging from 'Mini Guinea' to 'Mighty Mouse' to 'Stub' to 'Pony Boy'. He has a well-deserved reputation as a street-fighter whose first punch is a hard shot to the nuts. He is respected as a crafty bettor on football games. He has a nasty temper and is second cousin to G Town John on his mother's side.

His thick, black hair is slicked back, a retro fifties look, ala Sylvester Stallone, his idol. Rowena likens him to the gargoyles etched in City Hall, only scarier.

He sits across from Rowena, staring at her chest, a smirk twisting from the left side of his mouth.

"Hello Joey," she says, purposely avoiding the nicknames.

"Yeah, hello Ro Ro. Bad news about Al. You and he were tight."

"Everybody liked Al. He was one of the good guys."

Joey laughs. "Not everybody. Who shoots a friend?"

"A false friend. Why were you in his bar yesterday?"

Joey leans back. "It was a hot day. I needed a beer."

"Funny how you and your cousin John show up at the same time. Did Al owe money to G Town?"

"Ask John. I mind my own business."

"You collect for John. Were you guys after Al or Moocher or both?"

Joey's eyes narrow under his creased brow. "What are you talking about?"

Rowena leans across the table, staring into Joey's eyes, looking for him to blink.

"Motive. You would cut or shoot Mother Theresa to collect a nickel. Is that why you and your cousin paid Al a visit?"

Joey held up both hands. "Whoa. Slow down Ro Ro. Joey ain't no killer. I liked Al. He used to call me short shot. I called him long shot. We were buddies."

Rowena is not about to buy BS from him at any price. "Bull. You were there to send Al a message, not Moocher."

"So how do you figure that?"

"Because Al is dead, and Moocher is alive, Knucklehead."

Sweat beads on Joey's forehead. "You got it all wrong. Moocher owed eleven large. John wanted him to pay up."

"How much did Al owe?"

Joey's eyes spread wide. "I don't know nothing about Big Al and any debts."

Rowena digs her forefinger into his chest. "Do I have to ask Biker to come in here and reeducate you on getting an ass whipping? Now I'll ask you again. How much did Al owe G Town?"

Joey flashes ten fingers ten times.

"A hundred large?"

"I did not tell you anything. Look at it this way. Let's say Al owed money. Killing him means you are out whatever he owes. Hell, he was the safest man in Mount Airy as far as owing money to John."

Rowena shakes a fist under his nose. "Safe? Safe? He was murdered. How safe is that?"

She drops her voice to a whisper, low and slow for emphasis. "Tell me, you fool, how safe was Al?"

Joey shrugs, "I guess he was in trouble for some other reason."

Rowena believes Joey may have a valid point. "I like you for killing my old friend. I like you a lot."

Joey leaps up. "Ro Ro. I am clean on this one. I swear."

"Really?"

"Very really. It's too hot in here. I need air."

"Fess up Joey. What do you know that you are not telling me? If I catch you holding back, I will swat you like a sick fly."

Joey's chest heaves, his face turns sheet white. "Ro Ro, you've got to believe me. I know nothing more."

"Believe you? Hah. I'd believe the devil before I believe you. Get out but do not leave Philly. I am declaring you as a material witness in a murder investigation. Got it?"

Joey backs away. "Got it, Ro Ro."

Biker enters, smiling as Joey scurries down the hallway.

"You lit a bonfire under his ass. He'll be running like a greyhound to G Town."

"There is a lot more to this story. I don't think I am

going to like the truth when I find it."

Docky fills the doorway looking troubled. "Hey Miss Ro Ro, why do you want me to go chasing your dead old man's ghost when I got to figure out what happened to Al?"

Rowena tells him about her visit with G Town.

"Now I get it. That G Town is highly likely to have filled my slab with more than one body. You look tired. Best rest up if you're going to tangle with G Town. That man is evil. I would give my false teeth to nail his butt."

"If he killed Al or had him killed, I'll nail him, and you can keep your choppers. I am going home to shower and lie down for a thinking session. Call me when you bring in the next turkey."

Rowena lathers her body under the warm shower water. Usually a shower soothes her, but her mind is running in circles. Her world is in chaos and the eerie feeling that her past is about to rise from the grave unnerves her.

She slips on an old pair of cotton pajama bottoms and a Phillies tee shirt and crawls under the covers. After Ricky died, she avoided men, feeling that a good-looking widow was an easy target for the lechers. She had a brief affair with a charming, divorced businessman who escorted her to England and Scotland. The tryst with Bart was a moment of weakness brought on by loneliness. She has the job and her friends but no children, no legacy except for her record of finding murderers. Problem solving of the first degree, a skill worthy of the best mathematicians.

Her cell rings.

"Hello, Biker. What's up?"

"We brought in the Moocher."

"I will be there in twenty minutes. Put him in the hot room. No water."

"Guantanamo-style."

"Reverse waterboarding."

"You are too freaking much."

Rowena dresses quickly. She is tempted to take five minutes to row her Chuck Norris gym, but she is more worried about her case than her physique.

Moocher owes a lot of money to G Town and probably others, including the hundred bucks she lent him at Christmas. Why did Al stick his neck out for a known loser? It was a bad gamble. Or was it a payoff?

She calls Biker from her hands free. "Boss. It's me. I changed my mind on how to approach Moocher. When Moocher gets there, offer him a soda, maybe a Tastykake, too. I want him relaxed and thinking he is among friends. This is one rat who likes honey as much as he likes money."

"Seduction, eh? Why not?"

"Call it persuasion."

"Hah. Now you are Miss Congeniality with a badge."

"I like Lady Macbeth."

"Figures. The schmooze is on."

"Have you located Jumper?"

"Nope. We will get his worthless butt in here."

"I am counting on it."

Chapter Four

Joseph Emmet 'Moocher" McKee was the seventh child of eight McKee children. The other seven were all girls, so Joey was a true Irish Prince. The only thing he did in the way of a chore was to bring in the mail from the mail slot in the front door of their row home and deposit it on the dining room table. Work and ambition are equal strangers to Joey.

By the time he reached eighth grade, he had developed his gift for weaseling favors and money from friends and neighbors. He'd borrow money promising that he would bet on only a sure thing and his friends would get their money back and half the profits. No one ever recalls getting a payback.

Now in his mid-fifties, Joey has patriotic eyes, blue irises over the white space, surrounded by a bright red rim compliments of daily shots of John Powers Irish whisky.

Luggage size bags droop from his bleary eyes to his cheek bones. He makes a bloodhound look suave.

Growing up, Rowena and Joey lived on the same block, walked to Holy Cross grammar school together, and shared gossip and secrets. He tried to kiss her once. She let him but when his hand squeezed her breast, she kneed him in the nuts, sending him rolling on the ground. All seven of his sisters thanked her.

Rowena finds Moocher sitting comfortably at the table, gnawing on a soft pretzel, mustard lining his thin lips. He greets her with a burp. "Oops. Sorry, Ro Ro. Mustard gets my innards in a ruckus, but I can't eat a soft pretzel without a dab."

She held off a retort about how he gave her the yips.

"No problem. Do you want Grey Poupon?"

"Poop on what?"

Ro Ro rolls her eyes. "Never mind. We are here for Al. It is a tragedy and a mortal sin against all of us."

Moocher stuffs the end of the pretzel into his mouth. He chews away, drooling. "Sure. T'was a terrible thing with somebody murdering Al. He was a good guy. Have you any idea who did it?"

"We are working the case from all angles. How much do you owe G Town John?"

Moocher chews slowly, avoiding her question.

"Take your time. You have a lot of time. Five years for withholding evidence and obstruction of justice."

Moocher rolls his eyes. "Boy oh boy. You can ruin a good pretzel. I owed Al ten large. He paid off G Town. T'was Jumper who owed G Town, big time."

"So, you had ten thousand reasons to kill Al?"

Moocher thumbs his chest. "Me? Slow down a trot. I ain't got the balls to kill a mouse."

"Why did Al buy you out?"

Moocher shuffles his black high-top sneakers making a squeaking sound that sends a shiver up Ro Ro's arms.

"I dunno," he says.

"Bullshit. Fess up Joey. Tell me why Al stuck his neck out for you."

Moocher leans over the table. "You got to keep this hush hush. Al took up with my sister, Joan."

"Joan is a freaking nun, and she weighs two hundred if she weighs an ounce."

"Beneath the habit, she's got all the goods you have."

Ro Ro blanches, as an image of Joan and Al copulating rolls across her mind.

"How long had this unholy affair been going on?"

"Years! She gets birth control from Planned Parenthood. Now, maybe you understand I had no reason to kill Al. He was my banker and Joan was the collateral."

Rowena laughs, "Moocher, my man. You got more scam in you than P.T. Barnum. Tell me, who do you think shot Al?"

Moocher scratches his chin as if contemplating the origin of dark matter. "T'aint scarcely sure, but I think your old beau Black Bart may have an inkling. Word on the street, he found Al, but I also heard Bart owed Al and G Town beaucoup cabbage. Mayhap fifty grand."

Rowena clenches her fists, ready to smash him square in his mouth. "Joey, if you're lying, I will kick your nuts so hard they'll wrap around your ears."

Moocher crosses his hands over his lap. "You got me once. I ain't going for twice. I told you the truth as sure as the sun rises in the East and sets in the West."

She is afraid to believe him.

"Tell me how Bart Malone fits into the picture."

"Whoa. Now you are asking me to chime the bell on a cop. That's a race horse of a different color. Besides, he was your boyfriend, wasn't he? You should know about the people you keep company with."

"Lectures from you on behavior are less than credible. So, cut the crap and tell me how Bart Malone ties into the bookmaking operation run by G Town John."

Moocher smiles like he'd just found a hundred-dollar bill on the sidewalk. "Miss Smart Panties doesn't get it. Al had his own set up. Bart was his cover, his police protection. Al ran numbers, lent money at high rates, and made book on all sports. And Bart got a piece of the action. None of this sat well with G Town."

Rowena waits until the revelation set in that Al was dirty, and Bart is dirtier. "So, when G Town visited Al's bar, who was he looking to send a message to?"

Moocher whispers, "Jumper Roscoe. He owed G Town. My guess is that Jumper shot Al to pay off his debt to G Town. With Al out of the picture, G Town had the whole megillah. Mount Airy, Germantown, and Chestnut Hill. Maybe some of Montgomery County, too. Wyndmoor for sure. You got to keep me out of this. If G Town finds out I mentioned his business, I'll be eating soft pretzels with Al."

"So, why are you telling me all of this?"

"Life Insurance. If you dress G Town John in an orange suit, I get a freebie on the debt and I feel a lot safer. I got an allergy to bullets."

Biker opens the conference room door, his brows furled. "Good news. We found Jumper. The bad news is that he shot himself and left a note confessing to shooting Al O'Grady."

"Holy shit," says Moocher.

Rowena shook her head. "No way Jumper killed himself. Please get Docky on the job. I've got to go see an old friend."

"Can I skedaddle now?" asks Moocher.

"Yes, but I may have more questions for you later. No road trips, you hear?"

Moocher backs out the door and shuts it behind him.

Rowena phones Bart Malone.

"What's up, Ro Ro?"

"Jumper is dead. Come to the station. I have new evidence we need to discuss. Hurry."

"Sure thing. I'll be right there."

"What're you up to?" asks Biker.

"Did Docky review Ricky's case?"

"Yes, he did. A copy is on your desk along with the CSU report on Al's murder. You read them, then tell me what's going on."

Ro Ro speed reads the report on her ex's death, memorizing each word as if they are implanted into her brain.

"The officer who found Ricky dead behind the wheel was Bart Malone. That is how I met Bart."

"Connect the dots," says Biker.

"I always do, boss. Now I need to read Docky's report."

"What are you looking for?"

"The most elusive thing in the world. The Truth."

Chapter Five

Rowena (Ro) was raised by two staunch Roman Catholics, Desmond and Hannah, who believed the Pope was infallible, sex was sinful, non-Catholics were doomed to Hell, and females had no need to go to college.

She attended Holy Cross, a Catholic grade school and Cardinal Dougherty, a Catholic high school. She lost her religion before she lost her virginity. An exposé on pedophile priests named six priests from Cardinal Dougherty. Rowena reasoned that such men could not put God in a person's mouth. When she commented to her father, he swatted her across the face with the back of his hand, splitting her lip. Hurt and embarrassed, she ran to her room. The pain was soul deep. She vowed to the dark room that no man would ever again get away with hitting her.

Ricky had broken her heart by cheating on her and making a fool of her. The only good thing he did was die from natural causes and leave her ten thousand dollars, enough to help her get an associate degree at the Community College of Philadelphia with a major in Criminal Justice. The degree helped her career. And Bart Malone helped her get the insurance money. Without it, she may have been a Walmart Greeter for life. She owed him, big time. She was about to pay him back. Maybe.

Bart saunters into the conference room, smiling as if he had hit the Powerball lottery.

"Hey Ro Ro. What's up, Buttercup?"

"My blood pressure is soaring, sit down. We need to talk," she says.

Bart sees the case file for Richard Rawlings. His smile fades.

"Why are you looking at that old case?"

Rowena taps the file, "I like history. When Ricky bought it, you were the detective of record. You convinced the CSU to declare the cause of death to be a heart attack. In fact, Ricky was bombed out of his mind. His drunkenness would have negated any insurance claim. They could have claimed contributory negligence, or suicide. You falsified the report to help me. Right?"

"Yes. I liked you and felt sorry for you. And I'd do it again for you. I had feelings for you and still do."

Rowena crosses her arms and sits back. "Wrong! The report photos show marks of a sideswipe by a white car on the passenger side. Police cars are painted white. You side-swiped Ricky and you covered it up. You convinced the CSU to ignore the dent, saying it was an old accident."

Bart slams his fist onto the table. "No. You got it wrong. Hey Ro Ro, you got the money, not me. Maybe you had him run into that tree. Maybe you killed him for the insurance money or had someone do it for you."

"Look Bart. This conversation is offline. There is no mic on or tape rolling. Who killed Ricky and who knew the truth?"

Bart looks away, staring at the blank far wall. "You are off base. I don't know what you are talking about. This is like fake news. How can you believe this cockamamie theory?"

"Why does the truth scare you so much? I'm going to repay the money and reopen Ricky's case. He was a jerk, but he didn't deserve murder."

Bart walks around the table, avoiding her gaze. He stops pacing and leans down by her shoulder. "It was an accident. We were both whacked on gin. Evil stuff, that gin. We drag-raced, but I misjudged the curve and barely nudged him into that tree. I can still see his eyes staring at me in disbelief. To this day, I am sick about it. Sick to my stomach. Can't we just let it go?"

"How do I let it go?"

Bart sits next to her, clutching her hand. "Forgive me, Ro Ro. I am a weak man; I am weaker than a child."

"You are a child. Just resign. Get out. Or give me the truth about Al O'Grady's murder. Why was Al shot? Was it a hit? Did *you* do it?"

Bart grasps her hand. "I did not kill Al. I swear to Christ in heaven, I didn't do it."

Rowena pulls her hand away, reaches into her briefcase and pulls out Docky's report on Al's shooting. She turns to page three. "Read Docky's comments. He dusted the bar stools and found footprints. Guess whose?"

Bart read the notes. "I'll be damned. The dumb ass should have posted his picture on Facebook and wrote that he killed Al."

"Bring him in and I'll forget the other report. And I mean alive."

"Okay. I'll do it."

Bart left unaware that Biker was trailing him.

Rowena needs a margarita, but she settles for a Keurig dark roast, no sugar, no cream. A weight was off her shoulders.

Chapter Six

Docky trundles along the Formica floor carrying a report on Jumper Roscoe.

"Here Miss Ro Ro is the initial take on Mr. Roscoe. He was shot with the same gun as Al O'Grady. Was not a suicide. Hell, Ray Charles could see it was murder."

"Thanks, Docky."

"Have you arrested the fool?"

"I sent Bart to arrest him."

"Who is gonna arrest Bart?"

"Biker, if Bart gets cute."

"That chair being out of line was the key. How did you cipher that out?"

"Call it feminine logic. I knew Al would never clean up and leave a chair out of line. Ergo, someone else handled the chair. Simple algebra works. And that man was the killer," she says.

Docky pats her shoulder. "Yeah. The dwarf used the chair to disguise the angle of the shot and his height, so we would be looking for a man of a different height. Smart idea, but, dumb execution. Knuckleheads are everywhere."

"I wonder who gave him the idea?"

Rowena phones Biker. "Where is Bart?"

"He went right to G Town's house. Little Tony is there. Bart is taking Little Tony out in cuffs. He's putting Little Tony in the car.

Tony looks like he is coked up. I'll stay on him. Oh shit! Bart just shot Tony. I'm going in. Send back up."

"Damn!" says Ro Ro, "He was always dirty."

She hears shots fired. "Biker! Biker! Talk to me Biker. Are you all right?"

"Yeah. Bart never could shoot straight. I brought him down. Get Docky out here."

Rowena rushes to her car and speeds to G Town John's home. She had tested Bart and he had failed. He'd

murdered Ricky as sure as Little Tony stood on a bar stool in his sneakers and shot Al while Bart watched him, guiding him through the murder. When Bart saw the report identifying Little Tony, he knew he had to shoot him. Jumper was the stooge. And G Town planned it all.

She finds G Town sitting on a bench in his backyard, a glass of red wine in hand. He is wearing a straw hat with a red, white, and green band. "Welcome, good looking. There was quite a scene out there today. Lots of shoot 'em up, cops and robbers' stuff. Want some dago red?"

Ro Ro walks behind him and slaps the back of his head. "Damn fly was about to bite you."

G Town rises quickly, chest heaving, eyes narrow like a cobra ready to strike, "Don't ever do that again!"

"I'm not done with you, Johnny Boy. You will slip up someday and I will chop you down like a dead tree."

"Yeah, sure. You will get yours."

"Why did you kill Ricky?"

"He got out of line. I had to teach him a lesson."

"I see. Go play with your tomatoes. But, just remember, Ro Ro Morse will get you as sure as God made little green tomatoes."

In sweatpants, a t-shirt, and low-cut shoes, Rowena pushes herself extra hard on the home gym. Harder, faster, stronger. She has to get in shape for the long haul. She has to bring down Germantown John.

She lays her nine shot Glock nicknamed Gloria, after the rock song she liked so much, on the floor. "You are my best friend."

"Alexa, play Janis Joplin."

'Busted flat in Baton Rouge,' by Janice Joplin starts to fill the room.

Janis was strong and defiant. You could break her heart but not defeat her.

"No one will ever break my heart again," says Ro Ro.

She pulls on the rowing bar. "No one."

A dark figure passes across the bay window. The figure takes a shooter's stance.

Ro Ro catches the shooter's silhouette in the corner of her eye. She throws herself off the gym equipment just as three shots shatter the window spraying shards of glass across the room. The bullets rip into the seat where she had been sitting. She grabs Gloria. Gun in hand, she kneels and fires into the night. Her heart pounds through her sweatshirt.

The figure is gone.

She calls Biker's cell phone. No answer. "This is Lieutenant Jones. Leave a message."

"Biker. Somebody just tried to kill me. Get a squad and Docky to my house, pronto."

She clicks the phone off. Her knuckles tighten around the handgun.

She rails at the shattered window. "You missed. I will find you. I will get you. It's you or me. Kill or be killed."

Epilogue

The full summer moon casts a pall over G Town's tomatoes; their sheen promises G Town a tasty tomato salad, drenched in olive oil, mixed with thin slices of onion and pepper, and a sprinkle of garlic and oregano. Amoroso's fresh rolls from the South Philly bakery to mop up the juice, and a glass of red wine to wash it down.

G Town puffs on his Dominican cigar, savoring the fruits of a good day's work.

His throwaway cell buzzes.

"Yo Boss," says Biker.

"Hello Harley. You did well today."

"Yeah. I didn't mind shooting that pompous ass, Malone. I made the world a better place. When do we take over O'Grady's?"

G Town does not like Biker, but he is useful. "My bank will call the note and cash in the life insurance policy he turned over. We own the business and the bricks. You'll see your twenty percent cut in the Swiss account in two months. Does Rowena have any clue that she helped us?"

"Nah. That's the main reason I don't assign her a partner. A partner would complicate things. It's best to let her think she's special and old Biker is her best friend."

"For her sake, she better not catch on," says G Town.

"Right. Nice doing business with you," says Biker.

G Town hangs up, plucks a ripe tomato, wipes the skin with his hands, making it shine. He bites into the tomato. Juice drizzles down his chin.

Sweet, luscious, and ripe, like Rowena, he thinks.

Story Two: Deadly Doo Wop

Chapter One

Ro was raised on the Philadelphia staples of cheesesteaks, hoagies, soft pretzels, and Doo Wop music. Philly spawned dozens of street corner groups in the fifties and early sixties. Blacks, Whites, and Hispanic groups rocked and rolled twenty-four seven.

Dick Clark's *Bandstand* gave America a daily dose of Doo Wop, Philly style. Disc jockeys Hi Lit, Joe Niagara, and Georgie Woods led the radio charge for Doo Wop.

South Philly legend, Jerry "The Geater With the Heater" Blavat, rocks on today, as does DJ Harvey Holiday on his Sunday night show on Oldies 98.1 FM radio. Though born well past the prime of Doo Wop, Rowena was instilled with a love of Doo Wop by her parents who carried on the Doo Wop tradition, resisting the British Invasion and Motown. She knew every Doo Wop song by heart. The only trouble with her music education is her off-key, nasally, singing voice. When she sings in the shower, the water turns off.

Standing over the battered, eighty-four-year-old corpse of Doo Wop legend, Junior McCall, seems unreal. She had seen Junior perform at the Tower Theater four times. His records played on the local Oldies radio stations. The smooth baritone voice echoes in her mind. And he sang Ave Maria at her wedding, a gift from her parents. Solving this case is a personal matter.

Junior lies face up on the living room carpet of his Mount Airy townhouse, his arms stretched wide, his face swollen, dried blood caked on his forehead, his temples, and ears.

Docky ambles in, whistling a tune alien to Ro Ro.

"Hello Miss Ro Ro. My my. Somebody whipped up on old Junior."

"Hey Docky. Yes. Junior pissed off somebody, big time. They beat him from side to side. You knew him from his days as a background singer, didn't you?"

Docky slips on his surgical gloves and waves Ro Ro aside. "Junior was the best bass baritone I ever heard. He had his faults like most folks, but he was a stud singer. Yeah, me and Junior go way back. Now, let me do my job."

Docky's team of CSU agents seal off the room and go to work collecting prints, blood samples, and taking photos. Ro Ro steps outside the tape, holding in her emotions, half angry, half sorrowful. "Send me the report today, please."

Docky squints behind his horn-rimmed glasses. "Detective Miss Morse will get a full report when CSU is done. Don't go rushing us. We got to be thorough more than be fast. Now git."

"I saw your report on the shooting at my house. Was it a ghost that tried to kill me?"

"Whoever tried to kill you was smart enough to take off his shoes and wrap his feet in trash bags. He also took away the shell casings. Your attacker was a pro."

"Or a cop?"

"I said no such thing. Now scoot and let me do my job."

Ro Ro salutes and heads out. She has work to do.

She calls Biker.

"Hello, Ro Ro. What happened to Junior?" he asks.

"Somebody used his head for batting practice. Poor Junior took a terrible whipping. No sign of forced entry. No weapon on the premises.

Docky is on the case. He and Junior go way back, so I am sure Docky will scour the scene. Who is his next of kin?"

"He has a son named Malcolm X Abdullah. Apparently, Junior's wife Gloria left him some time ago. I called Malcolm and asked him to come in to identify the victim."

"How did he sound?"

"He was less than broken up. You might say he wasn't surprised or upset. Kind of like he expected the call."

"Hmm. Please get him into the House. I want a sit-down with him."

"I already sent a car for him. He will be here when you arrive."

"Thanks, boss."

"You're welcome."

"Do you have any clue on Gloria's whereabouts?"

"No. We can ask Malcolm. I did check, and he has two charges for assault with intent. He beat both raps."

"He has juice behind him. G Town John made his bail."

Alarms go off in Ro Ro's head. "That scumbag pops up where and when you least expect. Who called in the murder?"

"We got an anonymous 911 call from a cell phone we couldn't trace. The voice was muffled, so we can't be sure if the caller was male or female, nor the ethnicity."

"Hmm, given that Al O'Grady was also murdered in his own place and the late Bart Malone called it in to divert suspicion from himself. Do you see a correlation?"

"No."

"Still, there may be a link to G Town."

"You have G Town on your brain," said Biker.

"Yes. I do."

Rowena hangs up wondering how a big-time hood and conman fit in with the son of a Doo Wop legend. Strange bedfellows, indeed. Why does Biker not connect the dots?

Chapter Two

Rowena sits across from Malcolm at a round, wooden conference table under muted high-hat lights that reflect off Malcolm's shaved head.

Malcolm X had already identified his father's body without emotion. "That's Junior."

"He was a good man," says Ro Ro.

Malcom grins above his pointy goatee. "Singing sweet does not mean a man is good."

"He sang at my wedding," says Rowena.

"Is that so? Was Mama Gloria present?"

"Yes. Where is your lovely mother living?"

"She moved back to Germantown a month ago. She lives with that jive ass honky, Peter La Greca."

"She lives with Pistol Pete? Hmm. I didn't know. Did Junior know they were a couple?"

"Sure did. The old man didn't like it one bit. Hell, I don't know why he was so pissed-off. Mama had more boyfriends than a rooster has chickens. They came in all sizes, colors, and shapes."

"We need to talk to her."

Malcolm takes out his phone. "Here's the number."

Malcolm juts out his bottom lip satisfied that Rowena has jumped at the chance of seeing and talking to Gloria. He offered her up too easily, thinks Rowena. She writes down Gloria's number.

"Call her now," said Malcolm. "Invite her and Pete over, so we can have a family reunion. My murdered father, my whore mother, her John, you, and me. And let's bring in Mister G Town John. That man is a cousin to Pistol Pete. Yeah, we can sit around the body and sing Doo Wop songs. We can start with, "In the Still of the Night," and then we can do some Lee Andrews, "Teardrops," and tie in "Goodnight, Sweetheart." That is a trifecta old Junior would have approved of."

Malcolm sits back, smirking. "I should have been a Dee Jay. I could have paired up with Georgie Woods, 'The Man With the Goods'. I could have called myself 'The Malcolm 'X-Factor' Damn!"

Rowena blanches inwardly at Malcolm's cynicism. There is a lot of hate behind his black-rimmed glasses.

Rowena slaps the table. "Great idea. I like it. Doo Wop in death. Murder in street corner harmony. Too damned cool."

Malcom turns his head away. She has caught him off guard. He learns that Ro Ro Morse does not shrink when challenged.

Ro Ro points a finger at him. "You are a creative man. So, cipher me this. Who wanted to kill Junior so viciously? CSU counted twenty-three wounds on Junior. That is a lot of swings for one man. Maybe it was a team effort. Got any ideas?"

Malcolm's eyes narrowed like a cobra ready to strike. "Maybe I do." "Who would be your top suspect?" "I would not want to reckon." "How about G Town? Junior owes him money?" Malcolm rubs his goatee. "I choose not to speculate."

"Just share your gut instinct."

"You are a pushy lady. I don't like pushy women."

"Me, pushy? No. I'm curious, that's all."

Malcolm stands, "I got to go."

"Wait, I will call Mama and Pete and G Town, so we can serenade Junior."

"Kiss off Detective," he says and hurries out the door.

He knows more than he said.

She calls Gloria, Pete answers, and she tells him to come in and bring Gloria, immediately.

Biker and Docky enter the conference room, each sporting furrowed brows. "We have some news," says Docky.

"Let me guess," says Ro Ro. "There were multiple attackers."

Biker nods, "Right, as always."

Rowena shakes her head. "What did Junior do?"

Docky holds his palms up. "Doo Wop was not always clean and pure. Y'all, 1 remember Bob Horn, the first host of *Bandstand*. He had drinking and underage girl problems. Sam Cooke was murdered most likely because he fooled around with a prostitute in LA."

"True business," says Biker. "Junior did some lame things to youngsters."

"Is nothing sacred?" asks Rowena.

Chapter Three

Rowena first met Gloria Altomare Jones through Rowena's dead ex-husband, Ricky, who lived next door. Ricky introduced Ro Ro to Junior via Gloria.

Gloria enters the conference room ahead of Pistol Pete La Greca, a cousin to both the Altomare family and G Town John Mancuso. The West Mount Airy Italians settled into a neighborhood along Mount Pleasant Avenue called "Goat Hollow". The immigrants from Southern Italy raised goats to feed their infants on goat milk. It was said the goat milk made them strong and hardheaded.

Gloria's long black hair hangs below her shoulders. She looks chic in her charcoal gray pantsuit. Her violet eyes glow like gems.

Pistol Pete is two inches shorter than Gloria. Built like a brick shit house, Pete's shoulders fill out his herringbone sports coat. Balding, he combs his hair straight back. His thick fingers could crack a walnut. The two sit, side by side.

"We are so sorry for your loss," says Rowena.

Gloria smiles at Rowena and squeezes Pete's hand. "No tears here. Junior and I split a long time ago. Malcolm verified the identity. So, why are we here?"

Pete sneers, "We don't like youse cops. Youse are always out to screw the little guy. Youse worse than street punks, and don't think I don't know that mirror is two-way. Who's on the other side?"

Ro Ro resists the urge to smack Pete across his face. "She's Snow White?"

"Very funny. It's probably that jerk off Biker who got you all riled." Pete flips the bird at the mirror. "Here's to you, Biker."

"Where were you two last night?"

"Home in bed," says Gloria. "We like to screw."

"I heard, and you like to share the wealth. Very Christian of you," says Ro Ro.

"Don't get smart," says Pete.

"Pistol Pete is a cartoon cowboy. An ugly little dude with a scruffy mustache. You carry the moniker, so just answer my questions, and forget the macho bullshit. Got it?" asks Ro Ro.

Gloria put a hand over Pete's mouth. "We were home all night, and of course we have no witnesses to prove our alibis."

"Understood. Who do you think had it in for Junior?"

Pete shoves away Gloria's hand. "Junior weren't no saint.

Lots of people had reasons to hate his guts."

"Pete, stop," retorts Gloria.

Pete glares at Gloria and then at Ro Ro. "You women think you are so damned smart. He used women like youse as rag dolls. Especially the real young ones. Tell them Gloria. Tell them that Junior was part of the Bandstand shenanigans, and more. Tell them the truth, so we can get the hell out of here."

Rowena's heart rate pounds. "Tell us Gloria," she says.

Gloria's hands are shaking. "My husband was a pedophile. I left him when I caught him bathing Malcolm. Only he was doing more than washing him. He was abusing him. God forgive me for ever marrying that pervert. I need a drink. I need a lot of drinks."

"Why didn't you come forth sooner?" asks Rowena.

"I didn't want Malcolm in the news. It would have destroyed him. His friends would have teased him. God knows what would have happened to him."

"Are youse happy now?" asks Pete.

Ro Ro leans close to Gloria. "You just gave us a motive for killing Junior."

Pete stands up; he curls his fists. "Hey. There is a bunch of ex Bandstand kids and others out there who wanted to cut Junior's nuts off. Check the internet. Go on and check it out. We ain't saying another word without a lawyer present. We are leaving. Come on, Gloria."

Gloria stands, tears streaming down her face. "I am glad he is dead. Glad. Now I can sleep without dreaming about what Junior did to my son and lots of other kids."

Ro Ro waggles a finger at Gloria. "Don't go far. We need to talk again and do bring an attorney."

"G Town John's attorney is our attorney," says Pete.

"Did G Town know about Junior?"

Pete shrugs. "Who knows what the man knows? Why'nt you ask him?"

"You bet, I will."

Biker enters and gets chest to face with the shorter Pete. "Hello Pete."

"Goodbye Biker," says Pete, as he escorts Gloria out the door.

"I cannot believe Junior was a pedophile," says Ro Ro.

"Did you see that movie Spotlight? Did you read the Inquirer story on the priests teaching in our schools? Hell, I can believe a Doo Wop street singer can be a pedophile. I've seen lots of freaks. I can name judges, politicians, entertainers. Six years in Vice turns up the bottom of the sewer."

"How about G Town?"

Biker cracks a toothy smile. "The dude is a chick magnet. Maybe you got something for him the way you keep talking about him."

Ro Ro stiffens from head to toe. Biker hit a nerve she does not like, nor dare admit. Physical power turns her on.

"I am going to do some Google searches. I will start with Malcolm and Junior, and anything with the keywords 'Bandstand', 'Junior McCall', 'Malcolm Abdullah', or 'child abuse'. And one more. 'John Mancuso'."

"Girl, you got G Town phobia," says Biker.

Ro Ro's inner antenna switches on. Why is Biker trying to steer me away from G Town? Curiouser and curiouser.

She runs multiple searches, looking for a common thread linking Junior to child abuse but no luck. She then runs searches on Malcolm X Abdullah, child abuse victims, and counseling. Bingo!

Malcolm runs a counseling center for child abuse victims called "False Music Academy." The Academy is located on 532 West Chelten Avenue, second floor, in Germantown, six blocks from the Fourteenth District. She does a property search and finds out the building is owned by G Town Properties. And G Town Properties is owned by You Know Who. The door to her office opens. "How is the search going?" inquires Biker. She kills the screen. She forces a smile. "Nothing yet. I'll let you know if I find anything."

"Please do that. Maybe you should call it a day," he says.

Ro Ro fakes a yawn, stretches. "Good idea. There's no sense chasing ghosts."

Biker nods. "As always, Ro Ro knows best. I am outta here."

Damned right I do.

"Good night, boss man."

She waits a full five minutes before she drives away from the district, circles to the left and parks across the street from False Music Academy. Biker's black Mustang is parked in front of the building. Peter La Greca emerges from the building and waves at Biker to come inside. Ro Ro feels the sinking rock of betrayal weigh heavily in her belly.

Lies, lies, lies, she thinks as she drives away, needing a shower and a glass of wine to help her sleep.

An hour later, wrapped in a pajama gram Snuggie, a gift from a man named Harry Smythe she dated twice before kicking him to the curb, Ro Ro opens her email. She deletes the junk mail. A query from the dating site Plenty of Fish catches her eye. A man named Eric likes her profile. She's written that "she does not suffer fools–men need not apply." As a police officer, she will lock up a married man, and fools will be sent to Norristown State Hospital.

Usually that statement scares off the phonies and triflers.

Eric replies, "Not guilty on all counts. The ball is in your court."

She replies, "Okay. You are innocent until proven guilty. Pick a spot for coffee in Chestnut Hill on Saturday morning. Starbucks?"

She falls asleep, wondering why she never quits looking for an honest man in a corrupt world.

Stubbornness leads to frustration.

Chapter Four

Ro Ro assembles a two-detective team for her raid on The Music Academy. Detective Walt Biel is an old-time cop. Built like a pro football offensive lineman, Walt is as smart as he is beefy. His partner "Iron Mike" Postello was an Italian version of Walt. The Pillars of Hercules.

They watch as Malcolm and twenty-two others clamber up to the second floor. They are mostly older people, some using walkers. Not exactly a hit squad, Ro Ro muses to herself.

Ro Ro double-checks the warrant signed by Judge Alfaro, a horny old Italian judge. Cleavage opens a lot of doors. "Let's go," she says.

The detectives burst through the closed doors.

"I am Detective Rowena Morse conducting a legal search of these premises regarding the death by homicide of Junior McCall. You are all subject to search as material witnesses. No one is under arrest or suspicion. Please empty the contents of your wallets, purses, backpacks. Any drugs will be confiscated. Any unlicensed weapons will be confiscated. Do not try to leave, or these detectives will stop you. Trust me, they can stop fast-moving trucks."

Malcolm fumes from cheek to cheek. "Show me the damn warrant."

Ro Ro hands it to him. "It's in order."

He studies it and hands it back to her. "Right as rain. What are you looking for from these fine people?"

"The truth. Junior got his brains beat in by a crowd of angry people. Maybe this crowd did it or knows who did it. And do not BS me that none of you know anything. I did the research. Junior was an abuser, but nobody has the right to take the law into their own hands. If some or all of you did a beat down, fess up now and I can help you. If you button up, I will have no choice but to press charges to the hilt."

She pauses for effect. Lots of eyes are cast downward. Others turn away. No one looks her in the eye.

"Okay. Have it your way. Take out your IDs. I want your exact whereabouts, 24/7, for the last three days. Do not dare lie to me. Lies make me Irish angry. Even my freckles fume."

While the detectives gather the info. Ro Ro pulls Malcolm aside. "Look Malcolm, I know G Town is behind this so-called academy. Tell me how he fits in. Money laundering is my first guess."

Malcolm's eyes flutter from side to side. "G Man got more spies than the CIA."

"Do you have something for me?"

Malcolm's hands shake. "Can't say here."

"Shove me hard," she said.

Malcolm pushes her hard against the wall and shouts, "Bitch!"

The two detectives grab Malcolm and slam him against the wall. Ro Ro slaps cuffs on him and drags him to the door. "You are under arrest for assaulting a police officer."

She yanks him out of the room and down a flight of stairs.

"Okay Malcolm. Tell Mama Ro Ro what's on your mind."

Malcolm nods. "I was ashamed of Junior. He were not the only Doo Wopper that fooled around but he was wrong. So, I started this academy with money he gave me. But the dough ran out. So, Mom borrowed from G Town John. G Town kept raising the Vig. Then he started shaking down the folks. Got so everybody was into G Town. Then Junior got a bug up his ass. He started his own shakedown. Things got out of hand. Junior started shooting his mouth off. Then Pete came into the picture. He said we should teach Junior a lesson. Make him a piñata, a symbol. So, we got Junior drunked up and we all took turns whacking him about the head and shoulders. Then Pete took out a Louisville Slugger and beat Junior over the head, right in front of all of us. We tried to stop him, but it was too late. Pete said legally we were all to blame. One talks, all go to jail."

Ro Ro drops her face into her hands. "Will you all testify?"

"G Town will kill us."

"No, he won't. Leave it to Ro Ro."

Malcolm shakes his head. "I will need more than good intentions."

"Work with me."

She calls G Town John.

Chapter Five

She pulls up to G Town's house and moves a half block away. She opens her email, happily finding a new message from Erik, complete with a photo. He is no movie star, a little overweight, follicly-challenged but certainly a decent looking man. And he is not a cop.

He has a Masters in English Lit. He has traveled to Italy, Ireland, England, and a lot of the United States. He should not be a bore.

G Town welcomes her with a leering smile. "Hey, Ro Ro."

"Hey yourself. Got wine?"

"Does a cat got fur? Red?"

"Indeed."

John pours a couple of glasses quickly and hands one of them to Ro. They click glasses, gently. "Cent'Anni," he says.

"You know what Peter did, don't you," Ro says and smiles widely. G Town says nothing but looks her in the eye, intently.

Peter arrives less than a minute later, sauntering into the kitchen. "What the hell is the cop doing here?" he asks.

Peter does not sit down. He stands still like a rat who just realized he has chased the cheese into a trap.

"What's the deal?" asks Pete.

G Town pours Pete a glass of wine. "Drink it, Pete."

"No, I sense a set up."

"Suit yourself. Here's what is going down. Ro Ro likes you for killing Junior. She wants you to confess to self-defense. The deed goes in as accidental homicide. No jail time. In exchange, I give up my interests in the Doo Wop Academy. We all get a walk. She has no evidence."

"Malcolm is my eyewitness. He and twenty others. Now do as I say, or I hand you to the DA with sworn statements from a bunch of senior citizens that you swung the baseball bat first. You did it, Petey boy."

Pete shakes his head from side to side. "I don't like it."

Ro Ro takes out her handcuffs, spins Pete around and clamps the cuffs on him.

"You have the right to remain silent."

"Whoa. Hold the ponies. Unhook me."

"I would rather lock up this armpit with ears."

"Hey stunod! Play ball or go to jail," says G Town.

"Why do I have to carry the freight?"

"That is what mules do. Cop a plea now."

Pete shrugs. "Hell, I'll beat this wrap."

"Tell it to the judge," she says as she drags him by the cuffs to the door.

Ro Ro closes the case. No way could she have gotten a clean conviction. At least, she could listen to Doo Wop without shuddering. Or could she?

Late at night, she lies alone, in bed, her gun at her side. Naked, feeling that she has lost an old friend, the music of her parents, the melodies of a simpler time, a more sanguine day.

The Five Satins crooned street corner sweet the song "In the Still of the Night."

A calm feeling eases her, a timeless calm, a sense of peace beyond all understanding, a oneness with God. Music that sounds like a prayer.

"Who tried to kill me?" she asks the walls.

Story Three: Murder in Tranquility

Chapter One

Valley Green Inn

To Philly people, the name conjures up the best of Philadelphia's history dating back to William Penn himself. The inn hosts a restaurant, banquet rooms, and dining tables and chairs on a wooden porch overlooking Wissahickon Creek, coursing through Fairmount Park, and eventually emptying into the Schuylkill River. Legend claims George Washington slept there.

On bright summer days, children toss chunks of bread to mallards from the creek side bank. The laughter of preteens and harmless ducks meld into a cacophony of youthful innocence. Harmony amid the chaos of a modern city.

The summer sun peeks over the pink and gray horizon as Ro Ro kneels beside the body of a young Black youth identified by the driver's learner's permit in his wallet as Darnell Wayne, sixteen, residing at 254 East Meehan Street, Philadelphia. He is clean shaven and dressed in black trousers, a white shirt and black tie. A garish red blotch of fresh blood smeared across his chest. He had been shot by a rifle fired from across the creek. Whoever made that shot was an expert. She'd check local shooting ranges for a list of experts.

CSU crew chief Docky Poteet taps her on the shoulder. "You better catch the scum bag what shot this boy," says Docky.

"I catch them all, don't I?" asks Ro Ro.

Docky nods. "Yup. Pay attention Miss Ro Ro. This boy is known to me. Darnell is the godson of your boss, Biker. He is a good one."

Ro Ro let the impact of Docky's comment sink in. "He was ambushed from over there," says Ro Ro.

"Yup. The question is why? That boy was no gang banger. He was headed to college. He takes the bus from Mount Airy to Germantown Avenue and Willow Grove Avenue and then walks over a mile to work at the Inn. I will do a tox screen but as sure as I am Black that boy is clean."

"Got it. Did you call Biker?"

"Yup. I suspect he will be here shortly."

Three squad cars had sealed the road and the officers had yellow taped the crime scene.

"Who found the body?"

"Some kid named Jason Moran, according to the officers. They took him inside. Apparently, Jason was supposed to meet Darnell, but when he got here Darnell was lying dead. I tested him for gunshot residue. No trace. The Officers escorted him inside the Inn. Wait until you meet the manager. He looks like he fell out of a cartoon. Yeah, a real Pee-wee Herman."

Ro Ro heads toward the Inn, mindful that the picturesque, tranquil creek side is now a crime scene. The ducks squawk for their crumbs of stale bread. Their feeding time is all day, every day, murder or no murder.

The eternal tranquility of the dumb ducks in this world.

Chapter Two

Ro Ro wants to talk to Jason but figures that waiting would unnerve him, so she opts for Pee Wee Herman.

Inn Manager Terence Stoudt sits across the white linen tabletop sipping chamomile tea from a flowery porcelain cup, his name painted in calligraphy around the rim of the cup, his brows knitted above his light blue eyes, his thin lips held up a pencil thin mustache, neatly trimmed and waxed.

"Tell me about Darnell," says Ro Ro, feeling like she is interviewing a mannequin.

"Darnie was a dear. He brought his smile to work with him every day. We all liked him." His high-pitched voice scratches under her skin.

"Did Darnell have any enemies or any disputes with his colleagues?"

"None I'm aware of."

"What about the customers? Did he spill soup on anyone or annoy a customer for slow service?"

Terence sips his tea gingerly, holding the handle with his pinkie raised. "No. He was a good bus person. As soon as he turned eighteen, we were going to make him a waiter. He had earned a step up in position. He wanted the extra money, so he could buy a car."

"How about romantic interests? Was he involved with any of the staff?"

Terence sits back, leaning to one side. He crosses his legs as if meditating. "There was some gossip about Terrence and our other bus person, Jason."

"I see. I understand that Jason found the body. Tell me about Jason."

"Oh, Jason Moran is a street urchin from Roxborough. The eldest of five, he often says with his Irish pride lit up like a Christmas tree. Would you like to talk with him? I can fetch him forthwith."

The old English terminology sets off the "I am dealing with a phony" alarm. Plus, he seems anxious to stop the questioning.

"I am not done with you, Terence. How long have you been the Manager at the Inn?"

"Four years. Why is that important?"

"This is a murder case, Terence. Everything is relevant until I find the murderer. Have you had any personal involvement with Darnie, as you call him, or Jason?"

Terence freezes for a tell-tale second. "No. Of course not. They are minors. Gay does not mean stupid. Besides, I was having tea in the kitchen until I heard the police sirens. Two members of the staff will confirm where I was."

"Was Jason with you?"

"No. I do not know where he was."

"Fetch him forthwith for me."

"Will do. Are we done?"

"For now."

Terence waves a salute. "Adieu."

Jason Moran has the freckled face and red hair of an Irish choir boy. But his piercing blue eyes suggest the clever instincts of a streetwise kid who could handle himself. Tall and wiry, his muscular arms, adorned with tattoos of a snake on the right and an eagle on the left, suggests a connection to a local gang or Neo Nazis. So, what is he doing employed at a prestigious place such as Valley Green Inn?

"Hello Jason. I'm Detective Morse. Please sit. I need to ask you a few questions. First, please, show me some ID to prove you are Jason Moran."

He takes out his driver's license and flips it onto the table, muttering, "Dumb slut."

Ro Ro's eyes light up. "I see you are eighteen as of yesterday. Happy Birthday and welcome to the adult world."

Jason flops onto a chair. "I don't know squat."

Ro Ro slams her fist on the table. "Just answer my questions truthfully, or I will run your punk ass into the Fourteenth District and hold you as a material witness. We can get you a couple of nice guys to keep you company for a few hours. Am I clear?"

Jason's eyes narrow to thin slits of palpable hate and fear.

"Answer me, punk, when I ask you a question. Is that clear?"

He smirks, "Yeah. You are clear."

"Good to hear. Maybe you are smarter than a rock. Now tell me how you found Darnell this morning."

Jason fidgets.

"We were supposed to meet to talk about Terence. The perv was hittin' on both of us. At first, we were going to threaten to report him to the cops if he didn't quit. Then, Darnell came up with the idea of blackmailing the prick. We told Terence we wanted fifty grand apiece. We were meeting today to close the deal. But, as I was walking up to Darnell, he crumpled like a busted balloon. I never heard the shot."

Professional hit, she thinks.

"Where was Terence?"

"Nowhere I could see. Man, it was like a scene from American Sniper. I ran to Darnell, but his eyes were blank. I knew he was dead. Then I ran away before the sniper could shoot me."

"That spot where he was shot is an easy shot. It was your idea to meet out in clear sight, wasn't it? Who in your gang pulled the trigger?"

Jason turns white as a sheet. "That is fucking crazy."

"Is it? I think you sold out Darnell for money from Terence. How much did Terence pay you to set up Darnell?"

"Hey, you are nuts," he said, lips quivering in fear.

"Those tats are symbols of the Eagles and Snakes gang. Their motto was "talons and fangs of pain." They were an offshoot of Hell's Angels, and I will bet a year's salary your old man has the same tats. Has to be somebody smarter than you that planned this kill. Tell me the truth before I call the DA and get you locked up for Murder One. DAs like Death Penalty crimes."

"I ain't saying another word. I want a lawyer."

Ro Ro takes out her handcuffs and slaps them on Jason's wrists. "You have the right to remain silent ..."

Biker enters, grim faced, angry. "What 's up Ro Ro?"

"This mutt set up the hit on Darnell."

"What? Have you got evidence?"

"Am I ever wrong? Jason, here, admitted to criminal extortion which is enough for a search warrant. And, when we question his co-conspirator, Terence Stoudt, he will fess up to the plot to kill your godson."

"Take him in." Biker starts and stops. "Did you say Terence Stoudt? He comes from old money. My father worked at their estate in Chestnut Hill."

The screech of car wheels signals the escape of Terence Stoudt in his red and tan Mini Cooper.

"That is Stoudt fleeing the scene. I will see you at the station house, boss," says Ro Ro.

"And please get a warrant for Stoudt for conspiracy to commit murder, illicit sex with a minor, and sexual misconduct with a minor."

"Will do."

"Did you find a motive?"

"Terence, the boss, was hitting on the young guys for sex. They were blackmailing him in return."

"So, Terence's old money was at risk."

"Yep!"

"Nice conduct."

Ro Ro drives to the Fourteenth, bothered by the fact that Biker seems more worried about Terence Stoudt's money than he did about Terence's role in Darnell's death.

Chapter Three

Ro Ro receives a text from Biker that evening. "Terence Stoudt and his attorney will meet you in the district at ten-thirty sharp."

The lawyer for Terence Stoudt is Gabriel Porto, mouthpiece for Germantown John Mancuso. Gabe has a Law Degree from Villanova, a penchant for fast cars and easy women. They have bumped heads before, and she knows he is smart and tough. Sitting in his two-grand suit next to Terence cast doubts on who is the real money man.

The two men sit opposite her at a wooden table, their backs to the door. Gabe flashes a wide, toothy smile. "Ro Ro! Good to see you, bella. How's life treating you?"

Does he wax his mustache with olive oil? He was an unctuous man, slippery handshake, shifty eyes and matted down, coal black hair parted in the middle. A walking, stereotypical ambulance chaser.

"Cut the Italian blarney. We Irish are much better at it than you. Just tell your scumbag client that I have a witness who will testify that Terence and he conspired to kill Darnell Wayne. Your boy was being pressured to cough up some of his long green to pay off Darnell. He wanted a cheaper way out and a longer lasting solution so, he convinced Jason Moran to help him set up a hit on Darnell. Here is a copy of Moran's confession."

Gabe reads the confession. "Pure hearsay. No corroborating evidence. It won't hold up in court."

"I want the shooter, too. And I want to know if, and how, John Mancuso was involved."

Gabe sighs. "Ah, you have ta give to get. What is your offer?"

"Terence's allocution will ease his part in the conspiracy and will name the shooter and anyone else involved. The DA offers fifteen years with a chance of parole after nine."

"I cannot go to prison. It is a death sentence," says Terence.

"All you have is the testimony of a scared teenager. Nothing corroborates his story."

"Ask Terence why he takes two thousand out of his bank on the same day Jason Moran deposits the same amount."

Gabe sighs. "Terence was kind enough to help an employee in a jam."

"A ten-year-old would see through that fairy tale. The DA will press for higher charges. Terence will die in prison with a broomstick up his hiney."

Terence gasps aloud. "Dear God, why me?" Terence collapses to his knees, sobbing.

"Get hold of yourself," snaps Gabe.

"ADA Casey is an impatient man. He wants your response in twenty-four hours, or we go murder one. Life with no parole."

Gabe drags Terence to his feet. "Up you go, Terence. Atta boy. We will get back to you."

Biker enters, as if on cue. "Please turn down the deal, so I get to watch you die for killing my godson."

Biker paces around the table, hands on his hips, his brow furrowed. "I loved that boy Darnell like he was my own son. You are right about getting the shooter. He's gotta pay."

"And don't forget the man who set this up for Terence."

"How do you see G Town fitting into this case?"

"Jesus, Biker. Terence knew G Town. G Town's lawyer is defense attorney for Terence. More likely, he's here to protect G Town who probably set up the killing."

Biker shakes his head as if trying to shake off a hangover. "Damn."

Ro Ro senses Biker has a closer connection to Mancuso than anyone ever knew. Is he in G Town's pocket? The thought chills her.

"Let's focus on finding the shooter and see where that leaves us," says Biker.

"I will squeeze it out of Jason or Terence as part of a plea deal. The ADA will buy into it."

Biker's cell phone buzzes a text message. He turns away and reads it and promptly deletes the text. Biker scratches his head, a sign that something is bothering him. "Yes. That's a good strategy Ro Ro. Keep me posted."

Ro Ro senses this case will give her the opening she needs to take down G Town. But Biker may be a problem. Ro Ro loves her job partly because the force gives her assurance that the police are the good guys. Biker has shaken that trust.

When she was nine years old, four boys who let her hang out with them changed her forever. She felt a camaraderie with them, a sense of belonging. Then after a pre-Christmas blizzard while playing in foot deep snow, the boys grabbed her and shoved her into a pile of snow. They bombarded her while she tried to fight her way out. Their laughter cut her as sure as if they had used a knife to slice her. "Sissy Missy," they shouted. Her trust in them was forever lost.

She never spoke to any of the boys again.

Chapter Four

Restless at midnight, Ro Ro decides to take a ride and listen to smooth jazz. The ride takes her into Chestnut Hill. She winds the car along the tree-lined dark streets, past the Philadelphia Cricket Club, lighted so well its grass tennis courts shine like newly minted dollar bills. The stately, colonial style brick building offers her a view of old money, Terence's old money and influence and power. All she has is the law and her badge. But that would be enough for her to live a good life.

As she approaches Saint Martin's Lane, Biker's Mustang crosses her path. She slows so he does not see her. She follows him to exactly where she fears he is headed, the home of John Mancuso.

Mancuso greets Biker with a hug, but Biker shoves him aside and charges into the house yelling, "Why?! Why?! Why?!"

Security cameras are placed all around the house. There is no way she can get close to the doors or windows without alerting Mancuso. It is clear Biker has sold-out. He has been her mentor for over a decade. Heartsick, she hunkers down, feeling tired to her toes. Half an hour later, Biker comes out, slamming the door behind him. He starts the Mustang and speeds away, unaware that Ro Ro is tailing him.

He runs a red light at Germantown and Willow Grove Avenues. His Mustang bounces along the cobblestone street. Biker is emotional but not reckless. What has him so excited?

Ro Ro carefully runs the red light and catches the Mustang stuck behind a bus at Allens Lane. She keeps her distance.

Biker pulls over at O'Grady's Tavern. A man comes out and hands him a large manila envelope. Pay day.

She tails him to his house, and then she turns around and heads for the residence of G Town John.

Motion-sensor lights flood G Town's porch as she approaches his front door. She feels exposed, vulnerable, and wary. G Town opens the front door, a quizzical smile across his chiseled jaw. His biceps bulge from his sleeveless tee shirt. His thick black hair piled atop his massive head. He looks like Rocky Balboa ready to win a championship.

"Well, what brings Ro Ro Morse to my home?"

"I hear you have good homemade wine."

"Come ahead. We will share a glass."

Sitting at the kitchen table under a bright ceiling light, Ro Ro sips her wine, wondering if meeting him alone is a mistake. Playing hold 'em has taught her that sometimes you must play on instinct.

"I won't keep you long. I'm here to make you an offer."

He sits back, displaying the body language of an interested man. "What kind of deal?"

"A business dealing. I want a piece of the action from you and Biker, and don't deny he's in your pocket. I know all about the O'Grady Tavern deal. You guys set up Bart Malone and used him and then killed him. Don't deny that either. This is good wine. Did you make it yourself?"

G Town leers at her, undressing her from head to waist. "Nah. My eighty-six-year-old Uncle Giorgio makes three barrels every year. When he dies, the wine dies. Why should I even think about paying you one cent? What do you bring to my table except great boobs?"

"If you don't throw in with me, I go to Biker and team up with him. And you go bye-bye. You would look good in orange."

"Ain't you something? Ricky did not deserve you. Let me mull it over."

"You have twenty-four hours. One more thing. I want the shooter of Darnell and don't say you cannot deliver him."

"Why is a skinhead punk so important to you?"

"I am a cop. Even a dirty cop wants a collar. I want him for myself."

"Let me sort this out."

Ro Ro finishes the wine, rises, and sticks out her chest. "Twenty-three hours and fifty-nine minutes."

She starts to leave but G Town pulls her around by the arm and presses his chest against her. He backs off when she pushes the barrel of her gun against his groin. "The only bang you will get will come from my thirty-eight. Her name is Gloria. It is not wise to piss her off."

G Town backs off, his hands up in mock surrender. "Non più."

Her heart beating like a tom-tom, she backs away, and her eyes lock with G Town's. His eyes are sharp as ice picks. He scares her, even though she holds the gun.

"Don't ever mess with me or I will make G Town stand for Girlie Town."

"I get you."

"You better."

At six AM, she rolls over just in time to hear her cell buzz the arrival of a new text. She reads, "Jeremiah Anselm Mathers, Jason Moran's stepfather living in Roxborough near Fairmount Park."

She has her killer's name and G Town in her pocket. *This will be a good day,* she thinks, *if no one kills me.*

Chapter Five

Backed up by a six-man SWAT team and accompanied by Biker and Docky's CSU team, Ro Ro stands behind the cover of a squad car, her bulletproof vest mashing her chest. She calls out, using a megaphone toward the stucco and frame house of Jeremiah Mathers.

"Jeremiah Mathers. This is the Philadelphia Police Department. We have a warrant for your arrest for the murder of Darnell Wayne. Come out now."

A minute passes before Mathers opens the front door carrying a twenty-gauge shotgun. He holds it waist high against his faded denim overalls. He wears no shirt to cover the tattoos spread across his shaven chest, arms, and grizzled face, sunburn red from a lifetime of cheap booze. The man is smiling.

"Go to Hell, you Commie bastards," he cries out. He fires a blast from the hip. A hail of police bullets brings him down in a bloody mass. One of the police bullets grazes Ro Ro's cheek. Blood trickles down. Biker stands behind her, grim-faced and glaring. It was a warning shot.

She must have scared G Town more than she had realized. Or was Biker the one afraid of her?

The whole affair is messy. G Town is an organized man. Biker is no fool. The extortion scheme was sloppily executed. Maybe the so-called brains behind the caper is someone else. Maybe Darnell Wayne had inadvertently caused his own execution?

Docky stands at her side. "Come with me," he says. "I want to see how the devil lives."

Ro Ro and Docky walk inside while the CSU team works the area around the body of Jeremiah Mathers.

A confederate flag drapes across the wall of the living room and a swastika painted in red and black garnishes the wall above the mantle over a faded red-brick fireplace.

The threadbare, gray pile carpet is smudged from wall to wall.

A deer head hangs above a flat screen television.

Dirty dishes and silverware cover the stained sink. A PC sits on the Formica 1960s style kitchen table. "Docky, I need to check out this PC myself. Tag it so we keep the evidence trail clean. I will return it to the evidence room."

"Okay. I'll tag it. Be careful. It is evidence and I am responsible for maintaining it."

Ro Ro takes the PC out the back door and edges past Biker, who is smoking a cigarette and talking to the CSU team. She has not seen him smoke in over two years. Her hope is that there is something in the files that will incriminate G Town in Darnell's murder.

She pops the trunk and slides the PC under a sandy beach blanket.

Biker calls out. "Morse. What are you doing?"

"We must close the file on Darnell. The family needs closure."

"We will try to match the gun evidence of Darnell's case to one of the guns we find here. That will cinch it."

Biker nods. "CSU will do their job. Head back to the House and do your report. Put it on my desk before you leave."

Ro Ro flashes a quick salute. "Yes, sir. See you at the House. Biker, may I ask why you are smoking again?"

Biker winces at her cynicism. "That is my business. Now get going, detective."

"Maybe one of these clowns tried to kill me?"

Biker's jaw stiffens like she has slapped it hard. "No way. Now get your report done."

Ro Ro relishes mining files for evidence. It's cyber hide and seek. Jeremiah has made it easy by taping the password "091101" to the side of the PC.

She notes the dozen or so porn shortcuts on the desktop and opens Word. She scrolls through the documents until she sees the title, "Valley Green ONE."

The document is a carefully mapped outline of the dimensions and firing points for the murder of Darnell. The plot measures distance and height from two points on the far side of the Wissahickon. So, was there a second shooter? Did the second shooter fire at Darnell?

Her stomach tightens. The date on the document is three months away. The shooting plan was for a Sunday in early September at noon when the creek side would be packed with kids feeding ducks. They would be the ducks in the barrel. Darnell must have found out about the plan, so they set him up in their killing zone. Terence was the patsy.

She returns to the files but finds nothing more. On a hunch, she checks the porn sites. The first six were standard X-rated softcore scenes. The seventh reveals a man dressed in black holding the severed head of a white child. ISIS! ISIS and Neo Nazis in cahoots! Valley Green is a perfect candidate for a terror attack. They'd ruined their own plan by killing Darnell. Stupidity had saved the lives of dozens of children. Maybe there is a God.

She shuts down the computer. She has to tell Biker what she found, but only with Docky present. She needs a stiff drink to drown the nausea and fear roiling in her stomach.

No one is safe in Philly. Not even in Valley Green.

Epilogue

For a week, the press hails her and Biker and Docky as heroes. Ro Ro is interviewed on four national television networks and honored by women's groups across the country. A promotion comes through accompanied by a nice raise. Mom and Dad would have been proud of "the little girl that could."

At first, she savors the limelight and attention from countless men who tweet her asking to meet. But she cannot believe the fact that she has been more lucky than smart. The recognition feels shallow like some ill-gotten gain flung on her by the gods of mindless luck. Like hitting the lottery. She cannot reveal that Biker is a dirty cop. That G Town John has probably set up Terence as a patsy. Her fame is gilded with lies.

Someone sends her a dozen black roses. Is it a signal that she is marked for death? There is a target on her back for sure. Who has her in their sights? G Town? Biker? ISIS?

She has learned the great lesson that Fame hides the famous from the truth but protects no one from evil.

Story Four: Murder on the Fourth of July

Chapter One

No city in America holds more Independence Day celebrations than Philly. For 102 years, Chestnut Hill has offered one special event at the Water Tower recreation playground. The day starts at nine am at the nearby Chestnut Hill Bocce Club, a venerable private club housed in an old two-story converted home on Hartwell Lane. The birthday party for America kicks off with the Grand Marshall of the Club leading a rendition of the Pledge of Allegiance. Several hundred kids from age 3 to 13, their bikes decorated in red, white and blue, parade down the street, organized by the size of the bikes from tricycles and big wheels to 16-inch bikes for judges to select three winners by category.

The parents and children then proceed to the Water Tower Recreation Center baseball field for races, pony rides, face painting, balloons, hot dogs, and bottled water. One lucky boy and one lucky girl each win a new bicycle.

A forty-five-minute magic show completes the half-day festivities.

The affair is paid for by local merchants via an ad book. The Bocce Club raises the funds and supplies about two dozen volunteers. Americana at its finest.

After the clean-up, Club members return for barbeque and beverages.

Ro Ro had paraded in the event at the ages of 8 through 11, but she had never won a prize for best decorations. Though, she never lost a race in the sprints or crab claws.

Sitting in the sun-filled rear yard of the Club with a light draft beer, Ro Ro soaks in the good vibrations of happy people, long-time friends, and laughing children. She picks out a picnic table at the far end of the yard where she could scout whoever comes in and still watch the guys playing horseshoes. She is tempted to challenge for a spot on a team but backs off. Better to watch and enjoy the banter and ball busting among the players. This is home and she was glad for a day off from murder.

The Club's President is Charlie "Chooch" Mauro. The grandson of immigrants from Calabria in Southern Italy, Chooch has led the Parade for nineteen years in a row. Ro Ro calls him Uncle Chooch, for he is a second father figure to her.

His good-for-nothing son, Gregorio, ogles her chest, his dark eyes glued to her. She waves at him, and he nods in return. They were grade school classmates until he got expelled for stealing money from the poor box, wine from the sacristy, and a gold cross from the rectory. Chooch slapped him silly in front of the priest, Father Kelly, and repaid the church for his son's thievery.

Gregorio's partner is Jim "The Jolly Green Giant" Markey. Dressed in his customary green t-shirt, he leers at her from eyes reddened by Irish whiskey and stout. Six-foot six and arms like tree trunks, he'd scare a mountain lion, she thinks.

As the day eases into evening, a warm breeze wafts across the rear yard, giving it the sensuous texture of the Mediterranean coast near the small town of Bova Marina, ten miles east of Reggio, Calabria, the toe of the Italian boot.

Germantown John Mancuso enters the yard. Dressed in a black t-shirt, a gold chain around his thick neck, tight-fitting designer jeans and black, pointy leather boots, G Town looks like a South Philly made man. He casts a six-foot shadow across the rear yard. Ro Ro is glad she is packing a twenty-two strapped under the right leg of her jeans.

Several men rush up to G Town John, shaking his hand, offering a plastic cup of beer to the local version of Darth Vader.

Chooch glares daggers at G Town from across the yard. Their feud goes back years from the time G Town allegedly date-raped Chooch's daughter, Angela; Ro Ro eases her beer aside. She needs a clear mind. G Town saunters towards her, grinning like a hungry hyena.

"You look hot, Rowena," says G Town, undressing her with the violet-colored eyes any woman would find irresistible.

"Cool off elsewhere, asshole," she says. "I don't deal with rapists very well. They get my Irish up and I get a distinct urge to castrate them."

G Town leans over the table. "I don't need to rape anyone. And if you are referring to Angie Mauro, she was screwing half the neighborhood."

Ro Ro throws her beer in his face. "Oops! Now you are cooler."

A hush falls over the yard. G Town John glares and then backs away, smiling.

Gregorio rushes over with a paper towel. "Here, Mister Mancuso."

Chooch yells out. "The dirty dago needed a bath."

Laughter breaks out. Ro Ro, previously an enemy to G Town, has sealed her enmity forever with this public embarrassment.

G Town scowls, "You are one nasty little girl who needs a spanking. Someday!"

G Town gives the giant a thumbs-up, shakes Gregorio's hand and moves to the inside of the Club. It saves him the embarrassment of losing face by retreating through the open gate he used to enter the Club yard.

Ro Ro stays half an hour and then leaves for home. It has been a good day, she thinks.

A pretty, dark-haired woman in tight jeans and a low-cut gold top runs up to her. "Ro Ro Morse! How the hell are you? It's Angela, Chooch's daughter." Angela was breathing heavily. A large handbag slinged over her shoulder. Her skimpy top and tight cut-off jeans are way too young for her, thought Rowena.

Angie embraces Rowena. "I rushed over to personally thank you for making a fool of G Town. One of my friends caught it on her cell and posted it online. Hell, it'll get ten thousand hits. The greaseball deserved a beer in the face. I should have added a shot. Thank you so much."

Rowena winces under the sweaty embrace and the fear that the press would send out a report that an off-duty policewoman was involved in an altercation with a known hood. It is bad press for the Club too. "My pleasure. But please try to get your friend to withdraw the post. Please."

Angela's eyes widen in acknowledgement. "I'll text her now." Opening her purse reveals a handgun, probably a thirty-eight.

"Done," she says.

"I must run," says Rowena.

"Thank you, again. I hope my friend doesn't get you into any trouble."

"No worries," says Rowena.

Why is it that stupid people make life so hard on smart people?

Home, she showers and changes into her pajamas. She turns on her smooth jazz and lapses into a nap. At eleven-forty-nine, her cell buzzes.

She rouses when caller ID flashes, Harley Jones.

"What's up boss?" she asks.

"We got a 9-1-1. Somebody shot and killed Charlie Mauro at the Bocce Club. Docky and CSU are on the way. Get over there pronto."

Ro Ro gasps. "What the hell!"

Is no holiday safe from murder?

Chapter Two

The Bocce Club was established as a legal not-for-profit private Club in 1933. The building was a private residence until the owners divorced, with the wife leaving for parts unknown. The Italians adopted the premises in the prohibition era as a place to drink homemade wine and play cards and bocce. Situated on a corner double-lot, the property value of the club is estimated to be over one million dollars. The club has over three hundred members, with each owning one share.

Today, the bocce courts are covered by a horseshoe pit. There are more Irish members than Italian.

The Bocce Club keeps a low profile, respecting the privacy of the neighbors. There are five televisions on the walls, so all sports can be watched simultaneously.

The oak bar seats sixteen patrons. There is a pool table at the front, a dart board toward a rear wall, and a shuffleboard table against the wall toward the rear yard. Pennants from all major pro sports teams and six local colleges, and a Marine Corps banner are spread along the walls. Photos of all past presidents hang from the highest level. The original 1933 Charter of the Club greets all those who enter. It may be the largest man cave in Northwest Philly.

Ro Ro has spent many a day and night in The Club as a child and daughter of a member. Until this moment, she had never had a bad minute there.

Chooch's body lies face down under a CSU tarp.

Docky nods to Ro Ro. "Hello Ms. Rowena. Our victim was shot twice in the back. We found two shell casings from a thirty-eight. That fact alone suggests an amateur did the shooting. No pro leaves evidence."

"Maybe the perp wants us to think it was an amateur. By now that gun is broken into a dozen pieces at the bottom of several sewers."

"Who called it in?"

"It was an anonymous 9-1-1 call, so I'm told. Maybe a throw away cell phone was used. The time of the call was just before midnight."

"Chooch died on the day he loved the most. "

"Yup."

"His daughter was here earlier, carting a thirty-eight in her purse."

Docky scratches his goatee. "Hmmm. You don't think Angie shot her daddy, do ya?"

"I will drag her in and ask her for the gun. If she denies having it, we have a suspect."

Two hours later, Angie Mauro and her lawyer Gabe Porto sit across a conference room table from Rowena in the Fourteenth District station house. Angie is red-eyed, her lips puffy and her face pasty.

"Sorry about your dad. I need to ask you a few questions."

Gabe leans toward Ro Ro. "My client is under extreme duress. Can't this wait?"

"I saw a thirty-eight revolver in her handbag yesterday as she entered The Bocce Club where her father was murdered. Angie, show me the gun."

"I don't have it. Somebody at the club must have stolen it from my bag. I swear that is the truth."

"Will you consent to a gunshot residue test?"

"She will," says Gabe, too quickly.

"Was anything else taken from your handbag?"

"Nope."

"Who do you think took it?"

"When I got home. I called my dad and told him. He said not to worry. He would take care of finding it."

"Who do you think took it?"

Angie squirms in her seat.

"She has no idea who took it," says Gabe.

"Did your brother take it?"

"I just told you. She knows nothing about who took the gun. Stop badgering her," says Gabe.

"Did 'The Giant' take it?"

"Stop it," yells Gabe.

"I want answers. She knows who took that gun. She is scared to tell me, but sure as Chooch is dead, she knows who took that gun because she gave it or sold it to whoever shot Chooch."

"You are insinuating that she had something to do with her father's murder. That is an outrageous and unfounded accusation. My client came here of her own free will. She does not deserve this persecution. We are leaving."

"After she passes the test, she can leave. Angie, why would anyone kill Chooch?"

"I don't freaking know. I don't know squat. I want to go home. Gabe, please take me home."

Gabe pats her arm. "Take the test so this she-wolf will get it in her mind that you are innocent."

"Okay, okay, okay. Listen, Ro Ro. You know I didn't kill my father. You know it."

Ro Ro senses that Angie is trying to tell her that Rowena could easily find the killer. Angie knows who killed her father.

An hour later, the GSR test came back negative. Angie got the news in the conference room from Rowena. "Can I go now?"

"Yes."

"First, I gotta go, though. Where is the ladies room?"

Ro Ro senses Angie wants her to take her and not just show her.

"Follow me. You, too, Counselor. You usually sit when you pee, don't you?"

"Wait! Get another female to show her to the restroom."

Angie pats his cheek. "Ease up Gabe. I am a big girl. Ro Ro and I go way back. Don't we Ro Ro?"

"Surely, you do. Anything she tells you without me present is inadmissible."

Ro Ro laughs. "Restroom immunity is a new clause in legal jurisprudence."

The two women enter the restroom. After checking, to make sure the stalls are empty, Ro Ro locks the door. "What do you want to tell me?"

Angie enters a stall. "G Town wants to buy The Bocce Club property, but Dad stopped it. Greg was in favor. The sale is worth two million. Each member gets one share, but G Town offered Dad a hundred grand to broker the deal and he would forgive Greg's gambling debts for another sixty grand. If word gets out I told you, I am dead meat."

Ro Ro sighs. "It always comes down to greed and G Town. Whoever he touches gets dirty."

"Me, especially," says Angie.

She returns Angie to Gabe. "Here is your client. She and I talked about her dad and what the Fourth of July meant to him as a great tradition. We will call you if any news develops."

"Call me, not her. Let's go Angie."

As they walk away, Ro Ro's head spins like a pinwheel in a gale until a dangerous but clever plan works its way into her mind.

Chapter Three

Ro Ro knew for nine months that her boss was in business with John Mancuso. Biker was street smart and well connected at City Hall. The alliance with G Town was a marriage of convenience among thieves. He had to know about the sale of The Club to a G Town front corporation. Or did he?

She sets an appointment with him to review Chooch's murder.

"Boss, I think I may have stumbled on to a motive for the killing. I was getting my hair cut when I heard one of the director's wives talking on her cell that The Club was up for sale. I didn't hear any details, like who was the buyer or for how much. Anyway, I was wondering if Chooch was a roadblock to closing the sale. He loved that club. His Great Grandfather and Grandfather were charter members. What would that joint be worth on the market?"

Biker leaned back in his round backed Captain's chair and rested his arms on the arms of the chair. Biker's brow furled in wrinkles of surprise.

"Really? I don't know a lot about real estate in Chestnut Hill, except that it's expensive. You may be on to something."

"It was hairdresser chatter, but women tell more truth in a hairdresser's chair than in a confessional."

Biker cracks a smile. "Yeah, I heard that before. Let me check it out with the boys at Licenses and Inspections and the Property department. What else you got?"

"We cleared the daughter of the shooting with a GSR test. She carried a thirty-eight in her handbag that day. I know because I saw it. She claims someone lifted it. The son, Gregorio, is a shady character. But I find it hard to believe he killed his father. The Giant was at the Fourth of July party. He is likely involved."

"You are forgetting about G Town John. You know, the guy you christened with a beer to the face?"

"Sorry, boss. He got my Irish up when he started his macho BS."

"You need an anger management class."

"I don't like G Town for the killing unless– Holy shit! What if G Town was the buyer and Chooch was blocking him? Does that make sense to you?"

Biker nods, looking past her like a man discovering truth he does not like. "Maybe. Let me think on it. Meanwhile, this is all speculation. Keep your thoughts to yourself and focus on finding evidence the DA can use in court, like the murder weapon."

"Got it. Thanks, Boss."

Chestnut Hill has a community newspaper called the Chestnut Hill Local. And an active Community Association to watchdog all new building construction and renovations. They keep out many chain stores to protect The Hill's history and culture. Ro Ro knows the editors at the Local. More importantly, she knows Tom Will, the Executive Director of the Community Association. Tom is a trustworthy man.

She calls him from her cell and tells him about the pending sale of The Bocce Club. She is surprised when Tom reveals that he knows about the possible sale but had been assured by Chooch that no sale would get past him. "Over my dead body," was Chooch's prophetic comment to Tom.

"You have a story for the Local. Club President foreshadows his murder. Please run it as a favor to me and the Community," she asks.

"Will it help you find the killer?" asks Tom.

"It may smoke out his son."

"I know Gregorio. Pig pens are cleaner than him. I will do it in tomorrow's special edition. Shall I tell the Board, as well?"

"Yes. But none of this came from me. In fact, I want you to hint that Gregorio was the source. You know, a line that reads 'a source inside The Club revealed under anonymity the details of the sale.'"

"You are a devil in disguise."

"I have been called worse."

The story hits the Local the next day.

Biker calls her to his office.

"I just saw the newspaper report on the sale of The Club. It points to someone inside as the source. Who could that be?"

"My guess is Gregorio. He is Club Treasurer."

"Makes sense."

"Shall I call him in?"

"Do it now."

Gregorio shows up two hours later with Gabe Porto at his side.

Biker and Ro Ro greet them in the conference room. Gregorio is humming "Little Bitty Pretty One," an oldie heard on recent television ads.

Gabe sits across from Ro Ro and Biker but stares at Biker only. "Why are you persecuting this family? They are burying their father tomorrow."

Gregorio needs a shave. His swarthy chest hair bulges from his open neck, plaid shirt.

"Gregorio is the Club Treasurer and who better to ask about the pending sale than the man in charge of the books and confidante to his father? Shed some light on this deal, please," says Ro Ro.

Smirking, Gregorio holds up his hands. "I cannot. I signed a non-disclosure agreement."

"So, there is an agreement," says Biker.

"There is a non-disclosure agreement regarding certain possible transactions. That is all we can say," says Gabe.

"This is a murder investigation. We will subpoena that agreement, and I know six judges who will authorize the subpoena."

Gabe shrugs. "Knock yourself out."

Ro Ro pounces. "We will also have our forensic accountants go over the books. If they find money laundering or embezzlement in any form, they will indict the Treasurer. By the way, Gregorio, can you, account for your whereabouts on the night your father was murdered?"

Gregorio pounds the table with both fists. "I was home in bed, sleeping off the sixteen shots and beers I drank at the club."

"Can anyone verify your alibi?"

"My sister Angie stayed over. She was worried about me."

"Angie was carrying a thirty-eight. You knew she had it because she got it for you, didn't she?"

"Why would my client need self-protection?"

"Because he owes G Town big bucks and if the deal fell through, Giant would squash Gregorio like a plump grape," says Ro Ro.

"The Jolly Green Giant is my friend. He protects me," says Gregorio.

"Show me some evidence of my client's crime or we are out of here," says Gabe.

"Give us the non-disclosure," says Biker.

"Get a warrant," says Gabe.

Ro Ro smiles at Biker. "I have an idea. Let's bring Jim 'The Jolly Green Giant' Markey in for a chat. Maybe he can shed light on Gregorio's need for his protection."

Gregorio's shoulders hunch like a trapped alley cat. "Leave the Giant asleep. He is a good man."

Ro Ro taps her speed dial. "Desk Sergeant. Put out a call to bring in James Markey. Send six officers so he won't feel lonesome."

Gregorio glares at her like a cobra ready to bite.

"You can go now," says Ro Ro.

Biker laughs after they leave. "That boy is one scared puppy."

"Bow wow!"

Chapter Four

Jim "The Giant" Markey smells like a stale keg of beer. His green Eagles shirt fits him like a rubber glove on a polar bear's paw. His boots are as dirty as camels' feet in a sandstorm. The odor fills the conference room so badly Ro Ro sprays air freshener for a full minute. No wonder Biker chooses to watch through the two-way mirror.

"Thanks for coming in, Jim."

"Kiss off, Ro Ro."

"We can do this fast and smooth or slow and bumpy. What is your relationship with Gregorio Mauro?"

His hands can bend a horseshoe or crush an Adam's apple. Behind those unblinking eyes, a brain is churning.

"I protect him."

"From whom?"

"From anybody that screws with him."

"Does that include G Town John?"

"It includes everybody."

"Even the police?"

"Yep. Even you."

"How about his father? Did you protect him from Chooch?"

Giant's eyes dart around the room as if he is looking for an escape route.

"I see where this is going. I did not kill Chooch. I never killed anybody."

"Suppose I told you Gregorio copped to hiring you to kill his old man?"

"That is a lie."

"Is it? The old man left Gregorio a half-million-dollar insurance policy. What was your cut?"

Giant's jaw tightens. "I want a lawyer. Call Gabe Porto and tell him to get his ass down here, pronto."

"Gabe is Gregorio's mouthpiece. He brokered the deal to pin the shooting on you."

"You're making this up. I want Gabe here now."

"Whoa big boy! I'm trying to keep your large ass out of a large electric chair. If you got something to say, now is the time to tell me."

Giant squirms for a moment. He wraps his huge hands around his head. "I did not kill Chooch. I did not kill him. You gotta believe me. I hurt people, but I don't kill people."

Ro Ro leans her arm on his massive shoulder. "Who killed Chooch?"

"Giant don't rat. I know squat."

"You know because you did it and Gregorio ratted you out. The ship is sinking, and so you'd better jump, you oversized rodent. Hurry. The water is rising and your big ass is going down like the *Titanic*."

Ro Ro texts Biker. "If he leaves, tail him. I will follow. He will lead us to the killer."

Giant lets out a groan. "Noooo. I am not saying a thing."

Ro Ro pats the back of his hand. "Jimbo. You can go. Go on. Just go. We will be in touch with Gabe."

Giant curls his lip like a hurt child. "I didn't do it."

"Doesn't matter. You have been set up. You are a patsy. Whether or not you did the deed, you will do the time."

Giant hisses aloud. "Patsy is it? We shall see."

Giant storms out. He climbs into his pickup and speeds away with Biker on his tail and Ro Ro not far behind.

Chapter Five

Giant speeds up Greene Street towards Chestnut Hill. Biker calls Ro Ro. "He's on his cell. He's probably setting up a meeting."

"Good. We can nab them both. My guess is that whoever he is meeting is armed. Nobody would take on that monster unarmed."

"Who do you think he's meeting?" asks Biker.

"Only one person could tame Goliath."

Giant turns off Greene Street onto Allens Lane and then on to McCallum Street. Right before the McCallum Street Bridge, Giant swerves left down a dirt road that leads to an open spot under the bridge and high above Cresheim Creek, a small tributary to the Wissahickon Creek. Cresheim Creek pours into two small pools, Dynamite and Polio. Dynamite was so named because legend had it that campers blew up a dam. Polio was named due to another local legend declaring it a source of getting polio from swimming in the creek water. Ro Ro pulls up behind Biker's car. Giant's F-150 is parked ahead next to a light blue Chevy Cruze. Giant is screaming. "You lied to me. You sold me down the creek. The two of you!"

Angela pulls a revolver and aims it at Giant. "Stop. Who told you that lie?"

"Ro Ro. She says Greg cut a deal. I was the patsy."

"You fool. She tricked you. Did she follow you here?" asks Angela.

"No. She was in the station house when I left."

"So, nobody knows you're here?" asks Gregorio.

Giant pauses for a second then lunges for Angela. He grasps her neck in his hands as her gun fires a shot into his chest. Wounded, he lifts her by her neck, crushing her Adam's apple. Gregorio picks up the gun and fires four times, hitting Giant twice in the chest. Giant staggers toward Gregorio but falls at his feet.

"Drop the gun," yells Biker.

Ro Ro races to Angela. She bends over the girl's twisted corpse. Oddly, lying there reminds Ro Ro of Chooch's dead body. "Gone," says Ro Ro.

Gregorio holds the gun. "I shot the old man, and I will shoot you too, I am not going to prison."

"You will die in prison," says Ro Ro.

"My old man was gonna send me to prison. But Angela and I figured everybody was better off with him dead. Hell, it was the least a father could do for his kids, you know, die for them."

Giant stirs, reaching a paw around Gregorio's ankle, and pulls him backwards off the side of the hill. It was a sheer drop of two hundred feet to the creek below. Gregorio's screams echoed all the way down.

Giant grunts. "I got them Ro Ro. See, I told you, I ain't no patsy," he says with his last breath.

"We got them all. Nice work," says Biker.

"I figured that the gunman was Gregorio. Why else would she bring the gun to the Club? My guess is that they gave the gun to Giant asking him to hide it for safe keeping. All Angie had to do was smile at him. The plan was to lead us to him, making him the patsy. It was a smart play, except I read it before they fingered Giant. A man that big does not need a gun to murder somebody. I will call it in. Docky will curse me for a week," says Ro Ro.

"Yeah. He will. At least Chooch's club will not be sold."

"That will piss off G Town John, big time."

Biker laughs. "Your silver lining?"

"Happy Fifth of July."

Ro Ro lies awake, restless, and fearful that she has precipitated the killing of three people albeit their apparent guilt. She is a detective, not God.

She logs onto Facebook. A new message from The Bocce Club flashes. John Mancuso declares his candidacy for the Presidency of the Club in the next election. Vows to clean up all corruption.

Ro Ro's work is never done.

Story Five: The Reunion from Purgatory

Chapter One

Ro Ro is excited about the grammar school reunion tonight. Philadelphia Catholic school kids identify with their grammar school classmates more than their high school classmates. She is going to see her old girlfriends and has heard that Jack Mallory, her first crush, is attending. She has found his Facebook page and photo. Jack has grayed at the edges, but his deep-set blue eyes sparkle over his square set jaw line.

"Handsome is as handsome does," she says aloud to her bathroom mirror. She's lost six pounds over the past month. She chooses a low-cut top. Her black slacks are a smidgeon tight but that is what she wants.

"I am a hussy," she says.

Holy Cross Church, School, Nunnery, and Rectory line East Mount Airy Avenue. The four structures are solid stone. The Convent was built after a passionate plea by then pastor, Father James Kelly. The man is gone in body, but his spirit dwells in the hearts of many parishioners.

Ro Ro times her arrival to enter the church after communion. She'd be a hypocrite to take communion. The Catholic Church has lost her as a member after the pedophile scandals of the Eighties.

As she walks up the marble front steps, a young nun approaches her. She does not smile or show any emotion. Her beady eyes flit from side to side as if she's hiding from someone.

"Are you Detective Morse?"

"Yes. Who are you?"

"I am Sister Mary Margaret Bolger. Mother Superior Saint Claire wants to see you in her room right away."

Ro Ro welcomes the opportunity to miss Mass completely. "Take me to her."

"Follow me."

The nun walks in tiny, rapid steps like a mouse skittering to safety from a hungry cat. The convent has no smell, but she senses an atmosphere of sterility.

Ro Ro enters Mother Superior's room to find the ninety-something-year-old woman lying half upright in her bed, her white hair dangling down her pale face. Her hazel eyes squint behind silver wire-rimmed glasses.

"Welcome Rowena. Sister Mary Margaret, please leave us and shut the door. Go downstairs. I want total privacy. Am I clear?"

Sister Mary Margaret nods demurely. "Yes, Mother Superior."

"You look well, dear girl. I have thought of you often. You were not the run of the mill Catholic girl. I have followed your exploits in the news. You have a reputation for cleverness and honesty, two characteristics that rarely go hand in hand."

Rowena likes the surprise compliment from a woman she has not seen in thirty odd years.

"How may I be of service to you, Mother Superior?"

Mother Saint Claire whispers. "I will be gone to God very soon. I must unburden my secret to you. Many years ago, I inadvertently overheard a confession by one of your classmates. He confessed to Father Kelly that Walter Norris did not commit suicide. The penitent confessed that Walter was tricked into hanging himself. That is murder, is it not?"

Rowena feels like the Mother has slapped her with a ruler across the face. "Yes. I suppose so. But why haven't you come forward for the past thirty years?"

Mother shakes her head slowly. "It was hearsay from a confessional. It would not stand up in court. Father Kelly would be bound by the Seal of the Confessional. Making a charge would yield no justice."

Rowena's head spins like a ceiling fan. "Why tell me now?"

"The penitent will be at the reunion. I saw the attendee list. You must catch the killer. God made you clever. Use your God-given brains and talent so this old girl can go with a clear conscience."

Ro Ro feels a headache coming on. "Mother Superior, can you tell me if the killer was male or female?"

"I have told you enough. Now you go about your business and make me proud."

Rowena knows better than to push the Mother Superior. "Yes, I will do my best."

"God bless you, Rowena."

Ro Ro trudges down the steps to the ground floor. The church crowd is emptying out. The late September sun casts a shadow over their smiling faces. She sees a dozen old friends, including Jack Mallory, chatting in front of the church. He was chatting up Barbara Nolan and Debbie Castro. The two women had been the class social leaders. Barbara has flaming red hair stretched down her thin shoulders. Smug as a queen on a throne, thinks Rowena.

Debbie has put on a few pounds in the wrong places. Her black hair is surely dyed. If anyone knew what has happened to Walter, it may well be one of the women, or Jack. They were the unofficial leaders of the class. The crowd headed to the side door of the school and the downstairs auditorium for the party.

Taking up the rear are Donny "Bobbie" Brandt and Jerry Butterworth. Donny pulls out a joint and lights it. He blows smoke toward the church. Jerry snatches the joint and tokes a long moment. They walk slowly; their heads close to each other. Donny grabs Jerry and plants a kiss on his lips.

The men giggle until Jerry spots Ro Ro. He glares defiantly. Ro Ro shrugs her shoulders as if to say, "So what?"

Jerry nods, smiles, and half drags Bobbie away.

Which one of her classmates had confessed to murdering Walter Norris?

Chapter Two

Ro Ro calls Biker.

"Biker. I'm at my grade school reunion, and I may have caught a case."

Biker laughs out loud. "Only you could find murder in a confessional."

"How did you know?"

"What?"

She tells him about the story Mother Saint Claire told her.

"Well, a Mother Superior is a credible witness, so I guess we can re-open the case on her word alone. You know nobody likes cold murder cases. But you deserve a look-see. What else can old Biker do?"

"Here is what I need. I need a list of all of Walter's classmates and their home addresses. His closest friends will be the ones he walked to school with every day. Ask Docky to read the CSU report to see if he can find anything out of the ordinary. Please ask him to check on the exact dates and times."

"Got it. I have a way to access the computer files of the Archdiocese. We have valid reason to suspect pedophilia which opens the files to criminal investigation. It goes back to the sixty-five priests we charged in the Eighties. I will get my resources on it right away."

"Boss, I'm at the reunion. Get me the info and I will stoke up a fire. Who knows whose ass I will scorch?"

"Gotcha."

The parquet dance floor of the basement sparkles in the center of the gym. A dozen round tables covered in white tablecloths and surrounded by metal folding chairs remind Rowena of the old days of dances, punch often laced with VO and for the mixers. Jack sits at a table with his back to her. Damn if he did not look handsome as ever.

Barbara and Debbie sit at his sides with Bobbie and Jerry flanking the ladies. Ro Ro heads toward the open chair.

"Hello, great people," she says to the table. A shower of greetings pours out as she sits down across from Jack.

"Just like old times," says Jack, a bottle of Yuengling in front of him. The others have wine glasses. The men drinking red and the ladies drinking white.

"How is Miss Marple?" asks Bobbie.

"Happy that I am here and not chasing some gun-toting crackhead down an alley in Germantown."

"That would scare my boobs off," says Debbie.

"Nothing could scare those knockers," says Barbara. "I wish I had them."

"Nice talk for Catholic married ladies," says Jack.

Jack rises. "Ro Ro. What are you drinking?"

"Seltzer, two cents cheap," says Rowena.

"Come on. You're not on duty," says Jack.

"Club soda is fine. Thanks, Jack."

Debbie does not like Rowena stealing Jack's attention. "Hey guys. I say the Eagles repeat as Super Bowl Champs. I'd bet on it. Any takers?"

They talk about sports and politics for half an hour before Father Kilrain taps the microphone next to the deejay. Father Kilrain is a graying, red-faced Irishman from North Philly. He has the pushed-in nose look of a street kid who fought rather than ran from trouble. He has the reputation of being a staunch Catholic conservative. He spread his arms wide under his black vestments.

"Welcome to all. Your devotion to Holy Cross is legendary and much appreciated. Before we say Grace, let us bow our heads as I read the list of those dearly departed from us and sheltered in God's heavenly arms."

He read the names but left out Walter Norris. Rowena stood. "Pardon me, Father. But you left out the name of William Norris from the list."

Father Kilrain turns brick red as he glowers at Rowena. "Those who take their own lives are damned to Hell."

"Excuse me, Father. But I am Homicide Detective Rowena Morse. I came here today as an alumnus but have recently received evidence that Walter Norris did not willfully hang himself. In fact, the perpetrator of Walter's demise is likely one of my classmates. So, let's give Walter reasonable doubt and read his name."

Stunned, the room echoes with cries of shock and disbelief. Rowena scours the room for any tell-tale looks.

Father Kilrain glares. "Miss Morse. This is an outrage coming here and talking like this. An outrage."

"So is murder an outrage. Please read Walter's name."

The priest's lips quiver in rage. "No. And, I must ask you to leave."

"Father, I cannot leave. The party is just getting started. Please go on with Grace before the meal."

"Son of a bitch. Some things never change," says Jack, smiling from ear to ear.

"Rowena. You have a hell of a nerve pulling a stunt like that," says Barbara.

"It is no stunt."

Father Kilrain looms over her. "I told you to leave. Now!"

"Nope. I paid my twenty-five bucks, and I am staying."

Father Kilrain's neck veins are nearly bursting. "Get out!" He pounds the table. "I'm in charge. You're out of order."

"What are you so afraid of, Father?"

"If Rowena leaves, we all leave," says Jack.

"Righto," says Bobbie.

"Damn straight," says Jerry.

A chorus of boos erupts. Shouts of "Stay, Ro Ro!" ring out.

Father Kilrain waves his arm in a circling pattern. "All of you get out now. I will not be bullied in my own parish."

Jack rises and stands nose-to-nose with Father Kilrain. "It is our parish, Father. Our parents and grandparents paid for every stone in the four buildings including the rectory you live in. So please collect yourself, tamp down your Irish temper, and say Grace. We are all hungry."

The crowd murmurs their approval.

Father Kilrain turns on his heel and takes up the microphone. "Bless us O' Lord for these gifts which we are about to receive from thy bounty through Christ, Our Lord. Amen."

Ro Ro nods at Jack. The man has stones. "Thanks."

Lunch is laid out buffet style for hot roast beef, meatballs, salad, rolls, with pound cake for dessert.

Munching on her meatballs, sans roll, to keep the carbs down, Ro Ro feels Father Kilrain's glare. She surmises that his anger is over the top. What does he fear? Maybe he was the priest in the confessional? Or maybe Mother Claire has spoken of the incident with him?

Barbara taps Ro Ro's wrist with a rose-colored fingernail long enough to classify as a weapon. "Ro Ro, do you really think Walter was coerced into killing himself?"

"I think it's a possibility. Peer pressure on a neurotic thirteen-year-old is a lot for a fragile boy to handle."

"Try being a homosexual in a Catholic family and school," says Bobbie.

"I see your point," says Jerry, twisting his gold wedding band.

"Hazing at Penn State is not a kid's game," says Jack.

"So, who did it? Was it Father Kilrain in the pantry with a stern lecture? Or Mother Claire with her ruler across his knuckles. It had to be someone in authority," says Barbara.

Debbie polishes off her second roast beef sandwich and washes it down with a gulp of wine. "I think Ro Ro called it right. Peer pressure is more likely. Walter was afraid of his own shadow. Anybody could have egged him on to do the evil deed."

Jack laughs. "I thought copping a feel was the evil deed."

Barbara lightly punches Jack's shoulder. "If that was so, Master Jack, you are going straight to Hell. These boobs have your fingerprints indelibly imprinted. How about you, Ro Ro? Did Jack ever scratch your boobs?"

"Only in his wet dreams," says Ro Ro.

Jack laughs. "Ro Ro. How did you know?"

"Rowena Morse knows everything," says Jerry.

Ro Ro's cell buzzes a text from Biker. "See the PDFs."

"Excuse me boys and girls. I need to step out for a minute."

"New clues?" asks Bobbie.

"I cannot say," she says, and leaves them wondering what she is up to.

Ro Ro hurries up the tiled stairs to an empty classroom. She sits in a wooden desk and opens the first PDF to a list of names and addresses for the class. She notes Walter's address and all who lived near him at the time of his death. The closest was Bobbie Brandt who lived four houses from Walter. Next came two classmates now living in other states. Barbie lived two blocks away. Jack lived the farthest, but his house was on a direct course from Walter's house. Barbie was close to Jack. Debbie lived three houses from Barbara. Jerry lived on the same street as Jack but one block closer to Walter's address.

She opens the second PDF which shows Walter's death certificate. He died on November the second, All Souls Day.

The third PDF is the CSU report. Cause of death. Hanging from a tree limb with a clothesline around his neck. No evidence of foul play. No bruises or other markings on the body. Ruling was death by self-imposed hanging. Walter surely hung himself, but what or who prompted him? She scans the rest of the list. The name James Kilrain pops up as the priest who performed last rites at the morgue.

Ro Ro sits for a long moment, cycling different theories of the crime. She has more suspects than she needs.

The Beatles song, "A Hard Day's Night" echoes up the hallway. She wants to join the party. But first, she has to ask a question of Mother Claire.

She finds Mother Saint Claire sitting upright, her wan face is marked by her misty eyes. Rosary in hand, she waves Ro Ro to come to her bedside.

"What do you want to ask me, child?"

"Mother, this is very important. Did the confessor indicate that he or she acted alone?"

Mother pauses, her eyes squinting as if she is reading small print. "I cannot recall."

"You must have known the voice. Tell me, was the voice a student's voice?"

"You know I will not answer that question. You must find the truth without my breaking the Seal of the Confessional."

"Your answer leads me in a certain direction. I think I know who coerced or, should I say, shamed Walter into committing suicide. Proving it will be difficult. Thank you, Mother Superior."

"I told you nothing."

"Indirectly, you told me everything. Good day Mother."

"Go with God," she says.

Ro Ro returns to the party as Billy Joel waxes eloquently in his recording of, "Only the Good Die Young."

Jack sits between Barbara and Debbie like a chick magnet in attraction. The dude has charm, brains, broad shoulders, blue eyes like Sinatra, and the air of self-assurance that she finds irresistible. Bobbie and Jerry are in a far corner of the room, sitting by themselves. Father Kilrain sips from a glass of red wine. He saunters toward her. "I thought you left, Miss Troublemaker."

"Why didn't you mention that it was you who gave Walter the last rites?"

Father Kilrain wags a finger in her face. "Is that important?"

"Yes."

"Why?"

"It means you were on call that night."

"I was a young priest. Newbies always get the rotten hours."

Jack appears at her side. "I hope you and Father Kilrain are exchanging Catholic charity with each other."

"I need a statement from each of you as to your exact whereabouts on the night Walter hung himself."

"How dare you accuse me of anything." Father Kilrain slaps her hard across her face. Ro Ro reels and falls backward into a chair.

The party comes to a screeching halt. All eyes focus on the priest. Ro Ro starts to rise as Jack steps in between her and the priest. "What the hell was that for, Father?"

"Impudence. Now get out of here."

Ro Ro rises. "I will go, but you can bet you will hear from me very soon. She runs a hand in a wide circle. "Walter Norris was murdered, and I know how and why." She strides away, her leather heels resounding with each firm step.

"Holy crap," someone calls out.

"Indeed," she replies.

Her cell rings just as Ro Ro enters her car. Caller ID announces Charles Poteet. "Hey Docky?"

"Girlfriend of mine. Old Docky checked out the crime scene photos and there be something mighty wrong. That boy died of a hanging but not from a tree. He was hung standing on the ground."

"Run that by me again."

"There was no stress put on that rope by a tree limb. My thought is that two people done tied a rope around his neck. One person ran north and the other ran south and poor old Walter was strangled on his feet. Then they hung him up and made it look like he killed himself. They made a noose, but the marks on his throat don't match the properties of a noose. How about that?"

Ro Ro lets the news sink in. "What kind of knot matches the marks on his neck?"

"Most likely a Scout's Knot. We used a Bowline Knot in my youth, when my daddy and I went fishing on Wissahickon Creek."

Ro Ro absorbs the new information and recycles her theory of the crime. It was willful murder and not coercion.

"How come CSU didn't see it your way?"

"They saw a boy hanging from a tree and chalked it up as one more depressed kid looking for the easy way out of life. Black letter suicide. Forensic science has come a long way in the past thirty years. I have a ton of tools and knowledge that my predecessors never dreamed of."

"Thanks, Docky. I need to think this through. Please send me a report and copy Biker. And see what you find on Mother Superior Saint Claire."

"Will do. Miss Ro Ro. Will do."

Walter was not coerced by charm or fear. He was hanged because somebody feared him.

What crime did Mother Superior overhear?

Chapter Three

Rowena learned early in her career that to find a killer you need to understand the victim. What did Walter do to cause someone to kill him?

She happily finds that Walter's mother, Ellen Norris, is still alive, though his father has long since passed. Walter was their only child. Ellen agrees to talk to Ro Ro at her two-story stone home on West Idell Street in West Mount Airy.

Ellen is a pretty, seventy-something-year-old woman with white hair cut short. Dressed in slacks and a pullover pink blouse, Ellen looks fit. They sit at her butcher block kitchen table, each cradling a white, porcelain teacup garnished with painted red roses.

Rowena tells Ellen about Docky's findings. Ellen's posture stiffens as she fights back tears. "I knew my boy did not commit suicide. My God, what kind of person kills a boy and make the act look like suicide? My husband Jeff went to his grave thinking he had been too hard on Walter. He carried a heart full of guilt to his grave. In a way, the monster killed Jeff, as well as Walter."

Tears roll down her face. She dabs at them with a paper napkin from the holder on the countertop. A parakeet chirps from its cage in the nearby den, as if joining in Ellen's sorrow.

"I will find the perps who caused your family so much pain. But I need your help."

"Of course. Whatever you need."

"I was a classmate of Walter's at Holy Cross. We did not run in the same circles. Who were his best friends?"

Ellen shakes her head as if to clear her memory. "He liked Jack Mallory and the Brandt boy and the Butterworth boy and two girls with whom he walked to school every day."

"Barbara and Debbie?"

"Yes. That's their names. Walter was shy, but I think he had a case of puppy love for Barbara."

"I see. I don't remember Walter playing any sports. How did he amuse himself?"

Ellen smiles. "He loved to read. The boy adored Nancy Drew mysteries and the Hardy Boys. He always talked about becoming a detective. And he loved taking pictures. He snapped his camera at everyone and everything. He'd take photos of the neighbors hanging clothes which especially annoyed Emily Crispo, since she considered herself a sex object and did not want photos of herself being shown about the neighborhood. Hmm. I remember Walter saying that he had lots of pictures people would pay to keep secret. He said photographing the truth could make him rich. That Walter had some imagination."

"Do you still have any of those old pictures?"

"You know, I do. They are in a drawer in his old dresser. I have not looked at them."

"Do you have his camera?"

"Yes. I kept it."

"May I see that as well?"

"Certainly. Walter would not have minded. He loved to show off his work."

Rowena wades through the pictures which consist mainly of pictures of the neighbors and his classmates and a few of Father Kilrain and Mother Saint Claire laughing together. Her heart stops when she sees one of herself bending over, her skirt hiked nearly to her butt as she tied the laces on her sneakers. There are several more of Debbie's breasts jutting out from her uniform. Barbara and Jack are kissing in another picture, his right hand copping a feel.

Bobbie and Jerry were sitting on a park bench holding hands. The two boys were ogling each other.

Candid camera.

"He was quite a photographer, wasn't he?" asks Ellen.

"Ellen, these photographs may provide a motive for why someone killed Walter. If he had other photos that he wanted to sell, where would he keep them?"

"These pictures are replicas of a harmless hobby of a thirteen-year-old boy."

Ro Ro takes Ellen's wrist. "There may have been others that were not so harmless. Walter may have been blackmailing someone."

Ellen pulls her arm away. "How dare you accuse Walter of being a blackmailer. I thought you wanted to clear his name. Now you are dragging a dead boy's reputation through the mud."

"Ellen, please listen to me. These photos may help us find his murderer. In a way, Walter is helping us find his killer. You see that, don't you?"

Ellen throws up her hands. "This is all too upsetting. I am calling my lawyer. Now, please leave."

"I will leave but first call your lawyer while I am here, and I will confirm with him that these pictures are evidence in a homicide case and any effort to suppress them is a felony for obstruction of justice and evidence tampering. I am only trying to protect you and nail Walter's killers. We can do this nice and easy by searching for more photos and negatives or you can go legal and force me to get a warrant and send a team of policemen here to search every inch of your home. It's your call. Easy or hard."

Ellen strides about the room, glaring daggers at Ro Ro. "You have a point. I will agree to a joint search."

"Good choice. Did he develop his own photos?"

"Yes. His lab, as he called it, is in the basement. He had a filing cabinet. It is still intact."

"We can start there and if we find the evidence we need, we will stop there and not check every room." Ro Ro holds out her hand. "Deal?"

Ellen holds up her hands. "Yes, but do not touch me. I already feel violated by your presence in my home."

They rummage through the desk in the photo lab but find no photos or negatives. Ro Ro has anticipated a quick find, but Walter was cleverer than she thought. The search is about to end when Ro Ro sees an old birdcage hanging from a ceiling hook. "How old is that cage?" she asks.

"That is Lulu's cage. She was Walter's pet parakeet. He used to whistle to Lulu and she would whistle back to him. He loved that bird. When Lulu died, I got a new bird. I have had a dozen birds over the years, but no other bird could fill Lulu's cage."

Ro Ro lifts the cage off the hook and turns it upside down. A large envelope is taped to the bottom. She opens it to find sixteen negatives.

"I think we hit the jackpot. I will take these with me and have them developed. Once we see the photos, I will contact you. Ellen, we may have found the motive behind Walter's death. We may have cleared him of the taint on his name as a suicide."

Ellen folds her arms across her chest. "Very well. But if you besmirch my son or my family, I will have you put in your own birdcage."

Ro Ro nods. "Please understand, I am just doing my job as a cop."

"And I am doing mine as a mother and a wife."

Ro Ro heads upstairs, wary that the hurt, angry woman behind her has become an enemy for life.

She calls Biker and briefs him about the negatives. "Please get Docky's team ready to develop the photos. I will be at the station house in ten minutes."

Her nostrils spread wide as the scent of the hunt catches her senses. The hunt is on.

Chapter Four

Ro Ro and Biker and Docky review Walter's handiwork. The photos are not blurred despite their age. She suspected a case of pedophilia would unfold. Kilrain has the demeanor of an arrogant child molester. The State had found another case of mass pedophilia in the Summer of 2018. She thought Kilrain belonged to the ring and he alone had managed to kill Walter.

Walter was a blackmailer. He had photos of half his neighbors making love. He had photos of his own parents screwing. He had Jack and Barbara going at it in a parked car behind the church, and Debbie and Jack playing hide the salami in Pastorius Park near where he had been killed. The forensic accounting team found old bank records in Walter's name going back to the time of his demise in the amount of $17,800. He did not get that money shoveling sidewalks or cutting grass.

Walter was no saint and he had made a lot of enemies.

"That boy Walter done set his own death sentence," says Docky.

"We have enough suspects to fill a penitentiary. Who did it and how do we prove it beyond a reasonable doubt? There's plenty, based on the number of people in these photos."

"Mother Saint Claire heard the perp confess. We can probably rule out the neighbors. It's not likely they were at the reunion."

"Good point, Ro Ro," says Docky.

Biker cracks a toothy smile. "Maybe this is one case you cannot lay on G Town John."

Ro Ro does not like the joke, especially coming from a man on G Town's payroll. "I went over the evidence report. The perp left his wallet, his money, and a pocketknife. One thing they took was his house key. My thought is that they wanted the pictures and only the pictures."

She calls Ellen Norris and asks, "After Walter's death, did anyone try to break into your home?"

"Well, we once came home after dinner and found the place ransacked, but nothing was stolen. I called the police, and they came and said it was probably kids looking for money or drugs."

"Was the door left open when you went to dinner?"

"We always locked our doors."

"Did you keep a key hidden somewhere?"

"Yes. We kept it in a lockbox with a combination lock. Why are you asking these questions?"

"It is a routine question."

"Routine my Irish butt. Did someone think … it's the pictures isn't it? Walter took pictures he should not have taken. Is that why he was killed? And if he was killed, then his death was not a suicide. My God, he was buried without the sacraments. I swear there is no justice. I am calling Father Kilrain. I want a requiem Mass said for Walter."

"We will get Walter the justice he deserves. Please do not reveal this conversation with anyone. Discretion is Walter's best ally. Father Kilrain will not understand. He will impede us. Do not call him. Trust me, Ellen, for Walter's sake. He will get his Mass, but you must not reveal our findings to anyone. And I mean Father Kilrain and Mother Saint Claire. Can I trust you to wait a day or two longer?"

Ellen starts sobbing. "I will do as you ask. Oh, just find my baby's killer. Find them, please."

"We will."

Ro Ro feels like someone has placed a heavy stone on her chest.

"Guys, I'm going home. I need time and sleep to sort out the theory of the crime. And a drink."

Ro Ro stuffs a copy of the photos into a large manila envelope. The film and the originals would stay in the evidence room.

She finds a corner booth at O'Grady's bar and settles in with a VO Manhattan, up, ice on the side. Halfway through the cocktail, Germantown John walks in. He spots Ro Ro, smiles and eases toward her. He is clearly carrying under his leather jacket. His violet eyes sparkle. His countenance and demeanor ooze with animal magnetism. She wishes he were a good guy.

"Hello Detective. Long time, no see. How are you doing?"

"Good until your sorry ass walked in. Get lost in traffic and make the world happy."

"Sarcasm is unbecoming from a good-looking woman."

"What do you want, G Town?"

"What I want is for us to be friends. I can make our friendship worthwhile."

Ro Ro's blood pressure spikes but she holds her curse words in. "You have enough cops in your stable. I am not for sale at any price."

"There is always a price. Sometimes it is money. Sometimes people value personal things or family or friends or their reputation. But everybody has a limit and a price."

The cylinders click in her head. "Yes, we are all subject to our weaknesses being exposed. Fear is a motivator second to only love."

"I put fear first, ahead of love. It's easier to manage. Less expensive, too."

"May I buy you a drink?"

"No, thank you."

"Always the hard case."

"Yes."

"That is too bad. I like you even though you threw a beer in my face and it went viral. That stunt was not good for my image. Certain people suggested I pay you back. But I am not a vindictive man. I let it slide."

"Thanks for nothing."

G Town salutes her and leaves, walking with the swagger of a street wise guy.

Ro Ro finishes her Manhattan, feeling the irony of a killer helping her solve a killing. She is about to call for a second Holy Cross reunion.

Chapter Five

Ro Ro stations two detectives in plain clothes on Boyer Street, around the corner from the school. She straps on her listening device. If she gets into any trouble, the back-up will know where to find her. The sun has set, and a brisk wind shakes the trees. She is purposely late for the meeting with Father Kilrain, Mother Saint Claire, Jack, Bobbie, Jerry, Barbara, and Debbie. The not-so-magnificent Seven.

She has a surprise that may cause the effect she wants: a confession.

They are seated at a round wooden table on metal folding chairs. The overhead lights are turned up as high as she can get the maintenance man to set them. No one stands to greet her. Father Kilrain growls a "hello." Mother Claire clutches her rosary stringing between her fingers.

"Good evening, Rowena," she says loudly.

The others murmur inaudibly.

"Hello boys and girls, Father and Mother. Are we not one big family? Too bad Walter could not make it. He got sidetracked thirty years ago. But, you all know that, don't you?"

Ro Ro sits down, pressing the audio button ON in her pocket. Showtime.

Father Kilrain clears his throat. "Walter Norris chose his own fate. The police confirmed his death as a suicide. Why are we here?"

"We are here because a new look at the criminal evidence has led us to the conclusion that Walter was strangled by two or more people putting a clothesline around his neck, tied in a Bowline Knot. The stranglers then ran in opposite directions, thus squeezing Walter's neck in a vise-like noose. After Walter died, the perpetrators hung Walter from a tree limb to make it appear he had committed suicide. But there was a problem. They hung him believing he had the negatives and photos on him with which he used to blackmail them. Walter left the negatives in a safe place. They are now in police custody. I have reviewed them. My goodness but weren't you all photogenic. Hollywood handsome."

Father Kilrain slams his fist on the table. "I had no part in any of this affair. Whatever these people did thirty years ago was on them, not me."

"We checked everyone's bank records. These people have been paying you to keep quiet. You sold the Seal of the Confessional for a lifetime annuity. You are a conniver and a blackmailer. You disgraced the Priesthood and buried Walter as a heathen. You let his parents suffer for your personal gain. Your greed is worse than their murdering a misguided boy. Damn you to Hell."

Mother Superior rises, the rosary shaking in her hands. "Is this true Father? Did you sell out the church? And did the rest of you do what Rowena claims?"

"Yes, we did," says Jack. It is all true. I am glad it is out in the open. I have been living in fear for thirty years. Do what you want with me. I deserve to pay for killing Walter. We all deserve to pay for our sins."

"Pay, my ass," says Bobbie. "She has no real proof we killed Walter. What was our motive?"

Rowena points at him. "You said yesterday the terror of being outed in a Catholic family is a fear no one could withstand."

"I am getting a lawyer," says Bobbie.

"Me, too," says Jerry.

"Me, three," says Barbara.

"Let's make it a foursome," says Debbie.

Father Kilrain turns on his heel, his neck veins swollen with rage.

"Come in, boys," says Ro Ro. "We got 'em on tape."

"You taped us?" shouts Barbara.

"How could you?" says Debbie.

"It's inadmissible," says Bobbie.

"My lawyer will get it thrown out," says Jerry.

"They cannot throw me out," said Mother Claire. "I knew about the recording. It is my school. As Mother Superior, I permitted the taping. That confession Father Kilrain heard was under the stain of sin. He received ill-gotten gain. I will testify I heard Jack's confession in which he implicated all of you."

She kisses her rosary. She walks up to Father Kilrain. "God, forgive me," she says as she slaps him across the face.

The back-up team enters shouting the Miranda warning. Jack smiles at Rowena. "You are too damned smart."

Ro Ro calls Ellen Norris. "Justice has been done. You can have your Mass for Walter."

Ro Ro takes statements and writes reports until one in the morning. She flees the station house hoping to make O'Grady's for a night cap.

The bartender mixes her a Manhattan. "On me, Ro Ro."

"Thanks, Matty," she says.

She has done right by Ellen. Screw that twerp, Walter.

The door opens as Matty is about to lock up. Germantown John enters. "We meet again. May I join you?"

"I am jealous of those with whom I drink. Sit down and do not try to schmooze me. Elvis, in his youth, would not be able to get me into his bed tonight."

"Who did you lock up?"

Ro Ro sighs, "My oldest and best friends. It was quite a reunion."

Story Six: Sweet Science Murder

Chapter One

At eleven PM, homicide detective Morse's cell phone announces a call from "Docky."

She is expecting him to confirm the death by natural causes of boxing champion and Philly legend, Sugar Ron Simms. The middleweight champion had been found dead two days ago in his Chestnut Hill mansion on Crefeld street. She has already received a tox report that declared Sugar Ron clean on alcohol and narcotics. Twenty-four-year-old athletes in perfect condition rarely die from heart attacks, unless they were self-induced. Homicide has been called in by the mayor who wants to cover all bases, and his ass, with the voters. Sugar Ron was a living legend.

His girlfriend, Tamika Holmes, reported the death. She and Sugar Ron hosted a dinner for Sugar's manager, Lonny Ford, his cut man Jacko Judd, and promoter Leon Rose. Their maid and housekeeper, Noreen Cooke, served the food and completed the clean-up.

"What's up, Docky?"

"My blood pressure just hit the top of William Penn's hat. I did an analysis of the stomach contents of the Champ. He was kayoed by potassium cyanide."

"What? How can you be sure? PC isn't traceable."

"The Champ has an odor oozing from his lungs that smells like almonds. The odor also oozes from his stomach. PC leaves that odor. I tested and found that the smell came from the breathing tract. But, I found no almonds. My belief is that his chest cavity was laced with potassium cyanide. His stomach, too. He may have been poisoned twice. He was murdered. That fact is as black as me and as white as you."

"Mother of God." She trusts Docky's opinion and integrity more than any man.

"Email me your report. And please take a full inventory of everything in the house, especially the food and beverages. Everything."

"Will do. Find out who killed The Champ. The city needs you to get the perp and fry his nuts on a skillet."

The dinner party has to be interviewed. She calls Biker.

"What's up, Ro Ro?"

"Docky's blood pressure and my killer instinct."

"That's scary."

She tells him about the cyanide.

"God, help me. Now my BP is soaring. We better get ahead of this before the media."

"You're right, boss. Let's get the dinner party in for questioning tomorrow, first thing. Knowing Docky's "dog with a bone" approach, he will probably work half the night, so we may get more info before the sun comes up."

"Right. I will send squads to their residences at eight thirty tomorrow.'"

"Please get 'em all into the station house and put them in the large conference room, so we can watch and hear their banter. Tell them they are all material witnesses to a murder. They are not suspects, and do not need lawyers. That dining room is a murder scene. I will interview them one-on-one in the small interrogation room. How about if we order in coffee and doughnuts to get them off guard, comfortable? Get their cells so we can track emails and they will not be able to talk with each other to compare notes. Those phones may contain evidence, so we are within our rights to investigate their contents. Get the DA to issue search warrants and search all houses, simultaneously. We are looking for poison and anything that can be used to poison someone. Okay by you?"

"Yep."

"Good night, boss," she says and hangs up.

She pours herself a decaf coffee, pours in a splash of non-fat milk and settles on her sofa to the soothing sounds of Smooth Jazz.

Her father had once taken her to the Blue Horizon boxing arena on Broad Street. She was thirteen and almost the only female in the audience among hundreds of men reeking of cigar smoke and cheap whiskey while shouting every profanity she had ever heard, and a few new ones. Her dad made her tie her hair up and bury her blonde tresses under a wool cap. She wore his baggy old peacoat to hide her anatomy.

The fights were savage, sweaty contests between fast punching, grunting young men, Philly style beatdowns. She counted three TKOs, two bloody noses, and two teeth knocked out during the matches. The whole time she wondered why in God's name her dad took her to witness this brutality with no complaint by her sainted Irish Catholic mother.

She felt faint when one fighter landed face-first, smashing his nose against the canvas. Blood spurted into the crowd. A man screeched, "What the hell? He got my shoes bloody."

The main event was for the lightweight championship of North Philly. Two young black men, their bodies sculpted into statues, faced off. They fought with a rapid-fire style, each slashing the other's face.

Then, one of the boxers launched a left hook to the other man's jaw, sending his opponent to the canvas. The hurt boxer struggled to his feet, only to receive another left hook that sent him into La La land.

Dad's face lit up like he had seen Irish angels. "Did you see those punches, Rowena? Pure poetry in action. That's why they call boxing the sweet science."

"Anybody who finds that bout sweet is sick," she said.

"You may see worse activities in your lifetime," he said.

On the ride home, she sat silent, her arms folded.

Her dad wore an old gray tweed Jeff cap hunched down to his large ears. His square jaw was set as if he had been ready for her reaction.

"Rowena. Do you know why I insisted on taking you to see the boxing match?" he asked.

"No, Dad."

"I want you to learn and remember that poor, desperate men will risk getting their brains beat out for money. Some will do it in a boxing ring. Others will take abuse from cruel bosses, so they can support their families. It's a dog-eat-dog world, my daughter, and nobody gets out alive."

"That's a gruesome thought."

"It is a gruesome world, indeed. I just wanted you to see what you may have to deal with some day. Let no one push you around and always fight to win. You cannot afford to lose."

"Yes, Dad."

The music changed to Chris Botti. His trumpet swept sweet sounds over her. Music is a sweet science, not like police work as a homicide detective. Was she living in a ring, smelling the sweat of desperate people killing for money?

The hunt for the truth is on. The bell rings in five hours for round one with her alarm-clock set to 5AM. She has research to do of police records, bank records, and tax returns on the victims as well as the dinner guests.

The state database will give her an accounting of the winnings from the championship fight and tax returns. No need to bring in the IRS. She will do the real data mining. Her math skills earned her straight As in high school and a BA Magna Cum Laude in Computer Science from Drexel night school. Her mastery of data analysis gives her the unique ability to explore the deep web.

Touch gloves and come out fighting.

Chapter Two

She starts her research at five thirty and only lets up at nine thirty. Sugar Ron Simms has a juvenile record that is sealed, but he had been clean since turning pro. Not even a parking ticket. He liked Scotch and according to his credit card receipts, his last liquor purchase included a case of Johnny Walker Black, two cases of wine, a bottle of Bushmills Black, a bottle of Jack Daniels, a bottle of sweet vermouth, a bottle of Grand Marnier, and a bottle of Amaretto. The man knew how to throw a party. He had the dinner party catered by O'Neill's. Two lobster tails per person, prime rib, baked sweet potatoes, lettuce, tomatoes, and Italian olives in a Caesar salad topped with croutons. Boston cream pie for dessert. Sugar's purse was twenty-six million on the fight which he split with Leon and Lonny. The cut man Jacko Judd got $15,000. Tamika got a stipend of $25,000. Nobody was left out, but the fat cats got the fat part of the purse and pay-per-view fees. There was more money to be had if he lived, so why would any of these people want to kill him?

Noreen Cooke got nothing. But a forty-something-year-old woman is not likely to murder a boxing champion in his home when she has nothing to gain.

So, what the hell is the motive here? And just how was it done? And, why now?

There has to be more to this tale than the eye can see.

The people who were in the house for dinner sit at the oblong conference table munching on donuts and sipping coffee.

Tamika looks drained behind her smeared-on make-up. Her braided hair hangs shabbily down to her shoulders over her black leather top. Her jeans were tighter than a wet swimsuit. Her black leather boots need a shine.

Noreen looks bewildered in a plain, gray pantsuit, baggy and in need of a pressing. Her puffy face sags. She looks like a lost dog in a cage of lions.

Lonny Ford's double-breasted sport coat, over a custom fitted white dress shirt, adorned with gold cufflinks, looks like a man used to success. His slicked back, thinning gray hair glistens under the fluorescent lights. Lonny had been a leader in the old Hortter Street Gang. He had earned his bones by stealing the book of his best friend, Eddie Rinder. Eddie was later found under the Walnut Lane Bridge. The police ruled it a suicide. The officer who found Eddie was Biker.

Leon Rose is a cunning Jewish man who could charm the habit off a nun. Leon dressed in a plain brown suit, open collar white dress shirt. His bulbous nose earned him the nickname "Schnozzer." Leon has promoted dozens of fights. Rumors abound that he has fixed more than one championship bout and had bet large on the underdog. He has ties to Germantown John Mancuso. Mancuso has more tentacles than a dozen octopi. He and Leon are a scary, evil pair of crooks.

Jacko Judd lives hand-to-mouth. He rents a furnished apartment on West Coulter Street in Germantown. He likes horses that run slower than dead men. Ro Ro feels he did not have the brains to poison a rat, let alone The Champ.

She joins Biker, who has been listening in on the conference room discussion among dinner attendees.

"Hi Biker. Have you heard anything useful?"

"Nope. They probably know we are listening in, so if they say anything incriminating it will point to somebody other than themselves. What did you find from your research?"

"None of them had a financial reason to kill Sugar Ron. He was their meal ticket. They could have fed at that trough for years. There's a motive, but it is not in the bank or financial records. I expect to hear from the life insurance company, but I suspect his insurance is a lot less than what he could have earned for them. The man was worth more to them alive than dead."

"Hmm. Keep digging. How do you want to play them?"

"I'll take Tamika first, then Lonny, then Leon. Then Jacko and Noreen last. As I finish each interview, have a uniformed cop escort them away. In fact, take them home. I do not want anybody hanging around to intimidate another witness. Let's keep the cell phones until we scrub them raw."

"Good idea. I will escort Miss Tamika to you in the small conference room."

Tamika wears two faces. Her red rimmed eyes cast the telling sign of sorrow. Her pursed lips and square set jaw line signal anger and defiance.

"Hello Ms. Holmes. May I call you Tamika?"

"You may call me Tamika. Just tell me what the hell happened to Sugar?"

"We are not sure. We need to learn more about that dinner party. I read the food and beverage list. It looks like you had a great dinner plan. Did you help Sugar Ron do the menu?"

"I did the food with Noreen. She knows what he likes. Sugar chose the drinks."

"Sugar was ready for a real celebration. He whipped his challenger like the man was an amateur. Nobody in his weight class could beat Sugar. We checked the purse. He made a lot of money. We saw that he paid you twenty-five grand. That is a tidy sum, but a pittance compared to Lonny and Leon's take. How about life insurance? Are you Sugar Ron's beneficiary?"

"Damned if I know. Listen, Miss Detective. That man was priceless to me. I am carrying his child. My heart is broken into ten thousand pieces. Screw the insurance. And screw you."

Ro Ro feels the anger is real. So is the love behind it.

"When are you due?"

"I am three months pregnant. Sugar never knew about the child. I wanted him to focus on the fight. He loved boxing. It was his way of proving he was the best. It gave him dignity as a black man. Respect was more important to him than the money."

"How was his relationship with Lonny and Leon and Jacko?"

"Lonny was his manager. Lonny saw him as an ATM. Leon is only out for Leon. Sugar was an asset. When it came time for Sugar to lose his crown, Leon would dump him like a bad idea. Jacko was and is and always will be a leech. Sugar kept him on as a favor to Sugar's dead father. Jacko was a cut man for a man who had never been cut."

"How did Noreen get hired?"

Tamika leans back. "You know, I am not too sure. She had some link to Sugar's old man. She and the old man may have done the mattress two-step. Sugar had a shepherd's mentality. He took care of people. He had loyalty. That is a quality rare in most men. You getting the picture? Sugar was a special man. People stereotype boxers as dumb asses who have no brains, no heart. Sugar had both."

Tamika looks away as tears well up.

"What did Sugar eat and drink at dinner?"

"He ate what we all ate. He drank wine."

"Did Noreen serve each meal on separate plates, or did everyone pull from a common dish?"

Tamika's eyes narrow, showing she understands the meaning of Rowena's question. "She served us separately. She presented the lobster tails around a cut of prime rib placed in the middle of the plate. Each steak was cooked to order. Some liked it rare. Some liked it well done. Sugar wanted his medium rare. He had Noreen cook to order so everybody got what they wanted."

"I see. Was dessert also set on separate plates?"

"Yes."

"Hmm. Very interesting. Did they all drink the wine?

"Yes. We had a toast to Sugar."

"Yes. I love that chocolate. He ordered it from Termini's in South Philly."

"There was a heavy liquor supply. Can you think of anything Sugar drank that no one else touched?"

Tamika ran a hand across her face until her long fingers draped around her chin. "The amaretto. That was Sugar's personal drink."

Ro Ro's brain snaps to. "I have never had amaretto. What does it taste like?"

"It tastes like almonds. I cannot stand almonds. Sugar loved them. It was his personal snack."

"Did everyone know about his penchant for almonds and amaretto?"

"Oh Yeah. Sugar munched on them all the time."

Ro Ro's head spins round to Docky. Almonds and PC together. One shields the scent of the other. She has to talk to him. She may have found the means to the murder. Now she needs to find the motive.

Ro Ro stands up to end the meeting. "Tamika, you have been very helpful. I will call you again."

Tamika folds her arms across her chest. "You think someone poisoned my sweet Sugar, don't you?"

"Don't try to read my thoughts. I am gathering evidence. When I make an arrest, you will be the first to know. Please do not reveal what we discussed to anyone lest you ruin the investigation. Keep it quiet, Tamika."

Tamika nods and rises, her back straight. "You're one smart woman. I will do as you say. I want the bastard who killed my man to fry like a cut of catfish on a skillet."

Ro Ro calls Docky and tells him about the amaretto.

"Yes, it could be that whoever dropped PC into the amaretto knew the taste of one would shield the other."

Ro Ro is ready for the next dinner guest, Lonny Ford.

Lonny Ford fills out his light brown leather jacket like a GQ model. Muscular and trim, his mustache carefully etches under his aquiline nose and deep-set brown eyes. Lonny oozes animal magnetism and he knows it.

He carries himself with the swagger of a street wise guy.

"Good morning, Miss Detective. You look mighty fine this morning. Why am I so lucky to start my day talking to a good-looking woman?"

Ro Ro wants to slap the smile from his face.

"Why did you kill Sugar Ron?"

His jaw dropped. "What the hell kind of question is that?"

"A serious one. Answer it."

Lonny holds up his hands. "I get it. I heard you were a hard ass. I killed nobody, least of all my best friend and my main source of income."

"How much of Sugar Ron did you own?"

"Forty percent. Leon owned fifty one percent and Sugar Ron owned the rest. See, Old Ron was cool enough to accept nine percent of something rather than 100 percent of nothing. You dig?"

"Yeah, I dig. You bloody thief."

"Hey, I get what I can. It is business."

"You are a shrewd one, Lonny. Real shrewd. Now, why did you kill him?"

"Cut the crap. I did not kill him. I got me a bank account that could choke an elephant."

"Yes, I know. I saw your net worth."

"You snooped me out? Damn if you ain't the Sherlock in this town."

"How did you meet Sugar Ron?"

"I knew his daddy. They called him Suede. The man was smooth and good looking. He was like radar. He could pick up women from a mile away. Anyway, he brought his boy to me after Sugar knocked out some street punk a foot taller and thirty pounds heavier. Sugar hit the fool three times so fast the dudes watching swear the punches were so fast, if you blinked, you missed the punches. We got a future champ here. Please train him like he was your own boy. I owed Suede for saving me on a bad beef. He gave me an alibi. He was a stand-up man."

"How did he die?"

"He had a heart attack just like Sugar Ron. Jacko found him. Lots of women cried at that funeral, including Tamika's mother."

Ro Ro sits back, arms folded. The man can spin a tale.

"Tell me about the dinner party."

"First off, I offered to go to the Capital Grill on my tab. Leon insisted we dine in private for fear the public would mob Sugar Ron. Tamika argued for staying home. That woman is one jealous female. We had drinks, steak, lobster, and top-shelf wine. Sugar Ron said no one eats better than we do. He died a proud and happy man. Heart attack got him just like old Suede. Must be hereditary."

"Who drank the amaretto?"

"Sugar Ron and Leon tasted that sweet stuff. I stayed with the wine."

"If you did not drink it, how do you know it is sweet?"

"That damn stuff smells sweet. I got a touch of diabetes, so I watch what I imbibe. I got to save myself for all the young women out there."

"I hear Sugar modeled his style on Ali. Hit and move and don't get hit."

"You got it, Miss Detective. Sugar was sweet. Fluid. The man had style and heart."

"How does Jacko fit in?"

"Jacko was a friend of Suede. They went way back."

"How come Jacko's take was minimal?"

Lonny scowls, his eyes narrow into thin snake eyes. "Because I said so. Sugar ruled the ring. I ruled the purse. Jacko got a nibble of the pie. I owed him nothing."

Ro Ro notes the anger and contempt.

Ro Ro stands up, ending the interview. "That is all for now. Thank you for coming in. We will be in touch. Please keep our conversation private. By that I mean do not talk to any of the dinner guests just in case one of them is a murderer."

Lonny shakes his head. "It makes no sense killing Sugar. There is no percentage in it."

"Some things are worth more than money. I will be in touch."

"Not in the boxing business," he says as he leaves.

Ro Ro signals for Biker to join her.

"What do you make of Lonny?" asks Biker.

"He would kill his own mother for money. Bring in Leon."

Leon Rose eyes her from head to toe and back up again. He offers a handshake. Hello Miss Detective Morse."

She clasps his hand and squeezes hard. "Hello Mister Rose. Take a seat."

Leon's cologne is stronger than six bottles of Ro Ro's Dolce & Gabbana perfume. His nails are manicured, and his toupée fits neatly over his ample head. His beady eyes glint behind ivory colored, thick glasses. He grins like a schoolboy eying an ice cream cone.

He is the first man Ro Ro has interviewed with six gold rings, four on his left hand and two on the last two fingers of his hefty right hand.

"This is a terrible situation with Sugar Ron. Just terrible. The man had a bright future. But I do not understand why I am here talking to a homicide detective when the man died from natural causes."

"We are reviewing all possibilities before we make a call on the cause of death."

"That's a prudent approach. How can I help you?"

"Tell me about the dinner."

"It was okay. The beef was a little tough. The lobster was a bit overcooked. The wine was pedestrian. The company bored me. Otherwise, I had a sparkling evening. I must add that it was about the caliber I expected. Sugar Ron was a street urchin with no social skills and limited exposure to the refinements attributed to cultured people. He tried hard to be classy, but either you have or do not have class. Still, he was a decent man. I liked him. Does this analysis help you?"

"Sort of. Can you offer an opinion on who would want to poison him?"

Leon's jaw sags. "Poison? How? We all ate the same food."

"Not really. Each of you were served separate dinners. And, Sugar was the only one who drank the amaretto."

Leon purses his lips and nods as if he had offered the insight. "Good thinking, Detective. I heard you were a Schmarter."

"What was your relationship with Sugar Ron?"

"I owned a piece of his earnings, and I promoted the fights, so I got fees and royalties on television and pay-per-view revenues. Yes, I make a lot of money. But I had no reason to derail his gravy train. His demise was bad for my business. Why kill a golden goose when it shits money?"

"What about Lonny? Did you like him?"

"Lonny thinks he's a Romeo. He fell into a pile of green shit when he latched onto Sugar Ron. I made my bones years ago. Check it out. I own beachfront property at Avalon, Naples Florida, and Santa Barbara. You are welcome any time, Detective."

"If I visit your home, it will not be a social visit. Got that?"

Leon sits back. "Look, I am a busy man. Why am I here?"

"You attended the Last Supper, making you one of the last people to see Sugar Ron alive. That makes you a material witness to a possible homicide. We want your cooperation, not your bullshit. Now, tell me about Jacko and Noreen."

"You know about them? Hey, you are a sharp lady."

Ro Ro looks away to conceal her surprise that she has stumbled on to new information.

"How long have they been an item?"

"They were engaged until Jacko caught her in bed with Sugar Ron's old man. They got back together after the old man kicked. Love is grand."

Ro Ro smiles, "So I am told. Were there any bad feelings between them and Sugar Ron?"

"That is a damn good question. I do not know. I never paid much attention to the low life. You know, the deplorables."

"Deplorables can do surprising things. Stick around town, Rose. I will want to see you again."

"Sure. But next time my lawyer will be with me. You know him. Gabe Porto. He is the best."

Ah, Gabe, Germantown John's mouthpiece. Another surprise.

Leon raps his knuckles on the table. "I am signing out."

Ro Ro feels that a shower is in order.

Jacko Judd trundles into the room. His abundant stomach protrudes like a watermelon. Half of his gut overlaps the waistline of his baggy jeans. His checkered shirt looks ready to burst three buttons. His shaven head glistens, except for a red scar at the side of his left eye. His shaggy salt and pepper hair hangs rumpled, no apparent part on either side. He is a walking, unmade bed.

Ro Ro has seen men like Jacko. Usually, they hang out in dimly lit bars smoking cigarettes and drinking cheap whiskey, straight behind mugs of Budweiser or Pabst.

"Hello Mr. Judd. I understand you are the cutman for the world champion."

Jacko grunts, "Uh huh. The ex-world champ. He's dead, and dead men don't count, do they?"

"They count if somebody murdered them."

Jacko's neck twists under his squinting eyes. "I thought Ronnie died of a heart attack."

"We think Sugar Ron pissed off somebody and that somebody poisoned him."

"What the hell? Who would kill that man?"

"How long did you know him?"

"I knew that boy since he was knee-high to a pony. His old man and I were good buddies. We went to the racetrack together lots of times."

"How did his father die?"

Jacko coughs into the sleeve of his shirt. "Some say he drank himself to death."

"What do you say?"

"Me? I've got nothing to say."

"I saw the figures on the split of the purse. You got the short end of the pot. How did that make you feel?"

Jacko shrugs. "I did all right. No complaints."

"What do you think about Tamika?"

"She is all right. She is Noreen's niece, so that kind of makes her family."

"How so?"

"Noreen was Ronnie's aunt on his mother's side."

"So, Tamika was a kissing cousin?"

Jacko throws back his head, laughing. "She did more than kiss Ron. A lot more."

"She, too, got more of the take than you did."

"Yeah. But she did more than I did. I fixed cuts. She slept with him. I dooooo not sleep with men."

"Do you sleep with Noreen?"

"That's my business."

"I will take that as a yes. How is your health?"

"My health is good. Why all these personal questions? If you keep asking me these kinds of questions, I will get a lawyer."

"I just want to understand why you let Lonny and Leon and Tamika hose you. You've been loyal to Sugar Ron. You were friends with his father. You helped protect him. Yet, you get crumbs for your efforts. That cannot sit well with you."

Jacko's eyes narrow into slits like a child wincing in the face of a scolding parent.

He pounds the table. "I live my life my way. Jacko Judd is a man. I owe nobody nothing."

"Bull! They mock you and Sugar Ron let them do it. He did not care about you. He kept you on the payroll as a flunky."

"No. He respected me like I was an uncle."

"Uncles are family. They sit at the Thanksgiving table and share the meal. They don't lick crumbs from the kitchen floor. You damn fool."

Jacko smiles. "You are trying to bait me into saying something. Old Jacko is no punching bag. I am done talking to you."

Jacko rises. "Call my lawyer. His name is Gabe Porto. I think you know him."

Ro Ro nods. "Yes, I know Gabe. Do you know G Town?"

"Everybody in Philly knows Johnny Mancuso. And, Jacko has lots of friends in high places who you know. Don't try to play me. Never."

Ro Ro folds her arms. "We will become very good friends, Jacko Judd. You can bet on it."

Her words evoke an unexpected flinch from Jacko. The word "bet" was a tell.

Glaring, Jacko backs out of the room and right into Biker.

Biker grabs Jacko at the doorway. "You stay where we can find you," says Biker.

Jacko edges past Biker. "I will be around."

"You better be around."

"You struck a note with him."

"The word 'bet' scratches his brain. We need to find out if he owes G Town or another bookie any money. Send in Noreen."

Noreen Cooke looks tired, nervous, and defiant.

"What you want hassling me?" she asks Ro Ro.

"I want the truth about how Sugar Ron died. Don't you want the same outcome?"

Noreen sits at the table, staring at the far wall. "Please tell me I am in a nightmare, and I am going to wake up and my world will be in one piece again. I'm scared."

"What are you afraid of?"

Noreen wears a tiny gold crucifix necklace. She holds it tightly. "I am afraid God will come off the cross and thrash all of us money grubbing humans just like Jesus threw out the money changers. Money, money, money. I never had much and never wanted much. People go crazy when money is involved. People sell their souls for dollar bills."

"Please tell me what you know."

"I do not know much, but old Noreen has seen people chase after money and destroy themselves and their families."

"Are you talking about Sugar Ron's father?"

"Suede used to talk about money like it was a living thing. He called it lettuce, cabbage, bread, dough like it was the very substance of life. Sugar caught that money flu. He had the gold bug crawling in his soul. Now he is dead, and you people think somebody killed him. A beautiful boy is dead, killed in his prime. I have lived too long."

"Who killed him?"

"Evil killed him. Evil is real. Evil in the hearts of men is a force that will someday bring us all to ruination. I am so sad."

"Who killed him?"

Noreen wipes tears away. Her brown eyes droop over her baggy eyes. Ro Ro fears the tears are not genuine, the sorrow is feigned. "Moral indignation does not bring justice. We need facts. What do you know that I need to know? Help me, Noreen. For Ron's sake. Just answer a few questions."

"Okay. I will try."

"Who stood to gain by Ron's death?"

"Nobody. We all got a share of his winnings. Some got more. But, we all got something. Jacko says he was a seven-to-one favorite just like Sonny Liston when he fought Cassius Clay. Sugar was a sure thing."

A bell rings in Ro Ro's mind. "Did everyone bet on Sugar Ron?"

"Well, they were all talking about cracking the bookies by betting on Sugar. Lonny said it was found money."

"Tamika said that you prepared the meal plates individually. Did anyone assist you?"

"Hell no. I did the cooking and the clean-up."

"How about the drinks? Did everyone pour their own drinks?"

"I suspect so. Weren't a bartender around. What are you getting at?"

When a supposition does not work, it is faulty at the premise.

"I am just sorting out the details. Did you see or hear anything unusual?

"Let me think. Oh yeah. Ronny excused himself and went outside for a few minutes."

"Did he go outside alone?"

"I think so. I cannot be sure."

"Did he smoke cigars?"

"Gracious, no. He gave up smoking. He took up using those vape things."

"When did he start vaping?"

"A month ago, maybe."

"Thank you, Noreen. You can go now."

"Okay. God bless you, child."

The second Noreen leaves, Ro Ro waves Biker into the room. She calls Docky and puts her cell on speaker.

"Docky. Please look for a vape in Sugar Ron's house. And, check the oil for poison."

"Good Lord, Rowena. I was in the right church but the wrong pew. Nicotine poison may be the culprit, not potassium cyanide."

She holds her breath. "Bet on it."

She turns to Biker. "We need to find out who is into the bookies and for how much. We also need to find out who bet on Sugar Ron's opponent."

"Marty Ross was a seven to one underdog. Oh my god. I see it now."

Chapter Three

Ro Ro calls Germantown John's cell. He answers on the fourth ring. "My caller ID reads that I am talking to the best cop in Philly. To what do I owe this surprise?"

"Hello Mancuso. I'm working the possible homicide of Sugar Ron. I have come across some information you may find interesting, and I can use your help in sorting it out."

"What's in it for me?"

"How do you feel about people who try to cheat you?"

"You have my interest."

"Meet me in half an hour at Pastorius Park near the pond. We can find a bench and talk."

"It's a date."

"Hardly a date. And for the record, I will not be carrying a wire."

"I trust you, Rowena."

"That is a one-sided proposition."

She hangs up and guns her engine. She wants to arrive before he shows up.

Pastorius Park is a sixteen-acre tract founded in 1915. The semi-circle amphitheater hosts free summer concerts. The stage is up. Most days the park is a recreation area for dog walkers and pre-teens seeking a safe spot to smoke cigarettes or vape. Water spouting ponds give the park the atmosphere of tranquility.

To her dismay, G Town John has arrived earlier than her. He sits on a park bench. Dressed in a tight-fitting t-shirt, designer jeans and brown boots. He looks more like a GQ model than a bookie, loan shark, and all-around thug. He rises to greet her.

"Hello Ro Ro. You are looking well."

"Ditto. Thanks for meeting me."

"What is going on?"

Rowena feels okay talking to him, especially because Biker is in G Town's back pocket and probably already knows about the Sugar Ron killing.

"My guess is that you made a bundle on the fight. I believe someone tried to fix the fight by introducing pure nicotine into Sugar Ron through his Juul vape. But they screwed up the dose. He won the fight. The perp juiced the Juul and killed him, making his death look like a heart attack. "Docky" will confirm it. Here is what I need. I want a list of anyone close to Sugar Ron who bet against. You can call around to the bookies in the area and get me a list. That will give the basis for an indictment."

"Whoa! I cannot let it get around that you and I are amici. Lovers, yes. Friends, no."

"Forget about getting me into bed. This is a business deal. You find out who tried to screw you. I get the killer. Is it a deal?"

"I could get the list and take care of matters for you. Neat and clean."

"No deal. Why implicate yourself? If I take care of matters, there is no legal blow back. It's a fair deal."

"You got it all figured out."

"There is one loophole. Let's say you were the one behind the scheme. Let's say you bankrolled the project. If that word got out, you'd be taking bets from dead people only."

G Town throws back his head and laughs. "You are more devious than me. Give me a day or so to check things out."

She yanks the sleeve of his shirt hard, pulling his face close to hers. "Do not think about double-crossing me or lying to me."

G Town glowers, his violet eyes dark with anger. "Don't push me too hard. I don't like bullies, even ones as pretty as you."

She releases his shirt. "I just needed to make a point."

A young couple, probably seventeen years old, their fingers interlocked, walk toward them. The girl looks at her tall companion with adoring pale blue eyes, a reedy boy wearing wire-rimmed glasses, and sporting a pointy, partially grown in goatee. Her loose jeans show alabaster skin through a series of thigh high slits. They remind Ro Ro of her youth before she solved murders and dealt with evil men.

They whisper about old married couples fighting in public.

They pass on, snickering.

Ro Ro follows them, strutting a few paces behind until she overtakes them.

"Good day," says Ro Ro.

"What a handsome couple you make. How long have you been married?" asks the girl.

"We aren't married."

"A lover's quarrel perhaps," says the boy.

"Not even close. Someday this homicide detective will lock him up for life."

"Holy Moley," says the boy.

"You will learn someday that the world is not what it seems to be. Have a nice life," says Rowena.

Ro Ro peers over right shoulder. G Town is staring at her. She turns away feeling like there is a target on her back.

Docky sits across the table from Ro Ro in the small conference room. His grizzled face wears the look of a troubled man. Ro Ro has just told him about her meeting with G Town.

"Miss Rowena is a crazy lady. If G Town was behind the fix, and he thinks you will uncover it, he will do anything to stop you. I do not want to do an autopsy on you."

"He must have hired Gabe Porto to represent Jacko and himself. Jacko said he had friends in high places. I think he meant Lonny and

Leon. My guess is that G Town took the bets on Sugar Ron losing and laid them off on other bookies. If Ron lost, they still got the purse and they got seven-to-one on bets they never made. It is a brilliant scam. Only G Town could concoct the ruse. Jacko or Tamika probably spiked the Juul with the pure nicotine but over did it. I doubt Noreen knows anything. The problem is that if I tell Biker, he will warn G Town."

Docky shakes his head from side to side. "I just cannot believe Biker is dirty. I have known him for twenty years."

"My father once warned me that desperate men took desperate measures. I know Biker shot Bart Malone and made it look like a righteous killing. I'm not sure how to play this out. Do you have any ideas?"

Docky strokes his chin. "You can leave town."

"Did you find any prints on the Juul?"

"Nope. It was wiped clean."

"You did not find Ron's prints, meaning someone wiped it after he took the deadly dose of pure nicotine. Tamika had access to the Juul. She had a baby to protect as well as herself. She was in on the scam and probably covered the tracks. Can you pinpoint how long Sugar Ron used the pure nicotine?"

"Yes. He could not have survived more than seventy-two hours."

"He used it one night before the fight."

"That is what I calibrated. Damn if this puzzle does not have too many pieces."

"Let's see if the pieces fall in place when the conspirators sense I am onto them."

"You got cajones."

Ro Ro sighs. "I am a detective. It is my job to find the truth. It is a sweet science."

Docky pats the top of her hand. "Just don't get killed in the process."

Clad in her jammies, Ro Ro settles onto her sofa. She needs to wind down and there is no better relaxer than a glass of Merlot and Dave Brubeck's classic album, Take Five. Her father had introduced her to the album when she was seventeen.

Her calm is disrupted by Biker's phone call.

"Detective Morse. Who the hell do you think you are? I just got a call from Gabe Porto complaining that you harassed John Mancuso. Why did you not tell me, your superior officer, that you were going to interview Mancuso? This lone ranger act is getting old. I'm your boss, and you have to clear all interviews through me."

"I was only getting background information on bookmaking activity for Sugar Ron's fight. Mancuso is the biggest bookie in our district and parts of Montgomery County, so I thought he would be a valuable source of information. I figured he was an expert witness and I did not need approval to verify certain facts. Sorry, boss. I was just asking for betting information. I did not accuse G Town of anything."

"You know Porto is Jacko Judd's attorney and Mancuso's attorney, as well."

"Maybe I inadvertently pushed a button on Gabe's dashboard?"

"You are pushing my buttons. That is not wise. How would you like a transfer to another district?"

She wants to tell him to go to Hell but decides on discretion. "Lieutenant, I like and respect you and like working here. No way do I want a transfer."

"You are close to a one-way ticket to North Philly. Think about working dead druggies in the badlands. Good night."

The chord has been struck. She needs more wine for medicinal sleep therapy.

She texts an apology to Biker to document her contrition. She added, "I just talked to Docky. I will re-interview three people. Jacko, Tamika, and Noreen. They had access to the Juul. Docky says the nicotine poison was introduced two days before the fight. They are most likely the ones who tampered with the dose during that time."

Enough with the jabs. Time for a knockout.

Chapter Four

Tamika, Noreen, and Jacko sit around the conference room table with Ro Ro at the head. "Good morning. I invited you today to help us clear up a few things regarding the murder of Sugar Ron Simms."

Jacko interrupts her. "Murder? I thought he died of a heart attack."

"Who would murder that beautiful boy?" says Noreen.

Tamika slams her palm onto the tabletop. "My baby lost a father. I lost the love of my life. And, you are saying that it was murder. What the hell is going on?"

Ro Ro puts on her best angry cop look. "Murder makes me angry. When a person takes a life, it is a crime against all of society. When the instrument is poison, the murderer is not just criminal, he or she is a coward. In this case, the poison was administered in an electronic cigarette. To be precise, Simms died from a lethal dose of nicotine poisoning."

Ro Ro pauses to watch their reaction. Jacko's eyes drop to the floor. "Oh my God," he says, his jowls quivering.

Noreen gasps, "Sweet Jesus," then looks away.

Tamika stiffens ramrod straight. "Why? He took care of all of us."

"People commit murders for many reasons. Sometimes the murder is unintentional. It is a mistake. Sometimes it is an act of revenge or jealousy. Sometimes it is for greed. Mainly people murder people to solve a problem. It seems to be a good idea at the time. Now, I am going to meet with each of you as material witnesses, not suspects. If you know something, this moment will be your opportunity to speak up. Tamika, please come with me. You two stay put. There are two uniformed policemen outside. One male, one female in case you need a restroom visit."

Jacko raises his hand like a schoolboy asking permission to go to the lavatory. "Do we need a lawyer? I should call Gabe."

"Call him if you wish."

Ro Ro leads Tamika to the small conference room. They sit at opposite ends. A pitcher of ice water and plastic cups stand on a plastic tray. "I am sick to my stomach," says Tamika.

"Take a deep breath. Do you want water?"

"I would rather have a bourbon. You cannot believe I killed Sugar Ron?"

"My sources tell me he was going to leave you. The payoff from the fight was a one-time fee for services rendered."

Tamika's nostrils flare widely. "Who said that? I ain't no whore. I loved that man. And I do not know about vapes."

"Bull. You carry a vape. We recovered two Juuls from the house. I doubt Sugar smoked the pink one. You are the one who got Sugar Ron to use the electronic cigarette to cut down on his smoking."

"It was Lonny's idea to vape. He was afraid Sugar Ron was hooked on normal cigarettes. Smoking would kill his wind and his career."

"Who is the baby's father? Lonny or Sugar Ron?"

"How dare you ask me that. Lonny and me were done and over a year ago."

"And, you were cozy with Leon, were you not?"

Tamika buries her face in her hands. "I did a lot of bad things to survive. I did what I had to do."

"Was Sugar going to send you away?"

Tamika juts her chin out. "Yes. He was fixing to send me down the road. The man had no conscience. He was as ruthless outside the ring as he was inside. He liked beating on people. It made him feel superior."

"Did he beat you?"

Tamika laughs. "I wish he had smacked me around. Bruises are good for business. I would have proof of abuse. No bruises means no evidence. Okay, I admit he was a meal ticket, and when you are starving, a meal ticket is a wholesome way to get your fill."

"Did Noreen know about Sugar Ron leaving you?"

Tamika's eyes flit. "She knew. So did Jacko and Leon and Lonny. I was in the 'later on' file."

"Tamika, I have six squads canvassing smoke shops looking for purchasers of pure nicotine. They are Philly's finest. They will ferret out who bought the nicotine. Those joints have security cameras. Tell me now if you bought the nicotine."

Tamika folds her arms across her chest. "I bought it. That do not mean I spiked the Juul. You got nothing on me."

"We will see about that. I am holding you for further questioning."

Ro Ro Mirandizes her and orders the female officer to lead her to the lock up.

Ro Ro drinks two cups of water and asks her uniformed officer to bring in Jacko Judd.

Jacko shuffles into the conference room, his white sneakers squeaking, his laces loose over the front of the sneakers. His five o'clock shadow is early. He sits across from Ro Ro, glaring anger or fear or both.

"Good morning, Jacko."

"I want a lawyer. I want Gabe. I want him now."

"You can have a lawyer. You are not being charged with anything."

"I saw Tamika come into this room and get taken away. I do not want that to happen to me."

"How did you hear about Gabe? Did Germantown John refer you to him or him to you?"

Jacko pauses, as if his mind is solving the riddle of the Sphinx. "What is the difference? I want him to be here to represent me. I know my rights."

"I am sure you do. Answer me this question. Why do you need a lawyer?"

"I need a lawyer to protect me from cops like you who trick innocent people into saying the wrong things and end up getting railroaded to prison."

Ro Ro leans close enough to catch the scent of bourbon. "We know Sugar Ron Simms was poisoned from his vape. The Juul was filled with pure nicotine. That stuff could kill a lion."

"Why would I kill the man that feeds me?"

"You did not plan to kill him. You wanted him to lose the fight."

"That's crazy talk. Why would I want The Champ to lose?"

"Because you got seven-to-one that his opponent would win. You bet heavy with Germantown John. That's why he got you an expensive lawyer. He wants you to keep your mouth shut so you stay out of jail, and he can someday collect. Or maybe, he laid off your bet and bet on the opponent too to hedge the loss. It's just like when the Eagles won the Super Bowl. Philly fans took the Eagles with the points. The Books laid off the bets on the out-of-town schmucks. Either way, he wins. Smart books always cut their exposure. You see what I am driving at, don't you?"

Jacko pours a cup of water and gulps it down in one swallow. "That is a neat scheme. But it ain't true. I bet on Sugar at three-to-five. I never bet against myself."

Ro Ro shakes her head. "You are lying. You bet against him and covered your ass with the nicotine."

Jacko laughs. "Hah! That is a rich one. You know what the gab is on the street? The gab is that G Town and you are getting it on. And you are pissed because he dumped you. That is the word."

Ro Ro clenches her fists. "What a crock."

Her cell phone rings. It is Biker.

"Yes, boss."

"We tracked down the nicotine purchase to a store in Atlantic City. Guess who purchased pure nicotine three weeks ago? (A short pause.) Lonny Ford."

Ro Ro smiles for Jacko's sake. "I see. Please come get Jacko Judd and hold him as an accessory to murder."

Ro Ro hangs up. Jacko looks stunned. "What was that all about?"

Ro Ro reads him his rights. "Now you can call Gabe Porto. You are going to need him."

"What? I did nothing wrong."

"When you lie down with dogs, you get up with fleas. Prison has a lot of bad dogs."

She waves the uniformed officer to come in. "Please take Mister Judd to a holding cell and send in Noreen Cooke."

Carrying a threadbare brown and tan handbag in her gnarled hands, Noreen enters the conference room like she is being led to the gallows. Her drooping, red eyes hang over her high cheekbones. Her salt and pepper hair needs combing.

"Hello Noreen. How are you today?"

"I have been in the jailhouse more these past two days than in all my life."

"The investigation is proceeding rapidly. I just have a few points to cover with you."

"Okay."

"We are going on the premise that Sugar Ron was killed by accident. Somebody poured pure nicotine into his electronic cigarette. Their plan was to dope him enough for him to lose his fight and the doper or dopers could clean up by betting against him."

Noreen's eyes widen in disbelief. "Who could dream up a plan like that? The devil is alive, as sure as I am."

"I agree. The devil is alive. But Sugar Ron is dead. Mistake or not, The Champ is D. E. A. D."

"You said it was a mistake."

"That is what I first thought. You see, the appearance was the man was worth more alive than dead to the people close to him. Now I think there is more to this murder than money. I think the plan for Sugar Ron to lose was about power and control. As a champion, he was indomitable. But, if he lost, he was humbled and could be controlled. He could be managed. His ego would be shattered. His invulnerability would leave him. Like a little boy wandering alone looking for his parents."

Noreen runs a bony finger across her chin as if Ro Ro's words are food for thought. "That takes a mighty lot of thinking and planning. Who could cipher a plan like that?"

Ro Ro takes Noreen's hands. "You."

"Me? No. I ain't that clever. I am just an old woman waiting for a bus to heaven."

"Noreen, whoever filled that electronic cigarette, had to get close to Sugar Ron. Lonny bought it. He gave it to Tamika, who gave it to you. You would do anything for Tamika. She is your daughter, is she not?"

Noreen nods. "Yes. She is carrying my grandchild. Sugar Ron was going to dump her, just as I got dumped. I could not let that happen. He had to stay in the house. If he lost, he would heel like a tame dog. I wanted to make a man out of him. He needed to be a man more than to be a champ."

"Could he not be both?"

"No. He had his daddy's blood. They used to call his daddy Radar because he could pick up anything. He needed to need her. When he won, I got mad and stuffed his baked potato with the nicotine ... I meant to get him sick. He needed to learn a lesson. He was human. He defied God Almighty. He needed a dose of humble pie."

"He needs nothing now. You need a good lawyer. Gabe was hired to protect you and your family. How did Germantown John fit in?"

Noreen's back stiffens. "Jacko owed him big bucks. He told Germantown John to bet against Sugar. The payoff would cover Jacko's debts."

Jacko is a dead man.

"I need your statement. I will have a stenographer come in after I Mirandize you."

"Don't expect me to say more than I did it. I will not implicate Jacko or Tamika. I was the fool who did it all. Me. Just me. That is my terms. Me or you go prove the rest of them had something to do with my mistakes. I will deny their involvement. Old Gabe will make a good defense."

Ro Ro nods. "Reasonable doubt. You really thought through this situation."

"Damned straight. Now that I told the truth, I feel better. God will forgive me."

Ro Ro calls for the stenographer.

Ro Ro rests a hand on Noreen's bony shoulder. "In a crazy way, you are a champion."

Noreen laughs. "That sounds sweet as Sugar."

Alone with a glass of wine, her third, Ro Ro calls Germantown John's cell.

"Ciao, Ro Ro," he says.

"You beat another charge."

"I always win. You cannot beat me, so why not join me?"

"According to Jacko, you and I are already bedmates."

"I never said that to anyone. Make book on it."

"You can set the odds at around one-million-to-one."

"You'd be worth the payout."

Ro Ro laughs aloud. "Dream on."

"Stranger things have happened."

"True that. Goodnight, G Town," she says and hangs up.

Someday I will fry that smug bastard.

Epilogue

For a week after the arrest of Noreen for involuntary manslaughter, Jacko for accessory to manslaughter, and Tamika for accessory to manslaughter, Ro Ro finds herself in the uncomfortable position of rock star policewoman. She turns down offers to appear on Fox News and CBS local news. The Inquirer wants to do a feature story, but she declines. All three people charged pleaded guilty.

Lonny skates away clear from any charges. None of the three involved would dare implicate him. Ro Ro suspects Lonny had more to do with the nicotine than she had uncovered. She never figured Leon Rose as dumb enough or greedy enough to promote a fixed fight. Her cell caller ID reads, "Leon Rose."

"Hello, Mr. Rose."

"So, how is the Schmarter?"

"I am so good it hurts. What can I do for you?"

"I called to thank you for cleaning up that mess. You proved I was not involved. I appreciate you keeping my name clean. Nobody buys tickets to a fixed fight."

"That is what I figured."

"Glad you are smart as you are good looking."

"Thank you, Mister Rose. I appreciate the call. I must go."

"Wait. I want you to know that Leon Rose never forgets a friend. We have a common enemy. You know the enemy of my enemy is my friend. Our mutual enemy is Germantown John. If that dago ever causes you any grief, call me. I have ways of influencing people."

"I understand."

"Goodbye, detective."

"Goodbye, Leon."

She turns off the phone wondering if Leon is sending her a warning. Maybe boxing is a bittersweet science?

Story Seven: Death in Fame and Infamy

Chapter One

Every Philly neighborhood has its local heroes. In Ro Ro's youth, Neil Mann was "The Man." He stood six-two, his body crafted like Michelangelo's David. His clear blue eyes had shone like gems. He had starred in football, baseball, and basketball, and all at Cardinal Dougherty High School. He had also been valedictorian. He had earned a scholarship to play football for Joe Paterno at Penn State.

Then the car accident that would change his world happened on a snowy mountain road in his senior year at Happy Valley. His roommate ran his car into a telephone pole, killing himself and leaving The Man in a coma. Miraculously, The Man survived, adding to his stature as a larger-than-life hero. Broken in body and spirit, he never fully recovered and never played football again. The bright blue eyes dimmed from bouts of depression. He drank constantly.

Neil Mann lies face up on his unmade bed. His once trim, taut, muscular body has swollen under a huge belly. The blue eyes stare at the ceiling, unmoving. Ro Ro stands over The Man's bullet-ridden body wondering who would kill a man already dead in life.

The CSU's own Docky Poteet shakes his head slowly. "It is a shame what happened to that boy. I saw him play at CD High. He was a man among boys."

"Neil was God's gift to Mount Airy, and to me."

"How well did you know him?"

Ro Ro's mind bent back to a summer night when she had lost her virginity to a man god on a blanket in Pastorius Park.

"The first time is always special."

"Dang. He were one lucky dude."

"So was I. When was he killed?"

"My best estimate is eighteen hours ago. Midnight. Looks like a forty-four wound. No shell casings. No prints. The bullets are still in him. This killing was done by a pro."

"What did he do to scare somebody enough to kill him?"

Ro Ro scours his wallet and finds eleven dollars, a debit card from Beneficial Bank, and his auto license.

"Where is his cell?"

"The cell is in his right front pocket," says Docky.

Ro Ro extracts it. The Uber icon stares at her. "Mark this as evidence. I am taking it with me. It will give us a trail of his coming and going."

Docky takes a photo of the phone and notes his iPad. "What do you think you will find?"

"His cell is his diary. I will be looking for a hint of what he may have done to get killed."

"Good luck. Did he have family?"

"His mother, Claire Mann, is alive and well. I ran into her at the Chestnut Hill Art Festival last week. The woman is near seventy and still stops traffic. His dad committed suicide. He shot himself in the head. Herb Mann never recovered from Neil's accident. Herbert was a sergeant in the Fourteenth District. I will contact Claire and ask her to identify her son."

Ro Ro says a silent "Hail Mary."

"Please call me after you have finished with him. I will escort Claire to do the identification."

Ro Ro looks on at Neil's dead body with camera eyes, capturing the image of her dead first lover indelibly in her mind. Tears would come later in private. She has research to do. Banking information, credit card transactions, and the Uber trail to track. The computer does not lie.

At 2:17AM, Ro Ro shuts down her computer, satisfied that she has learned more about The Man than anyone on the planet except for his mother, Claire. Neil may have lived in near poverty for many years. He did not die penniless. His checking account had swelled to over one hundred and thirty thousand dollars in just the past six months. The Uber earnings were just over ten thousand, so how did Neil earn the other income?

The Uber account dropped from six hundred a week to two hundred. He was accepting less rides. Yet the weekly bank deposit amounts were nearly identical from week to week. The trip details show repetitive pick-ups and drop offs. She does a map search and finds a pattern of pick-ups and deliveries. Three recurring pick-ups are in Chestnut Hill. Three recurring drop offs are in Kensington-the drug center of Philadelphia.

He was not The Man. He was The Mule.

Ro Ro emails her notes to Biker. "Please contact drug enforcement to see if these addresses are known points of contact for dealers."

Has my hero stooped so low?

The ride home takes her by Pastorius Park. She had tasted sex here for the first time with a man she adored. But now he was as much a ghost to her as the memory of her virginity. We all lose our innocence. Is she about to lose it for the second time?

She and Claire Mann have a lot to discuss.

Chapter Two

Dressed in a steel grey pants suit, Claire Mann stands stoically at the side of her murdered son's body. Her athletic body honed by decades of yoga and jogging and golf at North Hills Country Club where she was a six handicap. Her white hair drapes to her shoulders. Not one hair was out of place. She was clearly The Woman who made The Man.

Docky rolls back the sheet covering Neil.

Claire's jaw sets firmly under her eyes. Her manner suggested a robotic firmness. "That is my son, Neil."

She traces her hand along Neil's face. "Why him God? Why him? Cover him please."

"Thank you, Claire," says Ro Ro.

Ro Ro takes Claire by the arm and leads her to her office. Claire walks in silence, seeming more angry than sad.

Ro Ro sits at her desk, across from Claire. "I know this is difficult beyond words, but can you think of anyone who would want Neil dead?"

"When he was a young boy, I knew he was destined to do great things. He ruled his world like a young god. He could do anything he set his mind to. My only fear was that a lesser person would bring him down. I feared some low-rent girl would get pregnant and make him marry her. I knew he drank, like his father, like the whole clan. That boy who drove the car off the road was drunk. How reckless. How stupid. My son's life was wasted. Is there a greater crime than murdering a boy without killing him? He was left a life without hope. Worse, he lived in a nightmare of smashed dreams. And, he watched his father disintegrate, all the while feeling that it was he who caused his father's death."

"Did Neil do drugs?"

Claire nods. "Yes. He took opioids. He got hooked after the accident. He called the pills his vitamins. I tried to get him into therapy, but he wouldn't go."

Ro Ro takes a deep breath, scarcely believing she can utter her next statement. "We suspect Neil was not only using drugs, but also transporting the opioids. His Uber job was a cover."

Claire curls her fists tightly. "Neil was not a criminal."

"His bank records show recent large and regular deposits. His Uber records show regular trips to known drug haunts in Kensington. Neil was involved in the drug business. Can you help us identify who he may have been working with?"

"I don't believe you. Rowena, I have always liked you. Many times I said to Neil that you were the kind of girl I wanted him to date. How can you believe Neil was a criminal?"

"Neil and I were good friends. He was three years older than me. That is a lifetime in teenage years. Look, I take no joy in raising these points, but the facts are the facts. Neil was no angel. His murder may have been caused by his dealing or transporting of drugs."

"I do not believe you."

"Think Claire. Who were his friends? Did he date anyone?"

"He had a woman he dated from time to time. Her first name was Renata. I am not sure of her last name."

Ro Ro blurts out, "Renata Castro?"

"No. I think her last name was Shields or Schiller or something like that."

Ro Ro snaps her fingers, "I got it. Schuler. Renata Castro married Jerry Schuler. Schuler was a dirty cop who was convicted for dealing heroin. Renata Castro was one of Neil's groupies."

"Are you saying there is a connection between my Neil and a heroin dealer?"

Ro Ro fears she has said way too much. "Heck no. I am just trying to make sense of Neil's murder. I need a motive. Money and drugs usually make viable motives. Don't read a lot into my comments. I am just scratching for leads. Can you think of any other women who were in Neil's life?"

"No. His only friend was Chas Gordon. Chas and Neil played football at Penn State. Chas adored Neil. Chas stuck by him forever. I called Chas last night and gave him the news on Neil. He took it quite well. Funny thing is he sounded as if he expected my call."

"How so?"

"He answered by asking me what was the matter? He did not even say his usual answer of 'Chas the Jazz here'."

"I see. Can you give me Chas's phone number?"

"Sure, Rowena. Please promise me you will keep Neil's reputation intact."

Ro Ro knows she cannot offer a firm promise. "I will do all I can to keep Neil's name pure as snow. Here is my card. My cell phone is on the back. Call me any time to talk, or if you remember something important."

They shake hands as Claire leaves, not having shed a single tear. Claire's emotionless demeanor troubles Rowena. Something is not normal about Claire. Claire expresses outrage, but her carriage shows a mechanical bent. A statue in a pantsuit.

Ro Ro types her notes into an encrypted file she has named, "The Murder of The Man."

She tracks down Chas and Renata and sends officers to bring them in for questioning. It is time to mine the Web.

The guilty can hide, but not escape.

Chapter Three

Rowena answers the knock on her office door from a six-foot-five and two-hundred-and-seventy-pound presence of Nar-cotics Detective Walter Hunt.

"Good morning, Miss Morse. You are looking marvelous as always," he says, loudly.

"Well, well, well, if it isn't the legend himself. Walter Gibraltar. I have been expecting you. Come in and sit down."

"Thank you, Detective Morse. Is there any coffee in this establishment?"

"Is it too early for Jamison?"

Walter taps the breast pocket of his suit coat. "You get the coffee. I brought my own sweetener."

Ro Ro laughs. "I should have known."

They settle over Styrofoam cups of black coffee.

Walter's shoulders fill his custom-made gray suit. He smiles widely, like a giant charming a child out of his candy.

"I heard about The Man. I played ball with him at Cardinal Dougherty. The Man could play. Do you have any leads on who killed him?"

Ro Ro pats his thick forearms. "Let's not toy with each other. We have strong evidence Neil was involved in drug trafficking. He was either a dealer, a mule, or a mole for you. Which reason brings you to my doorstep, handsome?"

Walter wags a finger. "You are too smart to be a cop. I can only say that the narcotics division is upset that Neil has croaked."

"Well, let me think about that comment. If he was a dealer, you would be happy. If he was a mule, you would not give a damn. That leaves mole. How long was he working for you guys?"

"This is confidential. I can only say that we paid a lot of money to get the goods on the Rudolf gang."

"Do you think they did the deed?"

"Most likely. Russians do not abide traitors."

"How did you hook Neil up with the Rudolf bunch?"

"Neil's old friend, Chas Gordon. His real name is Gordonov. He is a cousin of the Rudolf's. From the outside, Chas looks like Mr. Clean. But he bathes in the Rudolf cesspool. Neil found out about Chas's involvement and came to me personally. We concocted the whole Uber scenario and had Neil approach Chas with the idea of his running drugs. Neil needed the money. Chas bought the story. We were really close to nailing the whole operation. Neil was our star witness."

"And somehow, they caught on to Neil and wasted him. Interesting theory."

"We want these stiffs off balance. We want the press to hear that the police are looking into avenues involving somebody else."

"Who do you have in mind?"

Walter shrugs. "Germantown John."

Ro Ro laughs out loud. "That is too funny. I have been trying to nail him on real charges. He will go ballistic."

"I thought you would like screwing with that dago's brain. Meanwhile, we will help you nail the Rudolf gang."

Ro Ro leans away for a moment of thought. "What if they didn't do it?"

"Then, we are no worse off."

"You are a devious man."

"Guilty as charged."

"I am meeting with Chas today, and Renata Schuler, as well. What can you tell me about them?"

"Chas is as slippery as a wet eel. Do not get into a situation where you find yourself alone with him."

"Duly noted. What about Renata?"

"She has a mean streak. She sliced the face of a guy who pinched her ass. Will Biker be okay with our plan?" asks Walter.

"Let me handle Biker. Say nothing to anyone about the red herring."

"Huh? You don't trust Biker, do you?"

"I did not say that. Let's keep it all with me or no deal."

Walter eyes her before answering. "What the hell? We will play it your way."

"Let's." They shake hands. Walter holds on to her hand for a long moment. "Be careful, Rowena."

"You too, Gibraltar. Bye."

"Sláinte."

Ro Ro feels uneasy about putting out a false narrative but forgives herself. Screwing with G Town's head is justifiable deception in the cause of justice. She wants to tell Claire her son is still a hero, but knows that Claire may tell Chas. That slip would kill the plan. Telling her G Town may be involved may be a way to get the ploy going with Chas.

Chas "The Jazz was due in an hour. She opens her laptop and enters the name Charles Gordonov into her database.

Two uniformed officers escort a handcuffed Chas "The Jazz" into Ro Ro's office. Chas's black eyes glare at Ro Ro. His sallow complexion contrasts with his off-white skin. "Why am I being called here without my attorney?"

"Please sit, Mister Gordonov. Officers. Uncuff Mister Gordonov. He is a valuable witness in the murder of The Man."

"He resisted. We had to cuff him."

"Understood. Gordonov, would you like coffee or water?" she asks.

"I want neither. And stop calling me Gordonov. My name is Gordon. I am an American citizen and Gordon is my American name. Address me properly."

"Okay Gordo. We'll leave off the V. Do you prefer Chas "The Jazz?"

"What do you want from me?"

Rowena gets nose to nose with him. "I want the name of the shooter of Neil Mann."

"I don't know anything about that terrible incident."

"What was the nature of your relationship with Neil Mann?"

"We were college buddies. We played football together. We partied a few times."

"We know Neil was dealing in drugs. Did you and he have a business relationship?"

"No. We were casual friends. We did no business together."

"What is your occupation?"

"I am a business consultant."

"Are the Rudolfs your clients?"

"My client list is confidential."

"I will take that response as a yes. Did Neil confide in you?"

"No. We were drinking buddies. We talked football and women. He drove his Uber and I consulted with my clients."

"I tracked his Uber rides and found a pattern. Every Saturday morning, he made a pick-up in Chestnut Hill and went to three addresses in Kensington. Uber discourages prearranged rides with a specified driver. They don't want their drivers to get too cozy with riders lest they become competitors. The address in Chestnut Hill is your home address. You and Neil made recurring trips to known drug houses. Does the name Germantown John Mancuso ring a bell?"

"Sure. He is a legend. Everybody knows G Town."

"Is he a client of yours?"

"My client list is confidential."

"I will take that reply as a yes."

Ro Ro jots some things down on her pad of paper.

"I have two questions for you. Did Neil cross swords with G Town? Was G Town in the drug business with you?"

A sneer crosses his face. "I do not do business with non-Russians. I also avoid Italians. They are dangerous people. As to those weekly trips, I never went on any trips with Neil. He could have set the destination and pick-up location from a separate cell for whatever reason. Maybe he used my location as a blind. You cannot prove I ever rode with Neil on those trips you tracked."

Ro Ro hands him a copy of a search warrant. "Judge French disagrees. This is a warrant to search your premises, car and office. In fact, my team is doing the search as we speak."

"That is outrageous. It is illegal."

"Nope. It is a legal search. Please state your whereabouts for the past forty-eight hours."

"I will not speak without my lawyer. His name is Gabriel Porto. He will be in touch with you. I am leaving to go home before your stormtroopers ransack my house."

"Wait."

Docky enters, implements in-hand. "What do you want me to do with this hump?"

"Please test this man for gunshot residue and get his DNA. He is under arrest."

"What am I being charged with?"

"Suspicion of dealing drugs, and involvement with a known criminal enterprise. I have you on tape admitting G Town is a client."

"This is a joke. Porto will have me out in an hour."

Docky shoves a swab into Chas's mouth. "There we go. Now hold out your hands."

Ro Ro reads Chas his rights. She waves in the officers. "Take Mister Gordonov to a holding cell. Keep him isolated from other prisoners."

Chas curls his fists. "You bitch!"

"I suggest that you spend your energy praying those tests come back negative. Now, get out of here."

Docky chuckles. "That fool brought a toothpick to a gun fight. Doesn't he know GSR has a six-hour shelf life?"

"I doubt it. If he fired a gun, he will be looking for a way to deal."

Docky laughs. "You can lie with the best of them. Maybe you can get some fool to confess."

"Yepper."

"We retrieved the bullets. I will file a report once I have studied them further."

"Have you found something unusual?"

"Give me a few hours before I comment. Science has no basis in speculation."

"You're right, as always."

"Bye for now," he says.

Renata Castro Schuler is next on the calendar.

If Neil was The Man of the neighborhood, Renata "The Pinata" is the woman of the neighborhood. She introduced a lot of young men to the benefits of safe sex. Her promiscuity began at fourteen.

Her long dark hair hangs over her shoulders. In the summer, she wears short shorts and sleeveless tops over her firm, full breasts. In the cooler seasons, she pours herself into tight jeans, clinging sweaters and various shades of leather jackets and boots that raise her height from five four to five eight. She smokes thin cigars and drinks vodka neat.

Her mind is sharper than the stiletto she carries in her jacket or boots. Renata likes older men, strong men, like G Town, Neil, and a host of local hoods.

She married Jerry Schuler, turning a good cop into a dirty cop. Jerry's death left her with a pension and half a million dollars in life insurance payout. If Neil was involved with her, he was chasing the devil.

Renata's perfume announces her presence. She looks like an upscale hooker in a red leather jacket and matching boots. Her hair is neatly coiffed. Her red lipstick and dab of rouge on her cheeks only adds to the call girl motif.

Ro Ro notes the slight bulge in her right boot. The stiletto beat the metal detector.

"Hello, Ro Ro. Long time, no see."

"Hello Renata. You look great. Come, sit so we can talk about Neil."

Renata sits, placing a boot on a chair. Her designer jeans wrapped her thighs like cellophane. "I know Neil screwed you," she says.

"Somebody had to pop my cherry. Neil was the best choice. Who got yours?" asks Rowena.

"My cousin, Georgio. He was built like Adonis, but dumb as a statue."

"What was your relationship with Neil?"

"He needed a friend. I owed him a favor, so I took him under my wing. It was a payback thing."

"Can you account for your whereabouts for the past forty-eight hours?"

"I was busy shacking up with Sergei Rudolf."

"He must be in his sixties. How was it?"

"The man has been screwing for fifty plus years. He knows what to do and how to do it. His control is amazing."

"Are you in the drug business with him?"

Renata laughs. "I will take the Fifth on that one. Look Ro Ro. I cared about Neil. We went back a long way. I got jammed up once, after Jerry died. Neil got his old man to help me."

"Did you do the old man?"

"I was grateful. He accepted my gratitude."

"Did Neil know about your gratitude?"

Renata cracks a wide smile. "That old dude told his wife what we did. She was pissed to beat the band. Instead, she came after me."

"Come on, Renata. That is a tall tale. That old lady could not scare you."

"She had a handgun. She pointed it right at my boobs. She called me a slut."

"Describe the gun for me."

"It was big. She used two hands to hold it."

"Let's go back to your alibi. You realize shacking up gives you both an alibi. That is very convenient. I am not buying it."

Renata smiles widely. "Really? I didn't think of that."

Ro Ro sits back and folds her arms across her chest. She sits silently for a long moment to make Renata uncomfortable.

"Why is Ro Ro so quiet?"

"Just because I am a blond with big boobs does not mean I am a boob. You could not wait to shift suspicion to Claire. You were sleeping with Neil, not Sergei. Sergei is a diversion to deflect suspicion away from you. You better stop the BS and start telling me the truth. You got that?"

Renata lifts her chin in defiance. "I told you the truth. I'm innocent. That witch Claire would kill anyone who got in her way. Her husband hated her. Neil could not stand her bossiness. That is the truth."

Ro Ro slams the table with the flat of her hand. "Lies! Neil was up to his eyeballs with G Town John in the drug business. G Town and you have history. My guess is that you went to G Town to rat out Neil, so he would eliminate Neil and you would get his insurance. It is a repeat of the scam you pulled on Jerry Schuler. You are an evil woman. A Jezebel in cheap red leather. Now give me a real alibi."

Renata turns red. She utters, "Strega."

"Calling me a witch is not going to clear you. My focus is on you for this murder."

"I am saying nothing. I want my lawyer."

"Would that lawyer be one Gabe Porto?"

"Yes. How did you know?"

"Porto is G Town's mouthpiece. You are sleeping with G Town and got Neil to be his mule. You are dirty, Renata. Sporco."

Renata stands up.

Ro Ro signals for the uniforms. "Check out Mrs. Schuler's right boot."

Renata backs herself to the wall. "Don't touch me!"

"Hand over the stiletto," says Ro Ro.

Renata's nostrils flare like a rattler ready to attack. "Damn you."

"Give us the knife. Now!"

Renata slides the stiletto out of her boot and places it on the table. "I want it back."

Ro Ro buzzes Docky. "Come here so you can check Mrs. Schuler for GSR. She entered a police station with a concealed weapon. That is a felony."

Ro Ro reads her the Miranda warning as Docky enters, swabs in hand. "After Doctor Poteet does his duty, you can call Porto. Meanwhile, we will make you comfortable in a holding cell next to Chas "The Jazz" Gordonov. Docky, please stay for a minute."

Ro Ro waits for the room to clear and texts Walter, "I stirred Mancuso's minestrone pot."

"What did you learn from those two?"

"I think this case has a lot more hair on it. The reason I asked you to stay is I want you to look at the case file photos of the January 1994 accident near Penn State involving Neil Mann. Look over the photos and notes and report."

"What are you looking for?"

"I sense this murder goes deeper than recent history."

"Your instincts are usually right on. Give me a day."

Biker comes in just as Docky leaves.

"What's up, Ro Ro?"

"I am checking out a couple of theories regarding the crime. One theory involves drugs and G Town. The other involves a family tragedy. I'll keep you updated."

"Do that, and don't let your dislike for G Town get you off track."

"That's good advice."

Biker leaves. Ro Ro calls HR. She talks to the manager. "I need a confidential search of the roster for the Fourteenth District from 1990 to 2000. Who partnered with Herbert Mann and when? Please keep it between us."

"What's up?" asks the manager.

"Maybe nothing. Maybe everything."

In Philadelphia, everybody knows everybody.

Two hours later, Ro Ro, Biker, Gabe Porto, Renata, and Chas "The Jazz" sit around the conference room table. Gabe has met with his clients in private prior to the sit down.

"I understand that a search of my clients' homes, work places and vehicles was conducted in relation to the apparent homicide of Neil Mann. What evidence justified a search?" asks Gabe.

"They are known associates of the deceased and have motives to want to see the victim killed. They are also known to have engaged in nefarious activities in the past. We needed to verify their alibis and conduct DNA and GSR tests. They are both flight risks."

"You denied them access to an attorney."

"Your presence belies that statement. We Mirandized them. May I point out that Renata brought a lethal weapon into the district headquarters?"

"That is a bullcrap charge and you know it. What are you charging them with and what evidence supports the charges?"

"We are waiting on test results for GSR and DNA."

Gabe claps his hands. "We all know GSR has a short life expectancy. And DNA cannot prove anything until you tie it to a crime scene or weapon. Have you any such proof?"

"We will," says Ro Ro.

Gabe shrugs. "When? When elephants fly? Lieutenant Jones. What kind of policing goes on in homicide these days?"

Biker wags a finger at Gabe. "We aren't playing games, attorney. We acted properly. Now is the time for your clients to fess up and tell us who killed Neil Mann."

"My clients have nothing to say, except goodbye. We are out of here. And, if you guys try using anything found from the searches, we will have them repressed. Same thing on the test results. Let's go," says Gabe.

Gabe, Renata and Chas rise to leave.

"Wait. We will have the evidence ready in short order. I advise you to take no trips. Fugitives are usually looked upon as guilty," says Ro Ro.

"People are innocent until proven guilty, Ms. Morse," says Gabe.

"Tell your boss Mancuso I said hello," says Ro Ro.

Gabe sneers under his waxed mustache. "I will do just that."

Biker chuckles. "You damn sure know how to rile the other side. Do we really have any hard evidence to pin them to Neil's death?"

"Not yet."

"Stay after them. I'm going home."

"Good night, boss."

Walter wants G Town as a decoy. Why?

Ro Ro settles on her sofa to Diana Krall singing Gershwin, the smooth, sultry rendition, "They can't take that away from me" and the wine slips a satin sheet of calm over her until the phone buzzes. Caller ID reads: "Mancuso."

"Hello, Mancuso," she says.

"Hello, pain in the ass. I called to give you a heads up. You are chasing the wrong rabbit. I had nothing to do with Neil Mann's death. Any time you spend chasing me is time wasted on finding the real killer."

"Oh. And who might that be?"

"You are the detective. You figure it out."

"You can bet your Italian butt I will get the killer."

"Good. It is nice to hear the police are getting it right. I am an innocent man."

"Nobody is innocent."

"You have a point. I did not kill Neil Mann."

"Somebody killed him."

"Go find the bastard who did the deed and leave me alone."

He clicks off.

She pours three ounces of Merlot into a glass tumbler. The Man left one hell of a legacy for her to solve.

Chapter Four

Ro Ro has no partner, one more unusual aspect of her job. She understands most police officers treasure their partner, or they hate them. The partner is a confidante, a lifesaver, a point of trust in an untrustworthy world. They stand back-to-back against all opposing forces. Ro Ro trusts no one.

Poring over the list of partners from the Fourteenth District from the early nineties shows a seven-year partnership between Herb Mann and Clarence Hunt, Walter Hunt's Dad. The time frame matches the timeline of Neil's days at Penn State. How much had Herb told his partner, who, in turn, may have revealed to Walter?

She Googles Clarence Hunt, finding that he died of natural causes three years ago. Walter is his only son. She feels like she is holding a piece in a jigsaw puzzle, needing to find its connecting pieces.

Docky texts her. "Meet me in my office. News to report."

She texts, "Wait."

She scurries away to Docky's office in the basement. The office is a windowless corner space. The concrete walls guarantee privacy. Docky sits behind a metal desk. "Welcome to my dungeon," says Docky.

"Glad to be here. What've you uncovered??"

Docky slides a pile of papers and photos across the desk. "It's all here. The incident was an accident but there are several things to note. First, the accident was reported by an anonymous nine one one caller. When the police arrived, they found one boy dead. His name was Frank O'Malley. He died of severe head trauma. No seat belt. Neil was found outside the car, unconscious, on the passenger side. His chest injuries were consistent with being smashed against the steering wheel, meaning he was the driver. My guess is that a third person was in the car. That person tampered with evidence to make it look like O'Malley was driving the vehicle. There were footprints leading into the woods. That person was most likely the caller and the evidence tamperer."

Ro Ro's mind goes into overload. "Holy shit! Why didn't the police catch all of this?"

"Good question. My humble guess is that Neil's status as a football player and the son of a policeman was conveyed to the police by the caller."

Ro scans the report with photos. "What was Neil's BAL?"

"He was recorded at .18. The dead boy was stone sober, and that was odd for an Irish college boy, wouldn't you say?"

"Curiouser and curiouser."

Alice in Wonderland. "Neil in Happy Valley."

"One more point of interest. CSU gathered fingerprints from the rear seat. I ran those prints and found a match with our good friend Chas "The Jazz". He was in the system thanks to a DUI in Ninety-nine. He left the scene to avoid publicity. Shall I pass this info on to Lieutenant Jones?"

"Please continue to study the report and keep it locked up. I need to noodle this data. It opens up a line of thought regarding Neil acting as a mole for Walter Gibraltar."

"I see your point. I have more for you on the ballistics of the bullets we extracted from Neil's body. The bullets were thirty-eight calibers matching the thirty-eights police carried before the Department switched to Glocks."

Ro Ro's adrenaline surges." Docky, please compare the slugs pulled from Neil to the bullets from his father's suicide."

Docky scratches the tip of his goatee. "No way do they match."

"Humor me. The slugs should be in the evidence room. See if the gun is still there."

"What are you conjuring up, Lady Morse?"

"We may have a new theory of the crime. It's a theory I hope is wrong."

"That mind of yours works in unusual ways."

"That is why I don't have a partner. They're too slow, skeptical and only hold me down."

Ro Ro heads to her office, wondering what Herb Mann knows about the accident and what he told Clarence Hunt. The pieces of the puzzle were starting to fill in.

Partners can be a blessing or a threat.

Three hours later, Docky texts her. "Bullets match. No sight of Herb's gun."

"Damn!" she says aloud.

She calls Walter and makes a date that night for a meeting in Docky's dungeon.

Chapter Five

Walter's massive frame fills the doorway. Smiling, he pulls a flask out of his vest pocket and sits across from Ro Ro. He takes three shot glasses from his suit coat pocket.

"Where is Doc Poteet?" asks Walter.

"This meeting is just you and me. What flavor of Irish Whiskey did you bring?"

"Green Spot. Nothing but the best for you." He pours two shots. They click shot glasses and say, "Sláinte," in unison.

"What's up, Ro Ro?"

"There is an epidemic of lying in this case. It is so bad that the only one telling me the truth is a stone gangster named Mancuso. Walter, I want you to tell me how The Man got involved in your drug game. Do not bullshit me. There is no tape rolling and I am not wearing a wire. Just tell me the truth."

Walter's brow furrows above his serious frown. "My father passed the word on to me. You see, Frankie O'Malley was our cousin on my mother's side. Chas "The Jazz" also knew the truth. When The Man discovered Chas was running dope for the Rudolf mob, he came to me to stop the drug running. The Man wanted to get Chas straight. Well, I got the bright idea to use The Man as a mole, so we could nab the whole Rudolf crew. He could be a hero and make up for Franky getting the rap for driving the car. The Man wore a wire. About a week ago,

Chas got drunk and told Claire that her son was a drug runner. He was sick of hearing how great a guy The Man was. Chas was always jealous of The Man. He felt he was the real hero and not Neil. The crazy old lady called out The Man. He should have quit or told her the truth. But, if he tells her he is working with us, she might confront Chas and put him in danger. I swear I do not know who whacked The Man."

Walter chugs straight from the flask. "Herb Mann knew his son was guilty of homicide by drunken driving. It drove him over the edge. It's like father and son were destroyed that night. The ironic part is we were ready to arrest the Rudolf gang until The Man was killed. We lost our star witness. We have the tapes, but Neil's testimony would have sealed the deal."

"Mancuso was a red herring to keep me occupied."

"Yeah. We wanted the Rudolf's to not get scared away. Everybody knows you hate G Town. We figured you would leap at a chance to pin a murder rap on the dago. What else do you want to know, off the record?"

"You filled in the pieces."

"What's your next move?"

"I am going to find the missing gun that killed The Man."

"Do you know who did it?"

"Yes. Now pour me another shot."

The Mann residence is a modest stone construction, two-story, three-bedroom, and a one-and-a-half-bathroom home on East Allens Lane in West Mount Airy. A porch sporting a round table and four chairs overlook a rose bush and a circular garden.

At seven AM the next day, warrant in hand, Ro Ro and three officers, and a CSU analyst from Docky's office, knock on Claire Mann's front door.

Fully dressed in jeans and a gray sweater, a stern looking Claire answers the door. "What do you want?"

"We have a warrant to search the premises, your property, and your vehicle," says Ro Ro. "Go to it, fellows. Claire, please don't interfere."

"I'm a policeman's wife. He was disgraced by his son. I will not add to that sin by obstructing you. But whatever you are looking for, you will not find it here. I am an innocent woman."

Ro Ro takes her aside. "Come outside with me. It is high time you heard the truth."

They stand on the lawn near the rose bush. Ro Ro has rehearsed her account of Neil's role in the drug ring trap set by Walter.

"Your son screwed up by drinking and driving in the snow. A young man was killed, and Neil's life was ruined. He tried to make up for his mistake. He was not a drug runner. He was a police informant. Chas "The Jazz" lied to you. Neil was working with Walter Gibraltar to take down the Rudolf gang. Whoever killed him protected the Rudolfs."

Claire shoves Ro Ro hard, sending her five yards backwards. "You are a liar. Chas loved Neil. He protected him at the accident scene. They were like brothers. It was Neil that was rotten to the core. He drove my Herb to suicide."

"You fool. Chas is as corrupt as Judas. He fed you a line to ward off Neil, but he sent you over the edge."

"Liar!"

"Where is Herb's gun?"

"I have no idea. Do you think I shot Neil?"

"Yes. Now where is the gun?"

"This is madness."

"Your attorney may use insanity as a defense."

"Dear God, please spare me from this harlot."

"Confession will save you."

Claire turns away and races to the house screaming, "Get thee out of my house."

Ro Ro pulls her outside. "Stop before I arrest you for obstruction of justice."

Claire raises her fist and swings at Ro Ro, who easily dodges the swing. Her momentum sends Claire forward, falling to her knees. She rises and charges Ro Ro, sending them into a pile on the lawn. Ro Ro throws Claire off and grabs and handcuffs the older woman. "There. Now, stop your madness."

Ro Ro drags Claire inside, while a woman walking her dog takes a photo.

Ro Ro leads Claire to the living room sofa. "Sit and be quiet or we will arrest you for attacking a police officer."

Claire glares, her green eyes piercing through Ro Ro like ice picks. "Search, you witch. You will find nothing."

The search concludes at noon. No gun is found. Ro Ro calls Biker. "Boss. We did not find the gun."

"Dang! Come in and we can regroup. You made the local news for arresting the widow of a policeman and the mother of The Man. Some neighbor recorded the incident while she was walking her dog. It has gone viral. Our chicken butt DA is already apologizing and accusing you of police brutality. Nice work."

"I know she did it."

"We need evidence. Find the freaking gun."

Ro Ro bites her lip and heads to the District Office.

Biker sits across from her in his office. "Morse, this is a public relations disaster. I may have to pull you off the case. I may also have to assign you a partner, which means you will no longer work alone."

"A partner would slow me down."

"You need to be slowed down."

"Let's put a tail on her. Eventually, she will lead us to the gun. Ballistics show that the bullets from Herb Mann's suicide match the bullets Docky extracted from Neil Mann. She is the most likely suspect. She also had motive. She told me she blamed Neil for Herb's suicide. When a mother turns on a child, God cannot stop their need for revenge. She may kill again."

"Let me think about it."

"I need a warrant to search her locker at the country club."

"I will check it out with the DA. You said she will kill again. Who do you think will be the target?"

"Chas 'The Jazz' lied to her. He also corrupted The Man. In her deranged mind, he is guilty."

Ro Ro snaps her fingers. "Boss, I have an idea. Do not surveil her. Let her think she is safe. I'll keep an eye on Chas. If she goes for him, I will be there to nab her."

Biker shakes his head. "Take a few days off. Keep out of sight until the press finds another story. Then we can revisit your idea."

"In the meantime, Chas is a target. Put somebody on him, please."

"I will consider it. Go home, Ro Ro. Come back in three days."

Ro Ro senses that Biker has a good reason to get her out of the way.

"We will do it your way. Please, no partner."

"I am not sure I can get any detective in Philly to work with you, anyway."

"Thanks for nothing," she says.

Chapter Six

Over the next two days, Ro Ro squeezes every ounce of self-restraint she has to not contact either Claire or Chas. The press camps out on her doorstep for one day, then goes off chasing a story involving the killing of an illegal immigrant by an off duty cop..

Biker seems too eager to draw her away from following Chas. Why?

She watches the eleven o'clock news, happy she is not mentioned. She crawls into bed, strung out but grateful for the coming sleep.

At midnight, her cell buzzes.

"Hello."

"This is Claire Mann. Come to my home, now. Come alone."

"What's going on?"

Claire's voice sounds relaxed, resigned. "Come now, please. I have a present for you."

Claire hangs up. Rowena calls Docky and fills him in. "I have your back."

"Meet me at Ardsleigh Street and Allens Lane."

"I will. But I am a scientist. I do not have a weapon."

"You are a witness. You don't need a Glock. I will have a plan ready."

"What do you think she has in mind?"

"Maybe nothing. Maybe my murder."

"Oh, the joy."

After they meet, Docky circles the block and walks down the street on the opposite side of Claire's home, while Ro Ro walks up on the side of Claire's home.

Ro Ro knocks on the door.

"It's open," says Claire.

Ro Ro puts her hand on her sidearm. "I'm coming in."

Claire sits on the sofa facing Ro Ro. At her feet lies the body of Walter Gibraltar Hunt. A bullet has split his forehead in half. His blue eyes stare to the ceiling.

"There lies the devil. It was he who bedeviled and coerced my son and made me believe Neil was a crook. It was his father who teased and harassed my Herb to the point where Herb killed himself. It was he who deserved to die."

"Where is the gun?"

"Here," she says, pulling it from under her backside. She points it at R Ro. "I should kill you, too. You are the devil's accomplice."

"Put the gun down," says Ro Ro.

"I am going to shoot you and then myself. It is what makes it all right."

"What does it make right? Your family is dead, and your death is unnecessary. Neil was a good man. He was a hero. He deserved to live. He was helping rid the city of drugs. Now, I understand. What drugs are you on?"

"Chas gives me God's breath, a potion that makes you see God's will."

"How long have you been using this magic drug?"

"Since Herbie died. Chas is my angel. He made me understand why Neil had to die. Chas is my true heir, my spiritual son. He is my hero. He convinced me the Hunts were the devils."

"Entheogens!" shouts Docky. "Chas Gordonov fed her entheogens to control her. She was under his control. Like a puppet. She was entranced. You must shoot her, or she will surely shoot you."

Claire's hand is shaking. "Why did you lie to me? We agreed you would come alone. Liar!" She fires, missing Ro Ro by inches. Ro Ro fires and shoots her dead.

Epilogue

The press carries the story of the death of The Man and his mother as an indictment of a culture gone mad with drug usage. Ro Ro becomes a heroine, the woman who epitomizes the best of female courage. Chas is arrested as an accomplice to murder. The betting odds were that he would beat the rap.

Absolved, Ro Ro cements her position as the best detective in Philly. She takes time off. Settling onto a bench outside the Valley Green Inn, she tosses bread at the quacking ducks. Her father had taken her to the Wissy to fish for trout. She never caught one. But having her dad's full attention was reward enough. She wishes he were at her side.

A man sits beside her. "Is this seat taken?" asks John Mancuso.

"Up popped the devil."

"How is Philly's numero uno policewoman?"

"I am well. How is Philly's numero uno crook?"

G Town tosses a pebble into the water. "You are quite a lady. I admire a strong person. Strength is all that keeps people safe. Our vices corrupt our bodies and minds."

"Do not get philosophical. Class does not become you."

"Fate is the kingmaker. If Neil hadn't gotten into that accident, he may have become a leader. A president. A senator. Or, just a good father. Bad luck set all things in motion against him. Be careful, Rowena. Fate nearly got you. If that fool Chas had not set Claire after you, she would have beaten the rap and Chas wouldn't be under arrest."

"I have never seen you here at Valley Green. Why come here when I'm here? Did you follow me?"

G Town laughs. "I always keep an eye on you. Knowing where you are makes me feel safe."

Rowena stands up. "I gotta go."

"Let's do dinner sometime. I promise I'll be a gentleman."

"Ducks are ducks. You are you, and I am me. Nobody changes who or what they are."

"True that."

Rowena walks away thinking that in a different world she would have more than dinner with him. Is physical attraction an entheogen or untrustworthy hormones?

Story Eight: Murder at the Pool Between Good and Evil

Chapter One

In 1683, William Penn and Tamanend, Chief of the Lenni Lenape tribe of the Delaware nation, met in Shackamaxon Village to sign a peace treaty. The pact secured the safety of the Native Americans and the populace of Philadelphia, The City of Brotherly love.

The Philadelphia area has a rich tradition of the Native Americans. In Northwest Philly's Fourteenth police district lies a freshwater pool. The Devil's Pool. The pool lies less than fifty yards upstream along Cresheim Creek where the creek empties into the Wissahickon. The pool carries the longstanding reputation of a lethally dangerous body of water. Growing up, Ro Ro was forbidden to swim in the pool nestled between large rocks for fear its floor held a whirlpool that would suck a swimmer to Hell. The Lenni Lenape people believed it is the spot between good and evil. The Devil's Pool.

Today the pool is a favorite of teens, college students and young adults from Northwest Philly tempting fate by diving into the pool from the stone bridge overhead between large rocks guarding the edges. On hot summer days, as many as a hundred bikini-clad females and beer drinking young men crowd the pool area cheering on dare devils who leap from the stone bridge through a narrow opening into the pool.

The cliff divers of La Quebrada near Acapulco, Philly version.

The Friends of the Wissahickon Association oversees the pool. Their executive director, Megan Conrad Granato and Ro Ro graduated from Holy Cross Grammar School together. Megan is a pretty woman, divorced with two kids. Her reddish gray hair is swept back behind her round face. The early September heat roasts her inside her red and white striped pullover. The long sleeves signal psoriasis. She bites her lip to hold back tears as Docky's CSU team examines the remains of Ned Grissom. They tape off the scene while about twenty onlookers gather in the woods surrounding the pool.

CSU Chief Docky Poteet shakes his head from side to side. "Here is what the evidence shows. The young man landed face-first against the rocks on the west side of the pool. His body ricocheted into the creek and washed against the pool's edge. The body lodged in a crevice about six inches under the water. His jaw and neck were broken. His parents will have a tough time recognizing him. My guess is that he died around midnight."

"Who the hell dives into the eye of a needle hole in the dark?" asks Ro Ro. "Look. He's dressed in jeans, running shoes and a tee shirt. He was not planning on swimming. Did you find his wallet and smartphone?"

"Yes, on the wallet. He had eleven dollars on him. All one-dollar bills. His driver's license identifies him as Ned Roundtree. Address is 131 West Gorgas Lane. There is no insurance card, so I assume he had no car. This was not a robbery."

Ro Ro enters her notes on her cell. "What else?"

"We will test for drugs and alcohol. But, based on the angle of the fall, he either aimed his dive toward the rocks or, he was pushed from the right rear by a person or persons unknown," says Docky.

Megan pulls on Ro Ro's arm. The woman is stronger than most men. "Ned Roundtree could not swim. He had to be forced to climb up there. He also did not drink. He was native Lenape and hated alcohol. His father drank himself to death. Ned was neither drunk nor foolish. This act makes no sense," says Megan.

Ro Ro nods at her old friend. "Were you close to him?"

"He worked for us for three years. He used to call me Aunt Megan. God, you must find his killer."

"I will. I promise," says Ro Ro. "Who discovered the body?"

"Harry Jenks. He is a member of the Protect Our Nature Society. He hikes here almost every day. Harry is the big guy standing over there. The woman next to him is Monica Mason. She is also on the board of directors. The man to the right is Cletus Durrell. Another director."

"I need to talk to all of them starting with Harry. Introduce me, please."

Megan tugs on Ro Ro's shirt sleeve. "I am so glad I called you. I know you will get the bastards who did this."

Ro Ro nods, wondering why Megan uses the plural.

"Yepper."

Ro Ro motions for two uniformed policemen to come to her. "Climb up to that stone bridge and search the area. Look for smartphones from selfies gone bad."

Megan chimes in. "The area is a black hole for dropped cellphones."

"Eerie. It's like the past stopped here," says Ro Ro.

Megan points to the stone bridge. "That is really a gravity sewer. Drainage from Merck and other plants runs through it to a sanitation plant. If it bursts, the area will become a hell hole of waste."

"Thanks for sharing that. Have there been any leaks?"

Megan snaps her fingers. "Yes! About ten years ago, there was a chemical leak from the Merck facility. The Protect Our Nature team caught it in time and averted a catastrophe. Ask Harry Jenks about it. He retired from Merck."

Ro Ro gives Megan a thumbs up. "Will do."

Harry Jenks towers over Ro Ro by at least a foot. Built like an oak tree, his swarthy arms are folded across the chest of his red Phillies tee shirt. His scraggly beard hangs low. He looks like a man who kisses a beaver and it sticks to his chin.

Monica Mason is a short, thin woman. She nervously bobs on her white and pink Nikes. Her wire-rimmed glasses show off her clear blue eyes. Her white hair betrays her as older than she looks.

Cletus Durrell eyes Ro Ro's chest in a long, unabashed stare. Trim, his chest clung to his light gray tee shirt. His hairy legs boast well-formed legs. The man was an athlete in his past.

"Mr. Jenks. May I have a word with you? I am Detective Morse stationed at the Fourteenth District."

Harry nods. "I know you from the papers. You are the one John Mancuso saved from the bomb."

"Mr. Jenks, Let's talk over there. Miss Mason and Miss Durrell, I would like to ask each of you a few routine questions. Please wait."

"Will do, gladly," says Durrell, his eyes glued to her boobs.

Monica shrugs. "Sure Detective. I will be happy to help you."

"Thank you both. Mr. Jenks, let's talk away from the bystanders."

She leads Harry to a spot under a tall elm. The shade would be welcome. She glances to see Megan glaring at the covered body of Ned Roundtree. She looks angry, very angry.

"Please tell me, Mr. Jenks, how did you happen across the body of Ned Roundtree this morning?"

"My daily routine is to rise around five. Have a coffee and oatmeal. I then walk down Livezey Street from my home on Allens Lane and then along the Wissahickon Creek to Devil's Pool. It is a quiet place that time of day. I usually sit on a rock and let the quiet time seep into my mind. It's like going to a church without the walls and priests and sanctimony," he says.

"Back to nature. Just like the Lenni Lenape experienced. They were Ned's tribe. How well did you know Ned?"

"I knew him from his work at the Protect Our Nature team. I am a long-term member. There are about six hundred members. Ned was a fine young man. He traced his ancestry back to Penn Treaty days. His mother, June, will be very upset. She lives in Mount Airy. I suppose the police will notify her of Ned's accident."

Ro Ro's antenna perks up. "I didn't say it was an accident."

Harry turns pale. His jaw drops three inches. "You don't think it was murder, do you?"

"We're not sure. Can you think of any reason someone would want to harm Ned?"

Harry leans against the elm to steady himself. "No. Jesus help us. I am shocked."

"Tell me about the chemical leak from the Merck plant."

"It happened several years ago. Merck acted responsibly and quickly to clean up the problem."

"Were you on the Board of the Protect Our Nature at the time of the leak?"

"No. I joined the board later to serve as a watchdog. No one wanted a reoccurrence."

"Was Ned a militant for Native American rights?"

Harry looks away, sighs, and runs his hand across his face. He was stalling for time. "You could say that he was upset that the Lenni got the short end of the peace pipe. Philly is a great city with fabulous wealth. The whites won and the red people lost. Those were Ned's words at our last board meeting. He wanted justice in the form of reparations from the city."

"How did the board react to his desire for reparations?"

"He received a mixed reaction. The younger members were open to a discussion on the subject. The older members scoffed at the idea. Hell, the city can barely fund itself. Did they want a soda tax part two to fund an event from four hundred years ago?"

"What side were you on?"

"I sided with neither side. I suggested a compromise. I proposed we ask Merck and other companies to pay a tax on the gravity sewer running above Devil's Pool as a way of raising scholarships for Lenni Lenape descendants."

"That seems reasonable. How did Ned react to your proposal?"

"He said we were offering crumbs while eating the banquet."

"Ned had a way with words. Please give me your address. I also need to ask where you were at midnight last night?"

"I was home in bed listening to my wife's snoring."

She makes a note to do a full background check on Harry, including his bank records and criminal record. "Thank you, Harry. We will be following up. One more question. How do you know John Mancuso?"

Harry had the oops look like a kid who says too much to a cop.

"Everybody knows John."

"Everybody, meaning serious gamblers."

"I guess. I have to go."

"See you around, Harry."

Harry walks away, leaving Ro Ro with the feeling that there is more to Devil's Pool than swimming. She motions for Cletus to come forward.

Ro Ro Googles Cletus Durrell. Her guess was correct. Cletus played minor league baseball for the Phillies Reading farm team. He was an outfielder. He suffered an injury in a car accident that ended his career. He was married to Muriel Whitman. They lived on Valley Avenue in Roxborough. He had retired from Gordon Chemicals, one of the companies whose plant empties into Cresheim Creek.

He blatantly stares at her chest, a wry smile twisting his thin lips. "Hello Detective. How may I help you?"

"You can answer a few questions without staring at my breasts like a sixteen-year-old horn ball."

Cletus stops dead, as if she has hit him with a straight left jab. "Sorry Detective. I come from the Roxborough side of the Wissahickon. We are deplorable people, not at all like the lefties from Chestnut Hill. Bad manners are a way of life."

"I am from Mount Airy. We learned manners in grammar school. We also learned to respect each other. Now that we understand one another, I need to ask you a few questions and don't think about lying to me or bullshitting me, got that?"

Cletus salutes her. "Aye aye, Comandante. How can I help you?"

"What brought you here today?"

"I hike over here from Roxborough. I drive down Wises Mill Road to Valley Green. I cross over the creek at the Valley Green bridge and walk the path on this side of the creek. I jog back on the other side. It is my fitness regimen. I like being in shape. When you hit fifty, you need to work at being healthy."

"Did you know Ned Roundtree?"

"Sure. He was a real upstart. He had a chip on his shoulder the size of a manhole cover. Always yelling about white privilege and the red man getting the totem pole shoved where the sun don't shine. Pardon my language."

"You are pardoned. In this job I hear a lot worse. Harry said the same thing about Ned's activism. Who did he rub wrong?"

Cletus smiles like a toothy goat. "Just about everyone on the board. We are people who want to preserve our past. We love the park, the pool, the creek, and the culture. We don't relish some punk stirring up a lot of grievances from four hundred years ago. Old Billy Penn was a Quaker. He would not cheat anyone. A deal is a deal."

"Do you know his mother?"

"Yeah. I know June. She is a good woman. Her old man was a walking bottle of firewater. Two drinks and Charlie Roundtree was whooping up a fight. When he died, we raised money to bury him and pay for the funeral."

"What was your relationship with June?"

Cletus flinches. "We are just friends."

Cletus wore a wedding ring. "How did your wife feel about you comforting the widow?"

"My old lady trusts me."

"How did Ned feel about you?"

"That boy and I were like oil and water. He walked in his lane. I walked in mine."

"And, if one of you crossed a line, you crashed. Where were you last night around midnight?"

"I was home with my wife, Muriel."

"Do you have kids?"

"I have a son in the Army and a daughter living in Arizona. Why do you ask?"

"A man with children of his own is less likely to murder a friend's child."

"I heard you were a smart broad."

"How is your knee?"

"I get around."

"Do you have any idea who wanted him dead?"

"I thought it may be an accident?"

"The CSU says homicide. I trust science over rumor. I will want to talk to your wife to verify your alibi. What is your or her cell number?"

Cletus gave her both numbers. "Are we done?"

"Yes. For now."

Ro Ro does a Google search on Monica Mason. Her maiden name was Whitman. She was sister to Cletus's wife. Typical Philly. Everybody knows everybody. She had also worked at Gordon Chemical as an accountant. She had graduated from Penn State with a degree in forensic accounting. Divorced, her only child, Heather, was an Army sergeant. The site shows an early picture of Monica. Long blond hair draped down her shoulders. Her Betty Davis eyes alluring as fresh apples to Adam. She could have stopped rush hour traffic on Broad Street.

She waves Monica Mason forward.

"Hello, officer," says Monica.

"The title is detective. Hello Miss Mason."

"I meant no disrespect. I'm not used to dealing with police protocol. How may I help?"

"I understand that all three of you that I interviewed are members of the Board of the Friends of the Wissahickon. I swam in Devil's Pool in direct defiance of my parents. The local myth is that the pool is a dangerous, evil stream to Hell. What say you?"

"Water is water. I don't believe in superstitions."

"Murder is real. Ned Roundtree was murdered here. How well did you know Ned?"

Monica laughs. "Everybody knew Ned 'The Red'."

"That comment sounds racist."

"I was referring to his communist leanings, not his ances-try."

"Fair enough. Do you have any idea who wanted him dead?"

"I thought it was an accident?"

"Science says he was murdered. No myth."

Monica purses her lips to stop them from shivering. "I have no idea why he would be murdered. If every liberal pain in the ass was killed, we would lose half the country."

"Ned was hell-bent on attacking the chemical companies for abusing the environment. He also wanted reparations for the raw deal the Quakers pulled on his Lenni Lenape ancestors. Many would characterize him as a pain in the ass."

Monica twirls her hair around her manicured finger. "He was a cute man. Cuteness garners forgiveness."

"Then who thought he was uncute enough to shove him off the bridge?"

Monica casts her eyes to the ground. "I can't imagine someone killing a handsome boy like Ned. It's horrible. It is too freaking sad."

"Where were you last night at midnight?"

"I was home in bed by myself. My cat, Hermione, can vouch for me."

Ro Ro gets nose to nose. "Look cutie. This is a murder case. Frivolity is insulting and only makes me think you are laughing off something you want to hide. So, cut the clever answers. Do you have an alibi?"

Monica steps back, her fists clenched. "No."

"Please give me your address and phone number. I will be in touch."

"Do I need a lawyer?"

"Only you know the answer to that question."

The van carrying Ned heads away. No doubt to the lab for an autopsy. Ro Ro heads to the district office, anxious to hear Docky's findings.

She wants June Roundtree brought in for identification of her son's body and to answer questions. Ro Ro calculates the odds that the three board members meet as planned or by coincidence. Planning wins out.

She passes Megan sitting on a rock, smoking a joint, staring at the Wissahickon, a portrait of grief. Devil's Pool has captured another victim.

Chapter Two

The worst moment in a homicide detective's life is when a family member identifies their loved one's dead body. The sense of loss adds to the pressure on the detective to find the perp. The search for justice weighs heavily on the family and the detective. The moment binds the two in a spiritual tie. Truth becomes a mission, an obligation. In an ironic way, the quest becomes a reason to be.

June Roundtree looks much younger than her Google photo. Her jet-black hair is closely cropped. Tiny gold earrings dot her ears. Her taut, five-foot two-inch body looks firm under her paisley blouse and designer jeans. Her flat shoes squeak across the linoleum floor. She could have passed as Ned's sister. She married Joseph Roundtree on her sixteenth birthday. Ned was born four months later.

Ro Ro takes June's trembling hand and leads her to Ned's body covered by a white sheet on Docky's operating room table.

Docky stands tall, his hand on the sheet. "I am Doctor Charles Poteet. Are you ready to identify the person here?"

June wipes tears from her eyes with a tissue. "Please."

Docky swings back the sheet. June gasps. "Ned. That is my Ned." She sinks to her knees. Ro Ro and Docky help her to her feet.

"I got her," says Ro Ro.

She leads June upstairs, feeling a common grief and a determination to stop the tears.

June sits across from Ro Ro. A crimson ring circles her brown eyes. Her sadness reminds Ro Ro of a painting of the Pietà she had seen of the mother of Jesus gazing at her dead son's body.

"Why? Why was Ned killed?" asks June.

"We aren't sure. Here is what we do know. Ned alienated a lot of people by challenging them to pay reparations and to close the chemical plants near Devil's Pool."

June's face twists in confusion. "That's no reason to kill him. It ain't right."

"Can you think of anyone who wanted him dead?"

"No. He was loud and strong in his protest. He was young, and young men are impassioned."

"Killers are often motivated by fear. Who did he make nervous?"

"No one. At least, no one I can think of."

"I have a list of people who knew Ned. I will read them off. Tell me all you can about each one."

"Did one of them kill my Ned?"

"I am gathering evidence. No one has been charged. I am looking for a motive. Dr. Poteet will find the physical evidence. Together we will find the truth. You must tell me the truth."

"I will. I promise."

"Here is the first name. Harry Jenks."

"Ned hated him. He said the man was a bully, a beast who hated people of color."

"Was Ned afraid of Harry?"

"Ned was a born warrior, like his father. He feared no man."

"Harry worked for a chemical company that may have harmed the environment. Did Ned confront him?"

"My Ned confronted the world. He was angry at white people in general."

"What about Cletus Durrell?"

June's shoulders hunch like a wounded animal protecting itself from a predator. "Cletus is a different animal. He preys on weakness."

"Did Cletus hit on you?"

June looks away. "Often. I never gave in."

"Did Ned know about his advances?"

"Yes. He confronted Clete. Clete pulled a gun on Ned. He threatened to shoot Ned. I warned Ned to stay away from him. One does not hunt a wolf. A wolf makes for bad meat and will attack you in a pack. The wolf is evil."

"Monica Mason?"

"She is a witch. She teased my Ned. I warned him that a married woman is a mine field. Sooner or later you will take the wrong step. And your world will explode."

"My information showed she was divorced."

"Ned said the same thing."

"Who told you she was married?"

"Muriel Durrell. We are old friends. Did Muriel lie to me?"

"Maybe."

"Why would she lie?"

"I will find out. One more name. Megan Conrad Granato."

"My son adored her. She was like a second mother. She would never hurt Ned. Do you know she and Muriel are old friends? They were classmates at Chestnut Hill College."

"Surely, Megan knew Cletus, too."

"She introduced Muriel to Cletus."

"Were Megan and Cletus dating?"

"Yes. For a short period."

"How do you know all this history?"

"I am Muriel's hairdresser. Women tell hairdressers everything."

"Tell me about your husband."

"He was a handsome man. Fiery. He had bright, warm eyes a woman cannot resist. He was a magnet that drew in any woman he met."

"Why did you name your boy Ned?"

"Joseph picked the name. He said the name meant something special in Scotland. A Ned was a rebel, an outlaw."

"Did Joseph raise him to be a rabble rouser?"

June frowns as if defying Ro Ro. "Joseph raised Ned to stand up for himself. Back down to no one. Be a warrior, a true man."

"It is obvious from my research that you married Joseph when you were underage. Did you love him?"

"The sun rose on his left shoulder and set on his right shoulder. Just like Ned. They were my world, my universe. Can you understand that some men live in different dimensions? Our culture teaches us that leaders are born to destiny. Normal people fear the unusual people."

"So much so that they kill them," says Ro Ro.

They shake hands and part. Ro Ro feels a connection to June, a sisterhood of defiant women.

Chapter Three

Just before five PM, Docky texts Ro Ro. "Stop by my office. Important."

Ro Ro sits across from Docky. He holds a cellphone in his hand. "We found Ned's cellphone. He last used it around ten PM. He made calls to his mother, Megan Granato, Cletus Durrell, and Harry Jenks. Notice he didn't call Monica Mason. Why? Was she with him? His emails need your scrutiny."

"Where exactly did you find the cell?"

"It was in the weeds below the gravity sewer."

"Could he have been standing on the gravity bridge taking a picture from the phone?"

"Yes. That makes sense."

"Did you check the photos on the cell?"

Docky opens the photos. He hands her the device.

"What else did you find?"

"There is a thin crack in the gravity bridge. A pinhole at best. Chemicals we are trying to identify are seeping into the ground. My guess is potassium thiocyanate. It is commonly used in water treatment. It's deadly."

"Damn! The kid was right to challenge the Protect Our Nature Society. I wonder if Megan knew the poison was leaking into the soil."

"Check the emails. Ned informed all of them."

"The information is damning, but is it enough to spark a murder?"

"That'd be your call, Miss Ro Ro. Old Docky just serves up the facts. You make the case."

"I will research the water treatment companies to see if there is a financial link to anyone on the board."

Docky chuckles. "You and the internet are like bloodhounds chasing a wounded bear."

Ro Ro speeds away, eager to do intelligence searches on all board members of Friends of the Wissahickon.

She stops at Biker's office and updates him.

Biker smiles in approval. "Go get 'em, Morse. Follow the money and you will find the motive for the murder."

"I can use some help from Intelligence on researching bank records and credit cards."

"You got it. I will direct them to support you one hundred percent."

"Thanks, boss."

"Just keep me updated. I don't like surprises."

His support surprises her. He must have no financial interests to protect, she thinks.

Ro Ro downloads the emails to her PC. For the next four hours, she scours the emails for the received, forwarded, replied, and sends, making careful notes. The scent of the hunt flashes in her mind.

At ten past ten, she receives the findings of the Intelligence team: Jenks, Durrell, Mason and Megan are all on the payroll of Delaware Valley Treatment Properties, Inc. as consultants. They all receive monthly stipends of one thousand dollars. The payments go back over five years. They all have severe conflicts of interest. Bribery, too.

The emails from Ned to Megan suggest a much different relationship than aunt to nephew. Here's to you, Mrs. Robinson.

Ned was also involved with Monica Mason. His father and Muriel were old friends, too. Did June know about the affair? Did Cletus know?

Sex and money and fear and possibly jealousy mixed into a potent cocktail of human frailty.

Ro Ro calls Biker. "Boss, I need to talk to you."

"What's up?"

"We found enough motive for two murders. I'll show you the emails and the financial records."

"On my way."

Ro Ro takes Biker on the journey of evidence. At the end, he simply says, "Dang, if you ain't got them by the short hairs. Shall I have them served?"

"We have a financial trail. But not a clear evidence package to indict. Let's call them in as material witnesses. No lawyers. We want a conference. We will pressure them until somebody cracks."

"It's worth a try. We will get them in tomorrow, first thing."

"Add June Roundtree to the list. I want her to see and hear what went down."

"That makes sense. Maximum pressure equals maximum guilt."

"Right you are."

Ro Ro feels guilty in not disclosing the involvement of G Town John.

Chapter Four

At ten AM the next morning, the group summoned by Ro and Biker assemble in a conference room. Biker and Docky watch behind a two-way mirror. Harry sits next to Cletus on one side. Megan sits at the head of the table opposite Ro Ro at the other end. June and Monica sit next to each other, facing Harry and Cletus.

Ro Ro stands to take command of the meeting. "Thank you all for coming here. Our investigation has raised a series of questions. Some are best addressed in a group setting. Other questions are best to discuss in one-on-one meetings to maintain personal privacy. You are here as material witnesses, not as suspects. I asked June Roundtree to attend as well. In a way she represents Ned."

Megan folds her arms across her chest and leans back. "Excuse me, Detective. Isn't this an unusual setting for gathering witnesses?"

"Thank you for asking, Megan. Witnesses often forget details that other witnesses remember, so one witness feeds off another. If there are any discrepancies, we can resolve them on the spot. My first point involves the discovery of Ned's iPhone. You may say that a phone is an electronic diary. Calls and emails are tracked. It is as if Ned is testifying. The recovery of his phone gave Intelligence a window into his mind. Ned was troubled by the board's coverup of a chemical leak of thiocyanate in the gravity pipe above Devil's Pool. He told you specifically, Megan. He also told Cletus, Hank, Monica, and possibly others. Yet, nothing was done to address the leak, suggesting that the waste treatment company wanted the leak kept quiet. Certain board members were paid to protect the waste treatment company. One thousand a month was the going rate. We checked bank records and found the cash flow to each of your accounts. Ned was about to go public with the leak, thereby threatening the economic welfare of everyone in this room. That disclosure could lead to criminal charges. It is motive for Ned's murder. Or maybe Ned was killed by accident. Maybe on that fateful night, he was showing someone what he had found. Or perhaps, he did not realize that the person he was showing the leak to was involved in the scheme."

Ro Ro pauses to note the expression of surprise on the faces of all board members, save one.

"Confronted with that revelation, the person reacted and shoved Ned off the bridge to meet his death."

June pounds the table. "Which one of you thieves killed my son? Confess your sin."

Ro Ro motions for June to sit. "Please wait until I am done."

June glares at each board member. "I will get you."

"We are being threatened unjustly with bribery. I thought we were here to find the truth about Ned's death," says Monica.

"All in good time. The search of the cellphone revealed that two of you had intimate relationships with Ned. He had his father's looks and charm. And he was young."

"Sex is not a crime," says Monica.

"I am talking about jealousy. 'Hell hath no fury like a woman scorned.' An English playwright wrote those timeless words centuries ago. Jealousy and anger can also drive one to violence."

Megan glowers at her. "This is all conjecture. It proves nothing. Where is your evidence that any one of us pushed Ned to his death?"

"Fate intervened. Fate and technology. Ned was taking a picture when he was shoved. The cell recorded as it fell. One frame caught the face of the killer staring down as Ned plunged toward his death. One person who has led an exemplary life lost her mind for one second. One terrible moment. You may say the Devil made Megan lose her cool and send Ned catapulting to his death. Is that what happened, my old friend? He broke your heart?"

Megan buries her face in her hands. "Yes. Damn him. He used me."

"Don't blame him. Check your mirror."

June rushes at Megan, wielding a long, sharpened hair pin.

"Bitch."

She stabs Megan in the neck three times before Ro Ro grabs June from behind and tosses her to the floor. Biker rushes in with Docky. "I didn't see that coming," says Harry.

"Me neither," says Cletus.

Monica runs out screaming.

Ro Ro presses her blouse against Megan's wounds. June has hit the carotid artery. Megan is dead in less than a minute.

Ro Ro arrests June, feeling that she has been an unwitting accomplice to Megan's attack. The blood on Ro Ro's hands proves the legend is true. People should not swim in the Devil's Pool.

Story Nine: Too Honest to Live

Chapter One

Forensic Accountant Marty Fields straps his .38 Special handgun around his thirty-inch waist. He covers the weapon with a long, black Nike pullover. The shirt clings to his trim, athletic torso. He dons black running pants and Kelly Green running shoes. He places his cellphone in his right front pocket. His daily five AM run is a ritual. Marty likes order and playing by the rules, unlike the people he investigates who believe rules are for fools.

His wife Bernadette snores. Her black hair drapes her cherubic face. His Italian Madonna. They were college sweethearts having married eleven years ago, after graduating from Villanova. The twins would wake her soon. Five-year-old, Jenny and Jack, always awake with the energy of an erupting geyser.

He trots down Westview Street in West Mount Airy to Wissahickon Dive, heads west toward Livezey Lane, a secluded street that leads to Wissahickon Creek. His usual route is to jog to the creek, cross over the shallow water via stepping stones, then up stream to Valley Green Inn. From the Inn, he jogs uphill to Springfield Avenue, and circles home.

Marty needs a clear mind and a healthy body. He has enough evidence to smash a money laundering scheme that would send tremors through Philadelphia City Hall and earn him a six-figure fee. The people involved are evil. He needs the thirty-eight for self-protection.

He likes the tree-lined route, especially the stretch past Valley Green Inn. The ducks and mallards squawk, like neighbors greeting him, as he passes by. There are very few people awake, save for trout fishers and another dedicated jogger. The historic inn symbolizes an earlier time. Were people as greedy then as they are now?

"Yes," he declares to himself.

The September sun rises in the east, as Marty trudges up Springfield Avenue and then turns right. The roar of a car engine ahead of him sounds an alarm. The vehicle's front bumper pad, spikes jutting out, strikes him waist high, piercing his stomach and lower chest area. The SUV reverses, leaving Marty near death and bleeding. The SUV runs over his prostrate body, its tires aiming at Marty's head. The left front tire crushes his ribs.

In his final seconds on Earth, Marty finds a whisper of strength, enough to press his speed dial to Bernadette.

"Marty. Where are you Hon?" she asks.

"They got me."

"Who got you? Marty. Marty. Where are you?"

"I love you."

"Call 911. Hurry. Honey?"

Marty stares at the rising sun. Death at dawn seems so ironic. It does not follow the rules of life, the circadian rhythm of a new day.

Chapter Two

Ro Ro crouches over Marty's body. Docky stands over her shoulder.

"He's a young man," says Docky.

"Who is he?" asks Ro Ro.

"According to his wife, standing over there, he is Martin George Fields. He is thirty-three, father of two. He was run over twice by a vehicle, make and model to be determined. Note the puncture holes. It appears he was gored as he was run over and then run over again. He was carrying a thirty-eight, suggesting that he was in fear for his life. It is a freaking miracle he had the strength to hit the speed button on his cell. Intelligence tracked his GPS, and here we are."

Ro Ro rises, sensing that this is a murder with a message behind it. Whoever did the deed wants to send a message. "Don't tread on me."

Ro Ro steps over to Bernadette. She is standing grim-faced, her eyes staring blankly at her dead husband. She wears a Villanova tee shirt, faded jeans, and tennis shoes. Her hair hangs along her shoulders.

"Mrs. Fields. I am Detective Morse. I am very sorry for your loss. It is my job to find whoever killed Mr. Fields. I need to talk to you first, though. Are you up to answering a few questions?"

Bernadette Bacino Fields gasps a hollow sound, "Yeah. I will try. I am just so damn stunned. What am I going to tell my children? Marty was a great father. I planned to tell him tonight that I was pregnant."

She pats her belly. "This baby will never see its father. Damn, whoever killed my Marty. Damn them."

"He was carrying a gun. Was he under a threat?"

Bernadette's lips curl. "He was a forensic accountant. He caught the frauds. He was working on a big deal. Something to do with city taxes."

"Did he work alone?"

"No. He had a partner named Raj Patel. Raj does a lot of the computer work. He tracks trends and records. I help once in a while, but Marty insisted I stay home with the kids which was okay by me. I am an artist, so I can work freelance."

"Who was he investigating?"

"He never talked much about it."

"I need to look at his PC, cellphone, and talk to this Raj guy. Do I have your permission to review his records?"

"Absolutely. I have nothing to hide."

"I will have an officer pick up the PC and all business records."

"Please give me an hour to tell my children and Marty's family what happened."

"Sure. At any event, avoid publicity. Channel Six just arrived. We will protect your privacy as long as we can."

"Thank you, Detective Morse."

She reaches for her cell. "I will text you Raj's phone number."

"Do you need to notify him about Marty?"

"I cannot stand the shit. You deal with him."

"Duly noted. Where does Raj live?"

"He lives in Germantown. He has an apartment off Gypsy Lane."

"Did he and Marty have any issues?"

"Not really. Marty respected his intelligence and IT expertise. I thought he was a smug bastard who thought we were some lower caste people. He didn't mind taking a salary. Look, I must get to my children. They are at a neighbor's house. Can we talk later?"

"Sure. Here's my card. Please give me your cell number."

Bernadette hands her the cell. "Copy it, please."

"Done."

"What happens now?"

"The CSU will take Marty to the lab and then to the morgue. We will release him to you in a day or two when the CSU and coroner have completed their work."

Bernadette holds her face in her hands. "I cannot get my head wrapped around this scene."

"Understood. You have your hands full. You have been very helpful, Mrs. Fields."

Bernadette peers at Marty's corpse. The eastern sun casts a shadow over him. "He deserved a long, full life. He always looked for the truth. Can I expect you to do the same for him?"

"Count on it."

Ro Ro calls Raj Patel and relays the news.

"This is most distressing news," he says in a creaky voice.

"We need to ask you some questions, Mr. Patel."

Ro Ro hears the blare of a horn. Patel is not at home. Where was he at seven AM?

She wants to research him and Martin Fields before interviewing Raj. "Meet me at the Fourteenth District station in two hours, not before. It is located at 41 West Haines Street. Zip code 19144."

"I will put the location in my GPS and will be there as soon as possible."

"Where are you now?"

"I'm at home. I must shower and then I will meet you."

Why lie?

Ro Ro searches the deep web on Marty Fields. The man has no criminal record. In 2008, he graduated magna cum laude with a Bachelor of Science degree from Temple. He earned a Master of Arts degree from Villanova with a specialty in forensics accounting. After a two-year stint at Klein Recovery, he started his own company. His magna cum laude status from Villanova in 2008. He married Bernadette Bacino. She is an art history major at Temple.

His clients included the City of Philadelphia and two pharmaceutical companies. He owed four hundred and fifty thousand dollars in mortgages and student loans. His credit rating was over eight hundred. His bank account at Beneficial Bank shows a balance of eighty-six thousand dollars.

Raj Patel is a common name in India. Ro Ro traces his heritage to Bangalore, India. He majored in computer science at Villanova. He owes one hundred and seventy-three thousand in student loans and credit cards. His rating at Experian is 690.

He has never been married and has no children. His brother, Rohan, works in the IT department of the city. Had he influenced them to hire Martin?"

Raj sits across from Ro Ro. He carries his royal blue motorcycle helmet under his hairy, muscular arm. Wiry strong. His thick black hair is slicked back like a fifties rock star. Jet black, bright eyes glimmer under thick eyebrows.

"It saddens me greatly to hear that my friend is dead. The news reported it as an accident. What can you tell me?"

"I will ask the questions, Mr. Patel. First, I need to know your whereabouts this morning?"

"My whereabouts? I was home asleep until six-thirty when my alarm went off."

"Can anyone verify your whereabouts?"

"Am I being accused of doing something criminal?"

"I am a homicide detective, not a traffic policeman."

Raj takes a deep breath. "Wow. Are you saying Marty was murdered?"

"There was no accident. It was a willful murder. Now. Where were you this morning?"

"I told you. I was home alone."

"I do not believe you. When we spoke this morning, I heard a car horn. Do you sleep on the street?"

"I had my windows open. I don't have air conditioning. You must have heard a car horn from the street."

"Tell me about your work with Martin."

"We investigate large companies and government organizations. We find fraud or theft. We report it and get paid ten percent of whatever is verified as fraud or abuse. We do quite well."

"We know you have a contract with the city. What have you found?"

"That is confidential information."

"This is a murder investigation. Nothing is confidential. What are you investigating?"

Raj rises. "I am leaving this meeting. I will not violate my client's trust."

"Sit down. If you try to leave, I will have you restrained as a material witness, and I will charge you with obstruction of justice. Then, you will need a damn good lawyer."

Raj glares at her, his face is contorted in rage. "You are a she-devil."

"Sit down."

Raj sits. "What do you want to know?"

"What were you working on?"

"We found disturbing evidence of financial irregularities."

"Explain."

"We discovered that three city officials are electronically diverting tax funds from city accounts to an interest-bearing account in an off-shore bank. They leave the money there to collect interest and then return the funds electronically to the rightful accounts. They never touch the tax money. They glom the interest."

"Sweet move. How much interest are they collecting?"

"Over a quarter of a million a month. We were due to report the scheme to Sheldon Krause, the city controller, today."

"Who knew about your findings?"

"Just Marty and I knew. He did not tell Bernadette."

"Did your brother Rohan know about it?"

"Of course not."

"How did you get the contract?"

"Martin has contacts from his days at Klein Recovery."

"Why would Klein give up a potentially lucrative contract to Marty?"

"That is a good question. I have no answer."

"What are you going to do with the report?"

"I must issue it to Sheldon Krause."

"Does the Mayor know you are conducting an investigation?"

"I am not sure if Krause told him. There are a lot of loose lips in City Hall. My guess is that Krause kept his counsel."

"Who are the people named in the report?"

Raj wriggles in his seat. "This is very uncomfortable for me. I choose to not answer that question."

"This is a homicide case. There is a grieving wife and two young kids who have lost their father. Do not try my patience. I assure you a holding cell is more uncomfortable. We have especially interesting prisoners there right now. They would welcome your company."

Raj jerks his head back, as if she had belted him with a right cross to the jaw.

"You are not a lady."

"True that. Names and titles, now."

"Murray Fox, accounting supervisor. Sherry Smith, accounting manager. Cyril Doshkin, IT manager. He is the one who handles the security. He is a Muslim from Kiev."

"Do they know the contents of the report?"

"I never told anyone except Marty. He told Krause what we found. Maybe Krause said something to the people involved?"

"I want a copy of the report. Here is my PC. Download it."

"It's worth a lot of money in success fees."

"I will give you a receipt for it. You keep the master copy for your own interests."

"I guess that is a fair arrangement."

"It is the only game in town. Take it or leave it."

Raj reaches out his hand. "It's a deal."

Reluctantly, she shakes his hand.

"I am duty bound to warn you that if these people are responsible for killing Fields, you may be next."

Raj sighs. "You're right. What should I do?"

"Pack some clothes. We'll arrange for protective custody. Do not let anyone, including your brother, know your whereabouts."

"How long will I be in hiding?"

"Until I nail whoever killed Marty Fields and destroyed his family."

"I see. I will do as you say. What about the report?"

"You have the original. When you are safe, you can present it to Krause."

"He should be told I have it."

"I will deal with who knows what. The press will catch on sooner or later. I intend to move quickly."

"I have no doubt."

Raj turns to leave. Ro Ro signals for Biker to put a tail on him. Biker texts. "Got it."

Biker joins Ro Ro. "I put Anderson on him."

"Good. We need to talk to Krause immediately."

"Sure thing."

"I also want to talk to his brother, Rohan"

"We will bring him up."

"Please keep Rohan on ice until I chat with Krause. Let's get Intelligence to help me by checking the people named in the report. Dig into their credit cards, bank accounts, property holdings, Investment accounts, and employment history."

Biker smiles. "Thank the Lord for the Internet."

"And the deep web. Sherlock Holmes in space."

Ro Ro heads to her office. Her mind buzzing with possibilities. For sure, Raj would be under police eyes.

I will get the bastard, Bernadette.

Chapter Three

Sheldon Krause agrees to meet Ro Ro at the Fourteenth District station house. He looks shaken, sad even, as he sits across from her in her office. Sheldon stands six-foot two and weighs about two hundred and fifty pounds. His gut hangs over the belt-line of his khakis, his gray polo shirt bulging at the waistline. His white tennis shoes look large enough to house a small boat. His blue eyes shine like sapphire through his black rimmed glasses. Her research shows he graduated from Temple and was a member of the American Institute of Certified Public Accountants. The Mayor hired him from the private sector.

Sheldon rests his arms on her desk and leans forward, his brow knitted. "This affair with Martin Fields is very upsetting. I hired him to clean our swamp and he ends up dead. How can I be of assistance?"

"I have spoken to Raj Patel. I have his report. Have you seen it?"

"No. Marty prepped me by phone a few days ago. He was due to deliver the report to me today. His summary described the illicit activity and the role each person played. Marty knew how to ferret out the needle in the proverbial haystack. Do you think he was killed over this report?"

"That is the most apparent motive. The three people involved could be facing significant jail time. Plus, they would have to surrender all ill-gotten gains. That is a lot of motivation."

"I see. But, killing someone only draws attention to the issue. It's not logical."

"Desperate people do desperate things. What is your take on each of them, starting with Murray Fox?"

"Murray is a lonsman. He is not much of a mensch, but he is one I would consider capable of murder. He's married and has a couple of kids in college. He makes under a hundred K, so I am sure the student loans are piling up."

"How about Sherry Smith?"

"Sherry is a very attractive Black lady. She is married and has a boy named Amir who has a drug problem. I think Amir just turned twenty-one. He works in the sanitation division driving a truck."

"And Cyril Doshkin?"

Sheldon snaps his fingers. "Cyril is a piece of bad work. I should have fired him for hitting on every woman from the little old woman who cleans the offices to the admin assistants. He thinks Me Too means he gets to screw every woman in America. I will say this for Cyril. He is a genius on the computer. He has stopped several security threats from infiltrating our computers."

"He could make a lot of money in the IT world. What does he make with the city?"

"Cyril makes around sixty thousand per year. But I know he moonlights to make more. He also does not get a lot of supervision. In fact, he reports to Murray."

"Hmm. The IT guy does not report to IT? Isn't that unusual?"

"It is. But getting his talent was worth it. Until today. How is Bernadette holding up? Should I call her?"

"Let her grieve and deal with her children. We can serve her best by arresting whoever did this deed. Have you ever met Raj Patel's brother, Rohan?"

"Yes. He is buddies with Cyril."

Alarm bells go off in Ro Ro's head. "What kind of friends are they?"

Sheldon sits back, folding his arms across his chest and looking away. "I recall an occasion when Raj and Marty visited me to do an update, and Cyril called out to him. Yes. He said, 'How is my main man, Rohan?' and I thought nothing of it."

"What made you hire Marty Fields over a larger firm like Klein?"

"I wanted to keep a low profile. Klein's staff is well-known at City Hall. Marty was small potatoes but smart as hell. He could get the job done at a lower rate and more discreetly."

"What kind of cars do they drive?"

"I know Murray has a Land Rover. Sherry uses Uber. Cyril has a motorcycle."

"What kind of cycle?"

"I don't know much about them. It's a blue cycle of some kind."

Like the one Raj drove.

"Does Sherry's son have a car?"

"I don't know."

"For the record, Mr. Krause, where were you at five AM?"

"Home. My wife is my only witness."

"What kind of car do you and your wife drive?"

"Lucille has a BMW. I have a Chevy Cruze."

"You gave her the nicer car. You're a smart husband."

"She is spoiled, and I love spoiling her."

"Please keep the report confidential. It is evidence. I am giving it to you for your review and input. Our legal team will also review it. If we identify criminal activity, we must show it to the District Attorney."

"I understand. I will alert the Mayor."

"Please do so. We don't want to upset His Honor. Please ask him to keep it quiet."

Sheldon chuckles. "Wish me luck."

They shake hands.

Biker enters. "Shall we round up the usual suspects?"

"For sure. Bring them in as material witnesses to a possible motive. I think I will do a group interview. I want to see their interaction. The rats may turn on each other. Bring Rohan later. I will question him one-on-one."

"I will send plainclothes to fetch them. No sense in drawing unnecessary publicity."

"We agree, boss."

Ro Ro needs time to think and plan and prepare. The hardest thing to find is usually right in front of you.

Chapter Four

The five o'clock news cycle carries the story of Marty's murder as a hit-and-run. No mention is made of his report or that he is working on a fraud case for the city controller. Ro Ro hopes the killer perceives that he or she has gotten away with the attack, has fooled the stupid police.

The squads have rounded up the four suspects, placing the three city employees in one monitored room. She decides to address them as a group and then interview them separately.

Ro Ro has them escorted into the room. Murray Fox is a short, wiry man, grim-faced, his salt-and-pepper hair parts in the middle of his wide head. His beady brown eyes dart around the room, probably looking for microphones.

Sherry Smith looks haggard, stressed as evidenced by the bags under her brown eyes. She is pudgy, but not fat. Her mannish fedora sports a red feather. Her brown pantsuit hides her girth behind the jacket.

Cyril Doshkin wears a black leather jacket, matching the color of his slicked back hair and long sideburns. He has the face of a KGB agent in a B-rated spy movie: stern, scary and menacing, yet seductive.

She enters the conference room, sporting her best frown, Martin's report under her arm.

"Hello to all. I am Homicide Detective Rowena Morse. You are here as material witnesses to the motive behind the vehicular homicide of Martin Fields."

The room turns deathly quiet.

Murray raises his hand. "Did you say homicide? I thought it was a hit-and-run?"

"It is both a hit-and-run and a homicide."

"So, why the hell am I here?" asks Sherry.

"I ask the same question," says Cyril.

Ro Ro waves the report. "Here is Martin Fields's report on the money laundering scheme he uncovered. The report names you three as willing participants in skimming interest funds from the city tax accounts to your personal accounts. You all had a significant motive to kill Martin. We are interviewing you to talk about the homicide. The city fraud team and the feds will take you into custody after we are done questioning you on the homicide. Right now, you are not under arrest. However, I suggest you cooperate, so you can face the fraud charge without a murder rap hanging over you. A public defender is available if you need one."

Ro Ro stands by Sherry. "Please, come with me. I need to ask you a few questions."

Sherry does not budge. "I want a lawyer. I do not know nothing about no murder. Period."

"Please, come with me. Cooperating on the homicide will help you on the theft case. Come ahead for your own good."

Ro Ro escorts Sherry into the conference room.

Sherry sits, flinging her heavy red leather purse onto the table. "You scared me skinny. I have not done a damn thing."

"Where were you at five AM this morning?"

"I was home in bed with my husband."

"What kind of car do you drive?"

"I drive a Chevrolet Impala."

"Did you kill Marty Fields?"

"Hell no."

"Do you know who killed him?"

"Hell no, again. You be crazy, girl. And I do not know anything about stealing money."

"I don't care about theft. I am a homicide detective. If you withhold any information from me, I will charge you with obstruction of justice as an add on to the theft charges. You would not look good in orange."

Sherry casts her eyes down. "I need to talk to my husband. I need a lawyer. I am done talking."

Ro Ro escorts her back to the conference room. She stops at the door. "Thank you for help and information, Mrs. Smith. The ADA is waiting for you down the hallway. This officer will escort you. You did a lot to improve your situation."

Ro Ro taps Murray on the shoulder. "Come with me, Mr. Fox."

Murray stands wobbly on his feet, his fingertips touching the table-top, balancing his frame. "I am not a well man. I had a stent put in a year ago."

"This will not take long."

She leads him into the conference room. "Have a seat."

Murray's hands shake as he gingerly falls into a chair. "I did not kill anybody."

"Where were you at five AM today?"

"I was home with my wife, Ruth."

"What kind of cars do you and Ruth drive?"

"She drives a Subaru Forester and I drive a Cadillac ST."

"You live well for a city employee."

"So, shoot me for being good with my money."

"How about the city's money? The skimming was your idea, according to the report. The others went along for the ride. You took the lion's share of the gelt. You had the most to lose. Who did you hire to kill Martin?"

"I know nothing about anything."

"Bull! You know your own name, don't you? That is something. Murray Fox is properly named. Sheldon Krause caught on to you. He ordered the forensics accounting search. He got you, Murray. Now, tell me who you hired? Was it Cyril?"

"I want my lawyer. I will say not one more word without him."

"Get one for your wife, too. I am charging both of you, as will the feds. Does Ruth like to wear the color orange?"

"Damn you."

"God will damn you, not me. Tell me the truth."

"L. A. W. Y. E. R. I spelled it out for you."

"M. U. R. D. E. R. I spelled it out for you and Ruth. Our CSU is going over her car as we speak. "

"You won't find anything. She was home with me."

"Who did you hire for the kill? Maybe Cyril will fess up. I think he would sell out his mother."

Murray looks away. "I know nothing."

"Marty's report pins the planning on you. You planned the murder and made sure you had an alibi. Does Cyril have an alibi? He is your weak link. And Sherry will cave when I charge her husband. I checked. He has two felony priors. He will do life. Do you think he and she won't roll on you?"

"I am sick to my stomach. I need medical attention."

"Suck it up, Murray. You will get great care in Graterford Prison."

"You are a real bitch of a cop."

"Thanks for the compliment. Who did you hire?"

"I did not hire anybody. I am an innocent man."

"Billy Joel already wrote that song. You will sing it in front of a jury who will not be sympathetic to a money-grubbing prick who had a father of five-year-old twins run down."

"I want a lawyer."

Ro Ro escorts him to the conference room. Cyril is on his cellphone. He hangs up, abruptly. "You can go now, Murray, my friend. You have been of tremendous help. I will make sure the District Attorney is made aware of your cooperation. You will get a good deal. These officers will escort you. Officers, please treat my new friend as a friend of the Court. Farewell, Murray. Come with me Cyril."

Her cell bleeps a text. "Rohan is here."

She sends a text back, "Bring him to the conference room. I want Cyril to see him."

They pass Rohan in the hallway. Cyril and Rohan exchange glances. "You are next, Rohan. Come ahead, Cyril. I have a deal you cannot refuse."

Rohan's jaw drops open. He sneers at Cyril, spitting out a phrase in Arabic. Whatever he said, Cyril understands him, replying in Arabic.

Cyril sits with his eyes set like a man ready to fight.

Ro Ro presses her speed dial to Biker. "Sir, what kind of deal can we make with Cyril Doshkin? I hate to see a young guy go to jail for the rest of his life. I see. I got it. Yes sirree."

She hangs up from the fake call.

"Cyril, we are uncovering the truth like peeling an onion. It is your turn to tell us what you did. How much were you paid to run down Martin Fields?"

"I ran no one down."

"Where were you at five AM this morning?"

"I was asleep in my bed."

"Your cohorts say differently. They say you got wind of Martin's report from Raj's brother Rohan. They say the crazy Russian went berserk and threatened to kill Fields. Are you going to take the fall for the murder?"

"They lied to protect their own asses. I killed no one."

"Did Rohan kill Fields?"

"I do not know who killed Fields."

"That is not what the others say. They blame the Russian."

"You Americans see Russians in your nightmares. You are sissies."

"When those sissy American convicts get their hands on your sweet Russian ass, they will sissy you."

"I can take care of myself. I did nothing wrong. Anything I did on the IT platform I did at Murray's instructions."

"You were just following orders is a defense that did not work at Nuremberg. Why not tell me the truth and then I can help you? Be smart, not stubborn."

"You are bluffing me. You have no proof I killed Fields."

"Do you have an airtight alibi for your whereabouts at five AM yesterday?"

"I was home in bed."

"That is the standard answer. I do not believe you. You are a born liar."

Cyril laughs. "You should play poker. You bluff like the best of them."

"Okay, my Russian friend. The others have a deal. You do not, so who do you think is going down for murdering Martin Fields?"

Cyril leans across the table. "I know who did it. I want full immunity from all charges including the IT theft."

"I can arrange that. Tell me what you have."

"The Russians colluded with Donald Trump. Old orange hair did it." He laughs out loud. "Fake news. Fake testimony. Fake detective. I see through your bluff. Charge me or release me."

"The feds will charge you. Follow me."

She leads him to the conference room holding Rohan. "Thanks for everything, Cyril. Rohan is next in our little game of Let's Make a Deal. You got a good one."

Cyril blurts out in Arabic. Rohan looks askance.

She yanks Rohan by the collar. "Come on, pigeon."

Rohan is built like he's missed too many meals. He looks sallow, defeated like a man who has been whipped by bullies.

"Rohan, you are the only person in this caper who has a stake in both sides of the Fields report. Your brother has a stake, as does your friend Cyril. What can you tell me about Cyril Doshkin?"

"I know him a little bit."

"What kind of car do you drive?"

"I do not have a car. I ride a Harley Davidson."

"Your brother drove it here today. What kind of car do you drive?"

"I drive a Ford."

"Is it an SUV?"

"It is a Ford Escape."

"How appropriate. Did you use it to run over Marty Fields?"

"My vehicle was stolen yesterday. I reported the theft to the police. I don't know where it is. Here is a copy of the report I filed."

Ro Ro glances at the report. "Well, well, well. You covered your ass. When we recover the car, my guess is that our forensic team will match it to the vehicle that ran over Marty Fields. If that scenario plays, then whoever stole your car killed Marty. Sounds like an amazing coincidence. What is your alibi for five AM today?"

"I was home with my girlfriend, Nadia. Here is her phone number."

"You have all the bases covered. Or do you? What if I told you that one of the conspirators ratted out Cyril? They said Cyril planned the crime. You faked the stolen car report making you complicit. You are an accessory to murder. You will spend the rest of your young life in jail. Do you like anal sex?"

"I killed no one. I am a victim. My car was stolen."

Ro Ro checks her cell. "I have a new report that your car was found."

"What? You found my car. Where did you find it?"

"As if you don't know."

"I swear I don't know anything except that my car was stolen. That is not a crime."

"You don't get it do you? You are the pigeon, the one that will take the fall. You better tell us the truth, before we finish our investigation. Once we conclude the investigation, the facts will speak for themselves. It's your car that was used. You are screwed no matter who drove the car. Do you understand what I am telling you?"

Rohan buries his face in his hands. "All my life I have been taken advantage of by the ones I have loved. My brother is no exception."

"Tell me what happened."

Rohan stands, his fists clenched. "I am a man. I am not a rat. I am leaving."

She motions for Biker to have him followed.

Ro Ro takes a deep breath. The traps are set. Time to see which rat eats which cheese.

Docky calls. "We downloaded everyone's cell. Take a gander at Raj's photos."

Ro Ro looks at the pictures. "The sick, sleazy bastard is a voyeur."

"Yup! Now look at Murray Fox's photo set. Do you see anyone you know?"

"G Town John, Fox, and Sheldon Krause. That is quite a trifecta."

"Yup. Now check out Rohan's photos."

"Cyril and Rohan at the casino. It looks like Borgata."

"Yup."

"It seems that the old axiom about two degrees of separation in Philly is true."

"Yup. Everybody knows everybody."

"Tomorrow, I will be making some house calls."

"Yup."

That night, Ro Ro eats dinner at home. Pasta is easy to prepare as long as jarred marinara suffices to cover rigatoni. A loaf of Italian bread and a glass or two of Chianti completed the meal. Filled, she turns on her favorite Chris Botti CD and settles on to her sofa. She has grown accustomed to sleeping alone. When you wake up, you do not have to feel guilty or used or fearful that your bed partner is not trustworthy. Living alone does not necessarily translate to loneliness.

She texts Biker. "Please pick up Rohan. I will be in late this morning to interview him."

Now I can sleep.

Chapter Five

Ro Ro parks in front of the Martin home, a classic two-story structure made of Chestnut Hill stone. Embedded with garnets, the quarry stone glimmers in the sunlight. Ro Ro walks up the concrete entrance way to the front door. Bernadette stands in the doorway. "Good morning, detective."

"Thanks for seeing me."

They sit over the kitchen table. Coffee cups are filled from a four-cup coffee maker. The twins are playing on a swing set in the rear yard. "Martin's death has not sunk in yet."

"I will only be here for a few minutes. Did Martin always run the same route every morning?"

"Marty was an analytical man. He liked to place all things in the proper order. The route was his choice. He ran it one hundred percent of the time."

"Why did you dislike Raj so intensely? Did he hit on you?"

"He stopped by one morning after Marty had left for work and the kids had gotten on the bus to their day care school. He came to the door saying that he was supposed to meet Marty. He wanted to come inside. I hesitated, but he shoved the door open. I ran into the kitchen and grabbed my cellphone to call nine one one. He tore the phone out of my hand and tried to kiss me. I kneed him in the nuts. The horny bastard crumbled like a house of cards. I ordered him out."

"Did you tell Marty?"

"No. Marty would have killed him. I was not about to ruin our lives over one stupid move by that excuse for a man."

"Did he claim he loved you?"

"No."

"He obviously knew Marty's routine."

"O. M. G. You think he killed Marty over an infatuation with me?"

"I am still gathering facts. Has he called you?"

"No."

"If he calls you, record it on your cell."

"I will do that. How did you figure out his attempt to screw me?"

"He had pictures of you on his iPhone. The pictures were you sunbathing in your rear yard."

"Mother of God. He was spying on me."

"Yes. Be careful. I will post a squad car across the street for now. Please keep this information confidential. Please do not contact Raj. Promise?"

"I promise."

She bites her lip to hold off her tears.

Ro Ro leaves, feeling that every time she thinks people are worth saving, someone raises her doubts.

She calls G Town. He knows everybody.

G Town answers on the third ring. "This is a nice surprise."

"I am investigating the murder of Martin Fields and I need some answers about certain people. I think you know them."

"So that accident was not an accident with Martin Fields? What do you want of me?"

"Tell me about Sheldon Krause."

"Shelly 'The Jelly'. The man wiggles when he walks. He wiggles like a snake doing the hula."

"I saw a recent photo of you and Jelly at a party at your house. I recognized the tomato plants in the background."

"Shelly and I go back a long way. He is smart, slick and loves being the boss. We agree to never do business together. We are friends and know if we hook up around a pile of cash, one of us would end up badly."

"He hired Martin Fields. Why?"

G Town shakes his head from side to side. "I don't know. But, I will say that Shelly does not do anything that does not enrich himself."

"Is he a killer?"

"Nah. Shelly thinks he can outsmart and schmooze his way in this world. He used to say that the only muscle you need lies between your ears."

"Tell me about Murray Fox."

"Murray in a hurry. He is small potatoes. He's a Shelly wannabe."

"How do you know Marty Fields?"

"His wife is a Bacino. Her old man and my old man did business until the city screwed my old man in a frame up. Bernadette is a nice girl. Marty was a good kid. Whoever hurt them should rot in Hell."

"My job is to see the perp rot in prison, Hell on earth."

"Good luck in getting the prick who's responsible."

"I will get him. Count on it."

G Town chuckled. "A Mount Airy girl always gets her man."

"Damn straight."

Rohan sits alone in the conference room. Ro Ro has the air-conditioning vents closed. Ro Ro wants him to sweat about his future. After two hours, she confronts him. At first, he sits quietly, almost in meditation. As time passes, he starts walking around the room. Twice he opens the door, only to be confronted with a police officer who shoves him roughly into the room.

Showtime.

"Hello Rohan. How did you like sitting alone in a small room not knowing your fate? It is a lot like prison. You might say we are orienting you to your future."

"Why am I here?"

"You are here to confess to your role in the murder by auto of Martin Fields. Here is my theory of the crime. On the surface, it looks like a killing for financial purposes. It was not supposed to be a homicide. It was meant to look like an accident. The plan was to scare Marty. But the driver wanted more than money. He wanted Marty's wife. That is why he ran over Marty the second time. The first hit was for business reasons. The kill shot was personal. Raj hated Marty and was jealous of his marriage to Bernadette. He recruited your car, making *you* his accomplice. *You* gave in to save Cyril who *you* love. And, you and Cyril have political ties to Muslim groups needing cash. Stop Marty and protect Cyril. That is what Raj sold you. You bought your brother's lies. You handed him the keys to your car."

Rohan shakes from head to toe.

"No. I am innocent. I did nothing."

"You can save yourself. Tell me where Raj dumped the car. The car will exonerate you. Raj betrayed you for the love of a woman who cannot stand him. It was a useless, foolish love. He gave up everything for nothing. Do not make the same mistake. Tell me the truth beginning with the location of the car."

Rohan pounds the table. "All my life I have been used and abused. Yes. I will fight for myself. You got everything right. The car is in the parking lot of the Borgata Hotel in Atlantic City. It will be moved to a chop shop in New Jersey and destroyed."

Rohan exhales, his face brightening. "I feel free. I am no longer the pigeon."

Ro Ro nods. "Good man. I will get you a pad and pen. Write everything down. You are doing the right thing."

Biker enters, pad and pen in hand. "Tell it like it is, Rohan. We will pick up Raj Patel."

"My collar?"

"Your collar."

Ro Ro calls Sheldon Krause.

"This is Sheldon Krause."

"Meet me in Rittenhouse Park in half an hour, Shelly 'Bowl of Jelly'."

Silence.

"Did you hear me?"

"No one has called me by that name in a long time."

"Guess where I heard it."

Ro Ro sits on a bench on the western edge of the square. Sheldon ambles toward her wearing a straw fedora. He smiles as he sits next to her. "Hello Detective."

"We are arresting Raj Patel for the murder of Martin Fields. I cannot prove your involvement unless Raj gives you up. That is a distinct possibility."

"Why are you telling me this?"

"I want you to resign. I want our city swamp drained of you, Fox, Smith and Cyril. I want a clean city government."

"You are a romantic. There is no such thing as clean government. What is your price?"

"Your resignation."

Sheldon shakes his head. "How did you figure out the killing?"

"Raj was your weak link. He overreacted by running over Martin."

"I had nothing to do with the skimming."

"I know that. But with the evidence in your hands, you could grab it all by holding Cyril, Fox, and Sherry hostage. But Marty would not go along. He was supposed to bury the skimming for a piece of the action. Marty was too honest for his own good. You thought he was connected via Bernadette's father. You miscalculated. Marty was too honest to live."

"Prove your theory in court."

"Resign or I will go to the feds."

"Son of a bitch! Aren't *you* Joan of Arc."

"Resign by the end of the day or else."

Sheldon stands, smiling like a man who has just had an epiphany, a moment of truth. "You win."

He walks away as Ro Ro calls Bernadette. "I got them all. See you tonight."

She calls the Federal District Attorney.

"Ro Ro. This is Herman Weiss. What's up?"

"Sheldon Krause will resign today as city controller. Wait until it's public, and I will hand you old Jelly Belly's balls on a silver platter."

"Really? I can hardly wait."

Ro Ro walks through the park. The summer sun bathes the park in a warm hue, cleansing the air.

Today is a win for her and her city. Its government is a lot more sanitary.

Story Ten: Dark Angels

Chapter One

August in Philly bakes the city in a sweaty oven compounded by ninety plus humidity. Ro Ro's air conditioner has kicked off, leaving her in a hot bedroom. She takes a cold shower, opening her barred bedroom windows, turns on an old floor fan and prays for a breeze. Two glasses of ice water cool her innards. She falls into much needed sleep.

Boom. Thunder echoes through the predawn darkness.

An orange red flash spirals into the northern sky. Rowena's immediate thought is a gas explosion. Nobody survives a gas blast. Thirty seconds later, sirens scream. Her adrenalin soars beyond her tiredness.

It would be hours before the fire squad sorts out the cause of the firestorm. She turns on the television and makes a single cup of Colombia roast coffee. Common sense dictates she tries to sleep. But she cannot sleep with the sky burning a half-mile from her home.

At six-forty her cell rings. Biker is calling.

"Morse. I am at the scene of the explosion you probably heard earlier. Get over here to two twenty-nine East Gravers Lane."

"I thought it was probably a gas explosion."

"Docky thinks differently. And there is a dead body, so maybe it is a homicide. Get here pronto."

"What was it? A bomb?"

"Yep. Docky and the fire captain says it was loaded with C4 and there is hard evidence somebody used a drone to deliver it."

"Holy Moley."

The remnants of the stucco and stone three-story home on East Gravers Lane smoldered in the dawn light. The front wall of the home is smashed outward, covering the wooden porch in stone chunks. The upstairs windows lay shattered on the front lawn. The roof is open, its dormered windows blown out.

Four fire engines block the street. Neighbors mill around the yellow-taped perimeter. Two EMTs wheel a gurney carrying a body, its bare feet jutting out under a white sheet. They load the body into a van.

Biker and Docky wave her toward Biker's squad car. The smoky air chokes her.

"What have we got here?" asks Rowena, coughing in her handkerchief.

Docky is sweating profusely under his blotched white coat. "I dug up a camera lens. We have been studying drones and the glass I found is from a high-resolution camera. A drone was used to deliver a package of explosive material."

"Where the hell are we? Baghdad? Who was the victim?" she asks.

"We canvassed the neighbors. A father and son live here," says Biker.

"We collected a toothbrush, hairbrush, and clothing. We will identify the victim," says Docky.

"We are not sure if the victim was the owner or his son, or a guest."

Ro Ro points to a man, sporting a goatee running toward them. "My guess is that one of them is approaching."

The man races toward them, his taut body straining against his black tee shirt. Frozen, his mouth agape, he stares wild-eyed at the destroyed house. "My God. What happened here? What happened to my home? Where is my father?"

"Please show us some identification," says Biker.

He reaches for his wallet. "See here. My license. I am Ethan Campbell. My father, Judge Andrew Campbell, and I live here. Where is my father?"

Biker, Docky and Rowena exchange glances. Biker nods at Docky to talk. "I am CSU Doctor Charles Poteet. We have recovered a body from the rubble."

"Where is the body? I must see the body."

"The body is in yonder van."

Ethan rushes to the van. He pulls back the sheet and wails, "Noooo! Jesus be merciful. My father. My father." He falls to his knees, tears streaming down his face.

Biker and two uniformed policemen pull him away.

"Have two officers bring him to the station where he can calm down. I will talk to him and see what we can learn about who wanted him or his father or both dead and why. And find out where the mother is," says Ro Ro.

Ro Ro feels sympathy for the man who has lost his Dad and home. You do not expect Americans to die by drone bombing, especially in Chestnut Hill.

The times are changin'.

TV cameras close in on the scene. Reporters shout questions and stick microphones in her face. "Detective Morse. Was this a terrorist attack of some kind? Who lived here?"

Ro Ro puts up her hands. "Girls and boys of the fourth estate. Please hold off your questions. We are just beginning the investigation. When we know more, we will tell you. Now, let us do our job."

"Then, it is a homicide," says a reporter.

Ro Ro wags a finger at him. "Do not rush to judgment."

"You are a homicide detective and there is a dead body in the CSU van. Ergo, we have a murder," says another reporter.

Ro Ro smiles. "Write what you want, as usual."

"Say cheese." A camera clicks in her face.

Ro Ro turns away.

A roaring crash resounds from the collapse of a side wall of the home. Dust and flames leap toward a neighboring home.

The bystanders scream in horror. "Overkill!"

"Why kill that man this way?" says Ro Ro.

"I knew Judge Campbell. He was a bad judge," says Biker.

"How so?"

Biker sighs, "He was tossed off criminal court for taking bribes. He let some bad people off light."

The irony washes over Ro Ro. "Wow! I will do a search on him and see what turns up. Here is a funny thought. Would a bad guy kill a bad guy who did a good deed for him?"

Biker shakes his head. "The bad guys I know use guns to do a hit. Who the hell uses a drone?"

Ro Ro has a queasy sense that the answer may be terrifying. "There is no gunshot residue on a drone. And you can launch it from miles away."

"That is scary," says Docky.

"True that," says Ro Ro. "I need to talk to Ethan."

She beckons to a uniformed officer. "Get him to the district. And get pictures of the crowd. Maybe our bomber stopped by to check his work."

Ro Ro heads away, fearing that using a drone as a weapon has moved from ISIS land to Philly. She shivers in the heat.

God help us all.

Chapter Two

Ro Ro pores over the file on Judge Campbell. He was married to Elizabeth Shelly who died four years earlier. She swallowed a bottle of sleeping pills.

The case that brought down the judge was a straight-forward embezzlement case. To get off, he tried bribing a judge. His honor took funds from the trust fund of Clarence Shelly and Janet Shelly, parents of his wife.

Ro Ro writes a note. "What drove her to suicide? Was it public shame and embarrassment?"

The judge's lawyer was Gabriel Porto, Esquire, the mouthpiece for Germantown John Mancuso. G Town John would not use a drone to kill a welsher. The motive lies elsewhere.

She has Ethan escorted into her office. He looks like a man who needs a drink, but probably has had too much the night before. "Ethan, I am sorry for your loss. There's a number of standard questions I must ask you, so we follow proper police protocol. I will notate your responses on my laptop. First, are you sure the body you identified at the scene was your father's?"

Ethan sneers, "I know my own father. It was my old man."

"I know you are upset, but the less attitude you give me, the smoother this interview will proceed."

Ethan nods. "Sorry. This is a bit too much to absorb."

"Can you think of anybody who wanted him or you or both of you dead?"

Ethan blanches. "You included me as a target. I don't have any enemies. I'm an innocuous Temple graduate student."

"What is your major?"

"I am a math and physics major."

"So, you know about drone technology, do you?"

"Sure. We have a drone program. Robotics too. Doctor Liam Hagerty is world-class."

"Whoever fired that drone hit your house with pinpoint accuracy. Could someone from Temple have been involved?"

Ethan cracks a smile. "We are nerds, not murderers."

"We?"

"Yes, we. The whole program is unathletic techs who care more about physics than sports."

"Where were you all night?"

"I was with my girlfriend, Cheryl Ward. I can see life beyond drones."

"Was Cheryl shacked up with you all night?"

"Damn straight."

"Give me her cell number so we can check her out."

"She is on her way here. I called her and told her what happened. She's taking an Uber."

"I read about your father's legal troubles. Was he a gambler?"

Ethan looks away. "He was a terrible gambler. He could lose a one-horse race. He was addicted. He loved the action."

"My next few questions are necessary for me to understand your father better. Often the key to finding a killer lies in the life and nature of the victim. Please answer me truthfully so I do not chase any red herrings."

"I'll try."

"Why did your mother take her own life?"

Ethan looks away, letting out a long sigh. "My mother was frail in body and spirit. The disgrace my old man laid on her drove her to take all kinds of pills. She hardly went out. She quit golf, bridge, going to the theater, and family events. She went from a healthy, active woman to a zombie. She gradually disintegrated before my eyes."

"You blamed your father, didn't you?"

"Yes, I did," he says, red-faced, his brows knitted in anger.

"Who would gain financially from your father's death?"

Ethan shrugs. "Me. All he had was the house, a few hundred dollars in the bank, and the car."

"What about life insurance?"

Ethan snaps his fingers. "I almost forgot. He has a million-dollar level term policy."

Motive.

His cell buzzes. "Cheryl is here."

The office door opens to a short, pretty, dark-haired girl, stuffed into jeans, braless under a Temple tee shirt. She rushes to Ethan, clasping her arms around him. "Oh, Ethan. How terrible! Are you all right? How stupid to even ask. You must be a wreck inside. You could have been killed, too. Thank God you stayed over. Thanks God."

"I am Detective Morse. Miss Ward, are you stating that Ethan spent the night with you?"

"Yes. We are friends and lovers."

Ethan stands rigid. "Detective Morse, what more can I tell you?"

"Do you know John Mancuso?"

"I never met him, but I know my father lost a lot of money to him. He's a bookie. Wait! He is a beneficiary on the life policy. Dad owed him and that Lawyer Porto a lot of money. He used the life insurance as collateral for the debts. I know because dad said it was a reverse life policy. He was worth more to them dead than alive. Do you know those guys?"

"I am acquainted with Germantown John and his attorney, Gabriel Porto. It is no coincidence that Gabe represented both your father and G Town. That may have been a conflict of interest."

Ethan throws up his hands. "That is out of my league. I am just a dumb grad student. Look, my father was a jerk and a loser. But he was still my father. I didn't kill him. Cheryl just vouched for my whereabouts. I have funeral plans to make, and I need to get myself together. Can the police take us to the Chestnut Hill Hotel so I can book a room, shower, and get my affairs in order?"

"After we receive the CSU report and the Medical Examination Report, I may have more questions for you. "

"Fine. Call or text me your cell. I have nothing to hide."

"Stay strong, Ethan, and stay in Philly," says Ro Ro.

Ro Ro feels a headache coming on. This case offers a lot of new challenges. And Ethan seems too well rehearsed. Just how much does he despise his father? She calls Germantown John's cell and arranges to meet him in an hour. Her mental wheels were spinning like a runaway top.

Chapter Three

She finds Germantown John in his rear yard tending to his garden of tomatoes and green peppers. A fig tree offers a modicum of shade. He'd set up a small, round table covered by a red, white, and green tablecloth. A glass pitcher of iced tea, peppermint leaves floating, greets her.

His white, MAGA tee shirt clings to his burly chest. His khaki shorts, dirty from digging in the garden, holds his strong legs, bulging at the thighs.

"Welcome," he says.

He points to the table. "Let's sit here in plain sight. Are you wearing a wire?"

Ro Ro sits as he pours her a glass of iced tea. "No wires. I came to talk about the tragic death of Judge Campbell."

"That was a helluva way to go. The press reported he was nuked by a drone. I made the tea myself. I hope you like it."

"My mother used to add peppermint leaves, too. It adds to the flavor. We learned that you and the newly departed judge had business dealings. We also learned that you are a beneficiary on his life insurance policy giving you a financial incentive to croak him."

G Town laughs out loud. "Damn but I do like the direct, no bullshit approach. Yeah, the honorable judge and I had financial dealings. Yeah, I demanded collateral to cover his debt and my exposure. All legal, mind you."

"Mancuso, I do not envision you firing a drone into a crowded neighborhood. Not when a nine shot Beretta with a silencer is easier and draws less attention. How well do you know Ethan Campbell?"

G Town smirks disdainfully. "That squirt ain't got the stones to kill anybody. He was a momma's boy from jump street. You know, the kind of kid raised on comic books, always studying, never into sports. His old man told me a lot about his daughter Ethan."

"He called Ethan his daughter? God, the kid must have hated him. How about the mother?"

"She breast fed him until he was almost five. His Honor, Andy used to joke that the kid's got more sex out of her than he did."

"Did you know the mother?"

"Yeah, but not biblically. She was a cold milk bottle."

"Milk bottle?"

G Town snickers. "The old dagos call WASPS milk bottles. She was ice milk."

"She had a child. Andrew must have warmed up the milk at least once."

G Town raises his heavy eyebrows. "I suppose."

Ro Ro studies him to see if she can sense whether he is toying with her. The bastard likes to pass out phony info. Fake news, Italian-style.

"Who fired the drone? You or Ethan?"

G Town laughs. "That is the only dumb thought I ever heard leap from your pretty lips."

The whirring sound of a fast-moving drone splits the air.

"Incoming," he shouts.

Facing the house, G Town lunges across the table, smothering her with his body. A second later the bomb strikes the house. The house explodes, firing shards of glass, building stones, wooden pieces in all directions. She lies under G Town, protected by his body. Debris crashes on all sides. A piece of cinder block crashes into G Town's head, sending him askew, his skull opens like a can of tomato soup. His blood splatters her face, arms, head and legs. She shifts him aside and calls nine one one.

He's face down, blood flowing onto the grass. She checks his pulse. Alive.

She snatches the tablecloth and wraps it around his head. He'd saved her life.

"Do not die. Do not die," she says.

She screams at the shattered house, the hot sun, and the splatter around her. Someone has turned Chestnut Hill into Chestnut Hell. "Damn whoever did this!"

Evil is alive and well.

She gets into the emergency van with him and the EMTs. G Town is unconscious, barely breathing. "Hang on John. Hang on," she says.

Biker meets her at the ER for Chestnut Hill Hospital, his countenance is twisted in shock and anger.

"Are you okay?" he asks.

"I am fine. He saved my life."

"We got to get the bastards behind these bombings. Damn, damn, and damn again!"

"I assume Docky and his team are on the scene."

"Yes. He will find a clue to this mess."

Ro Ro walks in a circle around the waiting room to clear her mind. Docky always says there is evidence at all crime scenes. What did they miss?

The attacks were planned and targeted. Did Ethan have the cunning to plan this?

"I am going to the district. I need to get on the computer. I will have the hospital call me if there is any news. Please ask Docky to look for evidence of a timer."

"A timer?"

"Yes. And contact Gabe Porto. He needs to get into protective custody, immediately. Have a couple of uniforms bring him in. He may want to talk after this attack. Tell him it is for his own safety."

"Will do, Ro Ro. Do you mind telling your boss your theory of the crime?"

"Biker, please give me a bit of leeway. I need time to sort this out. It's like an algorithm with distorted logic."

"What do you mean?"

"It is diabolical. I need to find the devil in the woodpile."

"Go to it."

Chapter Four

She shuts the door to her office and Googles Professor Liam Hagerty of Temple University. Hagerty has worked on drones and robotics for years. His students have run experiments at Cape Canaveral, winning a national competition in 2018. Two members of the team were Ethan Campbell and Cheryl Ward. They have a lot to gain by killing Andrew and G Town. If Porto is also a victim, then all insurance would go to Ethan. Did Ethan have the stones and killer instinct to risk his life on a drone?

Hagerty has no obvious motive. He has no criminal record and is a tenured professor. Why would he participate in a murder plot? Ethan has the most to gain. Or does he?

The logical suspect is often not the obvious suspect. Someone else has a lot to gain.

Biker enters. "Porto is here. Fat boy looks like he wants to talk."

"Bring the fatted calf to me."

"Not here. Take him to the conference room so I can listen and watch you barbecue him."

"Good idea. Give me ten minutes to get there ahead of him."

Looking like a man afraid to breathe, Gabe enters the conference room. Ro Ro has arranged for bottles of water and an ice bucket on the table.

"Hello, Gabe. Glad to see you are still alive," says Ro Ro.

Gabe looks comical in his khaki shorts, green Sheldon Cooper "Bazinga" tee shirt, low cut white tennis shoes and knee length white socks.

"You have a sick sense of humor. How is Johnny Mancuso doing?" asks Gabe.

He grabs a water bottle, opens it and guzzles half in a long pull. "A man has got to stay hydrated in this heat. Why am I here?"

"Gabe, we have bumped heads but, in this case, I am here to help you. I owe G Town, big time. I was at his place talking to him in the back yard when the bomb hit. We were discussing life insurance."

"Life Insurance? What has that got to do with drones bombing innocent people?"

"Gabriel do not play games with me. You are not a suspect. I know about Andrew Campbell's use of an insurance policy as collateral on his gambling debts to John Mancuso. I also know you are a bene-ficiary as well, ostensibly for legal fees. But I think you were a part of Andrew's gambling debts. My guess is that you introduced him to G Town. Right?"

Gabe lifts the water bottle. "Salute! You are a smart dame. But what am I doing here?"

"Whose idea was it to use insurance as collateral?"

Gabe looks around the room as if someone else is there. "I can only speculate, but I believe it was Elizabeth's idea. She was the smarter one."

"Why did such a smart woman kill herself?"

"Maybe she did. Maybe she had help taking those pills?"

"Oh? Why is that?"

"A wife wants security. If she is alive, then she could block the deal. That is just a wild guess on my part."

"Did Ethan share that concern?"

Gabe chuckles. "That boy genius has the balls of a fish. He could talk computerese better than he could talk plain English."

"Do you know his girlfriend, Cheryl Ward?"

Gabe sits back, folds his arms and looks away, before answering in what appears to be very chosen words. "She gets around. That's all I can say."

"Did you sleep with her?"

Gabe smiles very broadly, his cheeks puff like a blowfish. "Flatter this old man all you want but I do not gossip. All I can tell you is that she knows how to get Ethan to do whatever she wants him to do. That's what Andrew told me. And she is a money hungry woman."

"Would Ethan kill for her?"

Gabe jerks back. "Whoa! I did not say he would kill anybody, least-wise his old man. And why would he take out G Town and me?"

"If he were the last man standing, all the Insurance would go to him."

Gabe slaps the table. "Dammit. I forgot that the survivor clause in the policy states that any beneficiary who dies within thirty days of Andrew, loses his benefits. They get passed on to the surviving beneficiary."

"Bingo!"

"I get it. But Ethan could not kill anybody. He would never take that chance."

Ro Ro feels the cylinders in his head click into place.

"I've gotta make a phone call. Wait."

"Who are you calling?"

"Be back soon. Stay put. Your life depends on it."

She reaches Professor Edward Hagerty on her second try.

"Professor this is Detective Rowena Morse. I am investigating the two recent drone attacks and need your professional opinion."

He's quiet, for a moment. "Okay, I guess. What do you want to know?"

"Are the students on your drone projects skilled in using timing sensors?"

"Yes. Do you think they are involved?"

"I am just getting technical information. No one has been charged. Second question. Do you have an inventory of sensors on campus?"

"I must ask you if you think any Temple students and faculty are involved in your investigation?"

"As I just stated, we need to check on a few technical details. Ethan Campbell and Cheryl Ward recommended we talk with you to get fact-based input. How long can the time delay be set ahead?"

"Indefinite."

"What type of drones do you use on your projects?"

"We use all kinds."

"What is the longest ranged one?"

"We use the DJI Mavic Pro Platinum. It can fly for about twenty-eight minutes. The range is just over four miles. It has collision prevention technology. "

"How many do you have at the university?"

"We keep an inventory report. Each student assigned a drone has to account for it. What is this all about?"

"The truth. Thank you, Doctor Hagerty. How many are signed out to Ethan Campbell and Cheryl Ward?"

"Each student is limited to two."

"Very interesting. How are drones launched?"

"The pilot sets up a trip by linking the drone to his command center. A laptop, a PC, or a smartphone serve as the guidance system. The destination is tied to the GPS. Launch parameters are dated. A command code fires the drone on its mission at a pre-arranged time."

"Does the command center keep a record of the trip?"

"Yes."

Ro Ro's hunter instincts snap into high gear. "Can anyone tamper with the settings?"

"Perhaps. The change would be recorded in the flight record."

"Professor Haggerty. You just got an 'A' from me. Please, do one more thing for me. I am sending a technology team into your lab to look at each PC, iPhone, server, and tablet to check to see if they were used to launch drones. If so, what were the points established on the GPS? It is a matter of life and death."

"Good Lord. I will comply but I must be here when they do their work."

"Of course. Log in each unit and shut the lab down until further notice. I will be in touch. Thank you."

"I am flabbergasted that my lab may be part of a criminal investigation. I must tell my superiors."

"If they object, I will subpoena and get a search warrant, so please get them to cooperate."

"Someone once said it is better to ask for forgiveness than permission. I will do as you ask. I have nothing to hide."

"The truth shall set you free."

"Or send me packing. Get your team here fast."

She left, her juices pumping.

Better than DNA?

Gabe is waiting for her. He has drunk four bottles of water. "I have just learned how this plan was done," Ro Ro says.

"Who is behind it?"

"I may know very soon. Gabe, here is what I want you to do. Go home and pack enough clothes for a week. Park your car in the driveway. Leave your television on and lights throughout the house. Call an Uber or a Lyft. Check into a downtown hotel. Think of the next few days as a vacation for health reasons."

Gabe's back stiffens. "You think I am going to be hit, don't you?"

"Bet on it."

"You are using me for bait."

"You may say that. I think I am saving your life. You can do what I ask or take a gamble and end up in Holy Sepulcher Cemetery. Your call."

"Who is behind this madness?"

"If I told you, you would not believe me. Please cooperate, for your sake."

Gabe sighs from his gut up to his head. "You better be right."

"I am your best chance to stop the attacks. Will you do as I request?"

"Yeah."

"Good man. Now go get a shower. You are a sweaty mess."

"I love you too," he says and leaves.

Ro Ro calls the hospital to check on G Town. He is uncon-scious and in serious condition.

She calls Docky. "Docky. Please see if you can determine the type of drone used in the attacks."

"I just confirmed it is a DJI Mavic Pro Platinum. It has collision pre-vention technology in the camera. The pieces were amazingly intact. We got lucky. You can buy it on Amazon."

"Do you have one?"

"Yeah. Even an old man needs toys."

"Have you found an iPhone in the wreckage?"

"We are still sorting out the debris."

"Call me if you find one. It may carry the electronic fingerprints I need to wrap this case up."

Biker walks in. "What is going on here?"

She tells him her theory of the crime.

"God in Heaven, help us all."

"We need to be careful. I think there is another drone out there ready to launch with deadly intent. We need to dispatch the tech team to Temple immediately to inspect the smartphones, PCs and laptops of Ethan Campbell, Cheryl Ward, Dr. Hagerty, and Gabe Porto. And G

Town's iPhone and any computer equipment in his home or car. Get a warrant for Ethan Campbell and Cheryl Ward's premises. We want their PCs, tablets, and iPhones. Get them to the tech team for analysis."

"Why? What are we looking for?"

"We are looking for a blueprint for murder. We should evacuate the homes near Porto's house without making the press aware of what we are doing. Tell the neighbors there is a gas leak. Use gas department vans to camouflage our activities. We should also position cars and camera all cars driving near Gabe's house. We may need a record of who was near his house and when."

"Are you sure of this?"

"Life is a gamble. Better to play the odds than to go all-in on a draw."

"Ro Ro, tell me why we have to do this now," says Biker.

"The perp wants the attacks to look like a series of terrorist attacks, but also wants to get his mission completed before the FBI gets involved."

"Clever. Very smart," says Biker.

"And ballsy."

"You convinced me. We will get it done."

Ro Ro needs a Manhattan but settles for the last bottle of water Gabe left behind.

She checks on G Town. No change. She fears that a life-long criminal will be remembered as a hero for saving her life. Fate works in mysterious ways, not unlike a reckless man who beats the odds at Russian roulette.

The tech team carries out their mission in short order. They find nothing to substantiate any attack from the Temple students. Ethan and Cheryl surrender their iPhones. Nothing incriminating is found. Her theory is holding true.

Professor Hagerty reports that five drones are missing from inventory. *Where are they?* she asks herself. *Who are the targets?*

She walks outside to relieve her tension. The sun sets in the sky beyond the district, casting a shadow across the brick structure. The night descends, moonless, threatening. The heat abates. A light breeze eases the intense humidity. A line from her school days crosses her mind. "Tender is the Night."

She packs up her laptop and heads toward Gabe Porto's house, a personal stakeout.

Half asleep, she nestles in the back seat of her car. Two fifteen AM. She calls the hospital to check on G Town. He is holding on, but in critical condition. If he lives, would his near-death experience change him? Would he grow darker in mind and spirit, or would the moment of truth wake him to his own mortality? And why did he instinctively rush to protect her?

The whirr of the approaching drone snaps her to attention. It approaches from an easterly direction, crashing into Gabe's home. The explosion rocks her car, sending debris splattering in all four directions.

Flames flash into the sky. She calls the fire department and then Biker and Docky. Her beloved Chestnut Hill has become Chestnut Hell. There was one more iPhone out there. Was there one more explosion coming?

Chapter Five

Ro Ro, Ethan, and Cheryl sit in the conference room near her office under the watchful eyes of Biker and Docky. Ethan appears nervous, flustered as he shifts from side to side. Cheryl sits back in her chair, her arms folded in defiance.

"Thank you for joining me," says Ro Ro.

"Do we need a lawyer?" asks Ethan.

"This is an informal discussion. If you, at any time, want a lawyer, just say so. "

Ro Ro takes out her iPhone. "It is amazing how much power is harnessed in this device. One can do many things, and even launch drones on a pre-scheduled basis. In fact, a dead man could launch a drone by scheduling a launch after he dies. Your father launched all three drones. He killed himself with drone number one believing that his suicide would go down as a terrorist attack. Dumb cops like me would never construe his plan. He was a gambler and liked his chances to go undetected. The second part of his plan was to eliminate G Town and Gabe so it would look like a terrorist attack had killed all three people. In so doing, his death would have been a homicide, thereby doubling his death benefit. And because he would have killed off Gabe and G Town, all proceeds would have gone to his only child."

Ethan slams his fist on the table. "That is a lie. My father did not kill himself."

Cheryl looks away. "Oh, dear," she says.

"The problem we face now is, did you two know about his scheme? Did you help him to arm the drones? Are there any more drones armed and aimed at other targets?"

"This assertion is preposterous," says Ethan.

"We need to know if there are more attacks coming. Your father is dead. G Town is in critical condition. Gabe is in a safe spot. Once I explain this theory to him, he may explain it to certain friends of G Town or G Town himself, God willing. They would be quick in exacting revenge on, guess who?"

"Jesus help us," says Cheryl.

"I suggest you pray for a rapid recovery for G Town. He saved my life and if he dies, I will go to any lengths to find his killers and bring them to justice."

Cheryl smirks, and says, "You cannot prove we had anything to do with the attacks. And, you cannot prove that Old Man Campbell committed suicide."

"Perhaps. But I can inform the Insurance company of what I suspect. They will withhold their payout until the investigation is concluded. We may never close the case because there is no statute of limitation on murder. Your father gambled and lost, as he did his whole life. He lost your mother, his career, and in trying to make up for his recklessness, he lost any chance of leaving you financial security. With suspicion hanging over you, who would hire either of you?"

"You have no proof we participated in this cockamamy scheme," says Cheryl.

"When we find the iPhone that set off the attacks, we can search it for flight patterns, fingerprints, and other telltale bits of evidence linking it to the perpetrators."

"It could be anywhere. The proverbial needle in a haystack," says Ethan.

"True. That is why we have hired Professor Hagerty to work out an algorithm to determine its location. He is using this problem as a research project for his class. They will calculate most likely launch spots within a four-mile radius of all three targets. It should not take too long to narrow down the search. Then, it will be only a matter of time until we find the iPhone and its owner."

Ethan sneers like a trapped animal. "What if you find it? We had nothing to do with these attacks. We are honorable people."

"Germantown John or his friends shoot first and ask questions later."

"I swear we had nothing to do with launching any drones," says Cheryl.

"Perception is reality," says Ro Ro.

She walks around the table and leans between them. "If someone turned up with the iPhone, and it showed no involvement by you two, you would dispel any thoughts of your involvement. The insurance money would be paid."

Ethan and Cheryl exchange glances. "If we handed you the supposed iPhone, we would be incriminating ourselves," says Cheryl.

"You are in a tough spot. Andrew Campbell's gamble has backfired. In seeking financial security, he has placed you in physical danger. How ironic."

Ethan puts his arm around Cheryl. "Give us a minute. Just turn off any microphones so we can talk confidentially."

"Sure. "

Ro Ro meets Biker in the adjoining room. "I think you got them going," says Biker."

"I'm not sure. I get the feeling they rehearsed. They had all the right answers to all of my questions."

"Who could have schooled them?" asks Biker.

"Their professor, Edward Hagerty for one."

"Really? A professor from a major university like Temple involved in a murder? I don't see it."

"Let me look into it."

Ethan waves Ro Ro to return. "Detective, we talked things over. We want to help. We will conduct our own search as a show of good faith and coordinate with Professor Hagerty. If we find the missing smartphone, we will give it to you as proof of our innocence. Please keep Mancuso's minions at bay. I did not kill my father. I loved him."

"You can go now, but do not leave the area."

Ro Ro heads to her PC. If there is a link between Campbell and Hagerty, she will find it. The X in this problem is not the solution to be found in a linear equation. It is a quadratic equation, at the least.

She is into her third hour of data mining when Docky enters her office. "What are you doing?" he asks.

"Looking for Darwin's missing link," she says.

"I always figured my in-laws were the missing link. Knuckle-dragging wastrels."

"In-laws? I thought you were a perpetual bachelor."

"I got married young and hung. My hormones ran faster than the Derby winner."

"Too funny. I am having trouble finding a link between Andrew Campbell and Edward Hagerty. "

Docky strokes his goatee, a sign he is thinking. "They both be Irish. They both be father figures to Ethan. Is Hagerty married?"

"He is divorced from Margaret Clark."

"The Irish be clannish folk. And they be mostly Catholic."

"All of that is true. But how do they fit today?"

"Ethan is one common link. Maybe Cheryl Ward links up too?"

"Good thought."

She Googles Cheryl Ward. Her mother is Margaret Hagerty. The professor is her uncle.

"You found the link. Cheryl is tied to the good professor."

"Keep digging," he says.

"Do not leave."

She searches the Hagerty family tree. She searches their real estate holdings. She focuses on a plot of land owned by the Hagerty clan in West Mount Airy, just off St. Georges Lane inside Fairmount Park. The home is very close to the Allens Lane Art center. An open field bordering McCallum Street. It is a perfect launch site.

"Docky, I may have something. Come with me."

"Where are we going?"

"To Maggie's Farm. In Mount Airy. It is less than three miles away. It is in drone range."

"Maggie's Farm is a line from an old Bob Dylan song."

"Come on. There is no time to lose."

"Don't you need a warrant?"

"No. I am searching for an iPhone covered under the previous warrant. The property is owned by Hagerty. It is covered."

"Cover your sweet ass by calling Biker."

"Exigent circumstances," she says.

She guns the engine and tears off.

"We are both getting fired," says Docky.

Ro Ro and Docky walk along the edge of the field where the open field backs up to the woods. A path leads into the woods. "This way," she says.

Docky follows, grumbling about lost pension.

They run into a small tent pitched in a clearing. Ro Ro opens the tent flap, finding a wooden tabletop. A drone and iPhone stand side by side. A package of what was likely C4 explosives is bolted to the side of the drone. Ro Ro gently eases the iPhone away from the drone. "This is the launcher."

She opens the app to check the GPS points. Her mouth drops as the GPS flashes a street address. 43 West Haines Street, Philadelphia, PA 19144. The headquarters of the 14th District. An attack on a police district would signal a terrorist motivated attack, deflecting away from a personal attack on Andrew Campbell. The casualties and collateral damage to families of dozens of police officers would be monstrous.

"Docky. Look at the address on the screen. The 14ᵗʰ District is the next target."

Docky staggers back holding his chest. "Sweet Jesus. Sweet loving Jesus. This be evil."

A timer buzzes. The drone stirs, lights flashing.

"It is turned on. Stop it!" yells Docky.

Ro Ro presses the off button on the phone, but the drone does not shut down. "It won't stop."

"Shoot it," says Docky.

Ro Ro reaches inside the drone and pulls at the bolted in package, but it will not budge. Frantic, she taps the Home button on the iPhone. An icon of a drone appears. She clicks on the icon. She double-clicks the home button and closes all open apps.

The drone lifts as Docky leaps at it, wrapping his arms around the wings, trying to wrestle it to the ground. The drone rips upward through Docky's arms. Ro Ro fires at it, and a few bullets slightly affect the drone and then it corrects itself. She empties her Glock at the camera, shattering it. The drone disappears seconds later. Then, as if sent by God, the drone reappears, nose-diving into the open field a hundred yards away in a fiery explosion.

The impact sends them both to the ground.

Docky screams from his shoes to his dreadlocks. Ro Ro lies flat on her back, looking up at the moonless sky wondering about the odds of surviving two drone attacks in two days.

"Docky. Please get your team here to get fingerprints on the tent and any fragments we can find. Maybe the geniuses got careless."

"Will do, after I pee in the woods. Excuse me."

She cradles the iPhone like it was a Holy Grail of truth. "Gotcha!"

Chapter Six

Rowena sits across the conference room table from Ethan and Cheryl. Biker watches behind the two-way mirror. Ethan has a five-o'clock shadow covering his thin face. The bags under his eyes look like wet tea bags. Cheryl sits tight-lipped; her arms are folded across her chest.

"Do we need a lawyer or two," asks Ethan.

"You can call one any time you want to. I asked you two to come here to explain our findings."

"What findings?" asks Cheryl.

Ro Ro pushes a report across the table. "Earlier today I shot down a drone loaded with explosives. The incident was at Allens Lane Art Center. I think you know the place. We found fingerprints on the drone, the tent where it was housed, and an iPhone. We want to take your prints to eliminate you as a match. Do you agree?"

Ethan snarls, "No way."

Cheryl jumps up. "Hell no. I want a lawyer."

"Are you afraid we will find a match?"

"There were no news reports of a drone attack," says Ethan.

"What are you afraid of?"

"I have nothing to hide," says Ethan.

"Then you will be printed and, hopefully, cleared. How about you Cheryl?"

"I want a lawyer."

"So, you have something to worry about?"

Rowena leans across the table. "You two got caught in a get rich quick scheme hatched by inveterate gambler Andrew Campbell. You could not resist the temptation to grab the money. Using drones was right up your educational alley. It looked like a foolproof scheme. Wrong! You are not the best and brightest. You are two young fools trapped into killing a man looking for an easy way out of life. You are going down."

Ethan's lips curl. "Suppose we do a deal."

"What kind of deal? What do you have to offer?"

"Two drones loaded and ready to fire."

Ro Ro cringes in anger. "Where are they?"

"Wouldn't you like to know," says Cheryl.

"I do not react well to threats."

"You give us total amnesty on everything, and we will give you the location of Numbers and Deuteronomy."

"The fourth and fifth books of the Bible. You had the gall to name stolen drones after the Holy Bible? You are sicker than the worst heretics."

"It is appropriate," says Cheryl.

"How can it be appropriate?"

"You do not get it, you bourgeois oaf?"

Ro Ro resists the urge to slap the smirk off his face. "You killed your father. You tried to kill John Mancuso and Gabe Porto to secure two million dollars of life insurance. You are using technology to hold the justice system hostage so you can get away with multiple felonies. What narcissistic fantasy possesses you to think this tactic will be allowed to stand?"

Smiling confidently, Ethan embraces Cheryl. "We have admitted nothing. You have no proof to support your accusations. There are no fingerprints or DNA as you implied, or you would have arrested us. You stated that the drones used in the attacks were from the Temple lab. The whole team touched those drones. You say you have finger-prints on a phone owned by my father. Of course, I handled that phone. I lived with him. The man you say set the attacks in motion is dead, so he cannot testify or corroborate anything. This is a perfect equation that cannot be mathematically or legally proven. It is pure genius."

Ro Ro laughs aloud. "You smug punk. You forgot about the Biblical law of an eye for an eye. Call it the Mancuso Law."

She waves at the two-way mirror. Gabe Porto enters the room, smiling like a Cheshire cat ready to munch on two mice. "Hello, young lovers," says Gabe. "It is very nice to see you alive, for now. I have friends outside waiting to give you a limo ride home."

Gabe holds up his iPhone. "Here is a picture of your two drivers. Sal and Manny. You heard of the Blues Brothers? These are the Black and Blue brothers."

Ethan's lips quiver. "This is coercion. It is illegal."

Ro Ro points to the door. "You are free to go."

Gabe squeezes Ethan and Cheryl in a strong hug. "Come along. Your five-star ride is waiting."

Ro Ro stands in front of them, stern-faced. "Here are your choices. Confess and tell us where to find Deuteronomy and Numbers or walk out on your own recognizance. I call the second choice Apocalypse, day of judgment."

Cheryl turns on Ethan. "You got me into this mess. You stupid ass."

She pounds Ethan's chest with both fists.

Ethan turns away. She pounds his back.

Ethan wails, "Dad. You drove mom to suicide, killed yourself and ruined me. Rot in Hell, dad."

Ro Ro slaps handcuffs on them. "You have the right to remain silent."

Ro Ro sits them down. She pulls two writing pads and pens from her briefcase. "Write your story, geniuses."

Gabe shakes Ro Ro's hand. "You are one tough tomato."

Ro Ro enters G Town's room. He is lying face up, a bandage covering his face and head. His violet eyes are shining through two slits. He is awake. Intravenous tubes feed antibiotics in his arm. She pulls a chair to his bedside. She says a silent Hail Mary. "Can you talk?"

He tries to talk but the tube in his mouth turns his words to babble. Ro Ro takes out a pen and pad from her briefcase. "Thank you for saving my butt," she says.

She lays the pad and pen on the bed by his right hand. "Write," she says.

He scribbles, "Did you get them?"

"Yes."

He writes, "Good."

"What can I do for you, John?"

He writes, "Make sure somebody picks my tomatoes before they go bad."

She bites her lip. "I will pick them."

He writes. "They remind me of you. Beautiful and honest."

Tears dribble down her cheeks. "God bless you, John."
She leans over and brushes her lips across his bandage.
He writes, "Sweet."
She holds back her tears.

God and love work in mysterious ways.